MORGUE DRAWER DO NOT ENTER!

MORGUE DRAWER DO NOT ENTER!

Jutta Profijt

TRANSLATED BY Erik J. Macki

amazon crossing

Previously published as *Kühlfach betreten verboten!* by Deutscher Taschenbuch Verlag, Germany. Translated from German by Erik J. Macki.

Published by AmazonCrossing, Seattle

www.apub.com

Amazon, the Amazon logo, and AmazonCrossing are trademarks of Amazon.com, Inc., or its affiliates.

ISBN-13: 9781477826409
ISBN-10: 1477826408

Cover design by Cyanotype Book Architects

Library of Congress Control Number: 2014910081

Printed in the United States of America

ONE

The Renault Kangoo van was wedged between the narrow piers under the bridge like a boil in a butt crack, but the driver's seat was empty. The fact that the driver had been able to get out was amazing, because the van did not look good at all. Well, OK. A shoe box on wheels never looks good, but my point must be obvious: the vehicle was now scrap metal, and the driver *should* have been hanging limply in his seat belt. With at least a whiplash hangover, if not a fatal kink in his neck. Though that would depend on the speed of the old junker when it slammed into the post. But no. No trace of the pier-kisser—just four passengers hanging lifelessly in their seat belts.

I teetered a little, as though someone had knocked my feet out from under me (virtually, of course): the four lifeless forms were *kids*.

The cops made it to the scene in no time, along with the paramedics—and the gawkers. Those vultures will find the location of any accident, and someone must have gotten a seriously secret tip-off for this one, because this unlit and potholed stretch of street that the Kangoo had veered off of ran along deserted train tracks and was favored only by canny locals bypassing major intersections and some stoplights.

It was already after seven on this cold, wet evening toward the end of November, so traffic was sporadic. All kinds of dog owners were home from work, now trotting their varmints over the bridge toward a tiny park on the south side that had taken on the function of dog toilet for the neighborhood. So the bridge overhead was extra full of gawpers. And whenever kids are involved, it makes everyone especially uptight, which is why all hell instantly broke loose.

"Get lost, you sick asshole!" one of the paramedics yelled at a particularly dedicated looky-loo who was filming the rescue operation on his touch-screen dildo.

More cops were requested, "to keep the oglers at a distance," as one uniform roared into his radio. So loudly, actually, that the oglers must have heard unless they were deaf as death. But they still didn't budge.

Two more flashing-blue-light buckets arrived, the chipmunks got out, two of them grabbed a roll of yellow barrier tape to block off the accident site, and two others climbed the stairs to the roadway of the bridge above.

"Identification, please," the taller one asked the spectators, who had been casually leaning over the railing so they wouldn't miss anything.

"What's that all about?" the documentary cinematographer inquired.

"As you're all witnesses here, I'm sure you've got something you'd like to share with us, so I don't see any reason to wait. And obviously the names of all witnesses will be recorded."

A few of them took off immediately, while others—such as the cinematographer—stayed put and started up a conversation about civil rights and police brutality against citizen defenders of accountability. I turned my attention from the hyenas to the four young victims.

The paramedics had removed them from the van and laid them on the ground, the little bonsais frighteningly still. I moved in closer, cautiously.

And then I heard them.

But before I continue my report, and for those of you who don't know me yet, I should catch you up to speed. My name is Pascha. My twenty-fifth birthday was a couple of months ago, but I was already dead then. I was murdered in February of this year, which is skating to its end just now. My soul left my body but never found the tunnel with the light, and since then I've been hanging around as a spirit on earth. There is one living person who I can communicate with, and that's a guy by the name of Martin Gänsewein, MD, a highly educated, practicing coroner for the city of Cologne, Germany, and also the person who, on the occasion of my autopsy, sliced me open from neck to ball sack. Since then we've sort of been friends. Mostly an involuntary arrangement as far as both parties are concerned, but since I lack alternatives on my end, I remain galactically loyal to the fuddy-duddy.

I can also communicate with other souls—at least, the ones with sufficient friendliness to pause and make the effort. Which they seldom do. At the moment of death, most souls leave the body and, without detouring, rush directly "into the light." There was one fat little nun named Marlene who kept me company for a while last spring, but otherwise I've been alone since I died. Because being alone on this plane of existence is about as lame as it is on the normal physical plane, I've spent tons—tons!—of time hanging out in emergency rooms and at accident scenes, hoping to find someone else to keep me company.

Which is what brought me here.

I hadn't counted on kids, however. And I've basically never dreamed of having anything to do with little snot-noses . . . When I was alive, I had this cousin who was born right on my eighteenth birthday, so everyone assumed I was bound to think he was the cutest thing ever. The two of us: bonded by destiny. Ha! I gave him a bond of destiny one time when I had to watch him. I strapped him to the leg of the kitchen table—naked on his potty—so I didn't need to change his damned diaper. Kind of worked up the family, that. But parents can get into a state of high hysteria about anything that has to do with their whiny offspring.

Anyway, now I was hanging out a few meters above the accident scene and could hear soft crying. Or whimpering. No idea what you're supposed to call the noises that were buzzing around me. At first I thought the sounds were coming from the gawkers, in their box seats on the bridge, who were about the same distance from the ground as I was, but it was clearly coming from the kids, whose bodies now lay side by side on the asphalt, totally motionless.

I froze. Paused. Listened.

More whining.

"Quiet!" I yelled loudly and, to my mind, rather authoritarian-like.

The whimpering stopped.

"Who are you?" I asked in a stern tone.

"I'm looking down at myself," came a wail suddenly from directly beside me.

"M-m-me too," sobbed another.

"Because we're dead," added a third, in a relatively composed but smart-ass tone. A girl's voice. Obviously.

The fourth voice just whined on.

"I want to go home," the second voice cried.

"Quiet!" I roared again.

I could sense the little souls wince.

Sorry, but I had to sort this all out. The whining was clearly coming from my altitude, not from the asphalt below. So were the snot-noses dead or not? The paramedics didn't seem to think so, because they were giving them injections. Dead people don't get shots, right? That would be wasteful.

And yet, the sproutlet souls were undoubtedly floating up around me. I didn't get it. So back to the beginning and take it from the top.

"All right, everybody take a turn. Who are you guys, and where do you come from?"

"We're from 3C. My name is Edeltraud."

"Edeltraud?" I asked and then roared. With laughter. I'd never heard such a stupid girl's name before in my whole life. Or in my whole death, for that matter.

I could sense her sulking, and at that moment her face appeared before me in a shroud of fog. The spirit girl looked just like the brat with dishwater-blonde pigtails lying on the street below, except now I could also see that her upper and lower jaws were wired with braces, and behind the crooked eyeglasses, her eyes were full of tears. Shit. Wailing womenfolk always mean stress.

"She doesn't like her name very much either," a boy's voice spoke up. "So I call her Edi."

"And what's your name?" I asked into the air.

"Joe." The littlest of the three boys appeared before me as a translucent figure. "Short for Johannes-Marius."

"So you're pretty familiar with abnormal names," I noted.

5

"I'm Bülent," said a dark-haired doughboy of a lad.

"Niclas." This one, rail thin and red haired, looked taller than the others. And now bursting into tears as well.

Oh, great. A know-it-all female brace-face, a pip-squeak who "understands women," a Turkish butterball, and a fire-alarm-headed wuss. What did 3C refer to? A special-ed class?

The little squad of ghosts hung their heads, unhappy and confused, as they watched events on the asphalt below with a mixture of fascination and horror.

"So as far as I can tell," I told the group, "your driver was wasted and hightailed it out of there after he rammed that clunker of a van into the piers."

"No." Naturally the objection came from the girl. "Ms. Akiroğlu—she's our teacher—was intentionally pushed off the road, and then the man took her."

"What man?" I asked, confused. "A paramedic?"

"Not a paramedic. A man with a hood. He kidnapped her."

This blonde brat was watching way too much *Law & Order.* Things like that do happen on that show. But not in real life. In reality, car accidents are caused by multiple factors. First, second, and third: alcohol. Fourth: dozing off at the wheel. Fifth: looking for your smokes in the passenger-side footwell, or groping the person in the passenger seat, or being groped by the person in the passenger seat. Sixth: fuck if I know. I'm sure the list could continue—speed-limit fetishists inevitably whip out their favorite factor: noncompliance with the posted speed limit. Whatever. I have never—and I really mean *never*—heard of a young teacher with four annoying whippersnappers being forced off the road and then kidnapped.

"What do we do now?" asked little Joe.

"I want to go home," Niclas whined.

"Good idea," I said. "Bye."

I expected the kids to get lost, but they kept swirling all around me.

"What?" I asked, annoyed.

"I *really* want to go home," repeated redheaded Niclas. "I mean back inside myself."

"Well, back into your bodies, open your eyelids, and off home with you."

All around me they bustled, pushing, moaning, and finally hanging their heads in disappointment.

"It doesn't work," said little Joe. "I can go close-up, but I can't get back in."

"All right, well, keep at it. *Hasta la vista.*"

All the good movies at the theater started at eight, and I wanted to be there. I still had enough time, so I started trundling toward the popcorn temple with the reassuring awareness of having effectively suppressed the wall of whining, but then I noticed they were sticking to me like gum on my soles.

"Hey!" I stopped and turned, kind of pissed. "What do you want from me?"

"Are you God?" Niclas asked.

Huh? Did I look like it?

"No! Of course I'm not."

"Do you know him?" he whispered.

"Now listen, you dumb-asses. I'm not the good Lord. He doesn't exist, actually. The good news is there aren't any killjoys up here with me either. No teachers, cops, or mothers. So we can whoop it all up like hell—uh, by which I mean, only those over eighteen. But right now, you puppies need to head back down to the paramedics. They'll take care of you."

I sensed their indecision.

"I'm staying with you," the chubby boy, Bülent, said resolutely. "You know what's going on."

No way, I thought. What—was I a wet nurse now? I had to think of something.

"Sorry," I said, "but that won't work. You need to stay with your bodies." This resulted in four question marks floating in front of me. "You need to be ready to jump back into your bodies at any time."

"Huh?" said Bülent.

"Pay attention, Kebab Boy." I was seriously pissed now. All I could hope was that their bodies down on the asphalt would wake up soon so I could get back to resting in heavenly peace. "You guys are lying down there in comas or whatever. You aren't dead."

The word *dead* totally shocked them. Evidently they hadn't considered that possibility.

"The paramedics are doing their thing to patch everybody up, and then your little souls will have to hustle, chop-chop, back into your bodies. From zero to one hundred in point zero seconds, if you get what I mean."

"What if we don't?" Bülent asked.

"Then you'll be dead."

Short pause.

"Like you?" Edi asked.

Hmm. Quick on the uptake.

"So you must have been too slow, huh?" Joe asked.

"No, I was murdered."

Breathless silence. They were flabbergasted. That possibility had not even occurred to them. I was pretty proud of myself. Being murdered is quite special, you see. Statistically speaking, only a select few ever accomplish this. Most people just kick it from driving into oncoming traffic on a motorcycle, or from a chemical overdose at a cancer clinic, or as a vegetable in an old folks' home. Really only a small number of people are ever killed deliberately. Like me.

"Just wait here until it's time to go back into your bodies. Have a nice day." I turned away again.

"How will we know when it's time?" Edi asked.

"Uh . . ."

"Oh, he doesn't know. He obviously hasn't figured it out yet himself," said Joe.

This was one clever crowd.

"I want to go home," the ginger-whinger repeated yet again.

"Stay cool, guys, and above all, stick with your bodies," I called over my shoulder. I wanted to get to the movie theater, finally, because the new Bruce Willis movie was opening tonight. There wouldn't be any popcorn for me, or chicks to feel up, of course, but at least I get in free.

I'd been on my way for a couple of seconds when I sensed the sproutlets on my tail again. I stopped. "Hey, seriously, you guys need to stay with your bodies."

"B-but we're all alone there," Edi stammered.

"Bullshit, Snow White. The paramedics are there, the cops are there, and tons of other people who willingly chose their shit jobs. So, one last time: bye-bye, babies!"

It didn't help. They kept following me. Hesitant and blubbering, but sticking to me like spilled rum and Coke on a bar top. I sighed. *Adios*, Brucie baby. You'll have to save the world without me tonight.

Back at the scene of the crash, I saw that the first aid was apparently complete, because the paramedics were getting the patients ready to travel, putting them on gurneys, covering them, strapping them into place, and rolling them into the meat wagon with the blue lights already flashing. The cops were still interviewing witnesses, while the crime-scene investigators were busy rolling their surveying wheels around, taking photographs of the skid marks, and searching the pothole-ridden road for evidence with powerful flashlights.

"OK, people," I said with a sigh. "I'll take you to the hospital. You stay close to your beds there so you'll be there when your bodies wake up."

The bonsais and I were still hovering over the scene as I heard the whoop-whoop-whoop of a police helicopter, flying in low with a spotlight, to help the searchers on the ground.

Uh-oh.

"Let's get out of here," I called to the kids, and we all began to move up and away from the helicopter. All of us but Niclas, who'd already been caught in the rotors' downdraft, his face starting to stretch out like taffy.

"Hey, Fire Alarm," I cried out. "Watch out for the helicopter!"

But Niclas lacked the power needed to escape the whirling rush of air. Now he was slowly but surely being sucked toward the chopper's blades.

Now, while it is true that we ghosts aren't made of matter, we're still made of something. Otherwise we wouldn't exist. It's complicated, the whole physics thing, and not really scientifically researched yet either. I mean, I don't know of any dead Einstein who would come haunt my world and fish for his Nobel Prize by running a couple of phantasmic experiments about souls trapped between the vale of tears and heavenly paradise. Which is the long-winded reason why I have no explanation for how rotor blades can physically suck souls in. But I could see for myself, live and in color, how Niclas was being sucked closer and closer to the spinning blades. I couldn't grab him and pull him back. I couldn't shove him out of the way, and I couldn't throw myself in his path. Well, fine. Maybe I could have done that, but I wasn't about to.

Niclas's friends were screaming like banshees—well, I guess they were screaming more *as* banshees—but Niclas remained totally silent. You might even say he was paralyzed, like a mouse cornered by a snake, or a groom at the altar. There were only a few meters left between him and the rotors. His face looked like a grainy old black-and-white TV screen when someone's fiddling with the antennas. His nose and ears sheared to the left and then to the right. His face grew longer and longer—and then the rotors sucked him up. What was left of him swirled into the chopper blades like water draining from a bathtub.

Then he was gone.

His three pals abruptly fell silent, and then the wailing began again. Yowling young 'uns pretty much make the most horrific sound in the world, but I lacked the strength to bawl them out just now. I was shocked myself, actually. Until I heard the gagging.

"Niclas?" I asked hesitantly.

"Uaärgh," came the response.

"Niclas?" Edi yelled so shrilly it nearly burst my skull.

We listened. The barfing sounds were coming from a whirl of colors some distance away, spinning sluggishly and uncertainly like a slowing top.

"I want to go home," the swirl whined.

Clearly Niclas.

"Pull another number like that, and that'll be the *end* of you," I said.

The others floated there next to me, staring as Niclas began to reassemble into his normal spirit form.

That is, until Joe called out, "Hey, the ambulances are gone."
Shit!

On my command, we all whizzed after the ambulances together. Since the tots weren't exactly on top of the intricacies of spiritual locomotion just yet, we flew slower than a lawn mower going uphill. But when it comes to traffic speed, the city of Cologne is reliably slow. The ambulances had turned on their flashers and sirens, but the crumbling asphalt along this poorly maintained stretch slowed their progress. When they finally made it onto the main road, things didn't go much faster, since Cologne drivers wouldn't dream of yielding just because there's a flashing light behind them. So we caught up quickly, and I checked inside the ambulances, assigned the kids to the right wagons, and followed behind the last vehicle in the caravan. Whenever one of the shrimpos got distracted before we made it to the hospital, I'd head him off and herd him back into line.

The paramedics brought the children's bodies to University Medical Center. We arrived without any more detours. I supervised the sorting—one ghost per body, each staying with his or her proper earthly form. Once we'd accomplished that, I gave them all permission to visit with each other briefly but strictly forbade them from leaving the hospital ward.

Then I zoomed off to the movies.

Strangely, though, for the first time in my life, I couldn't concentrate on an action flick. I even wondered if I should check in at the hospital again. But I wasn't in the mood. Actually I hate hospitals, I don't like kids, and those brats certainly weren't my responsibility. I tried to watch the movie for a while, although before I knew it, I'd stopped following what was happening on the screen. When the flick ended, I left the theater along with a hundred other people, who were apparently amazed at what they had just seen. Oh well. I would just catch Bruce Willis again tomorrow and take in all the awesome action then.

Is it giving away too much if I say right from the get-go that I never actually got to see it?

I spent the rest of the night at Martin and Birgit's. As a reminder for all of you early-onset Alzheimer's patients out there: Martin is the coroner who I can communicate with mentally. Birgit is his girlfriend. They've been living together since October 1 in an apartment that—naturally—Birgit found. I say "naturally" because Martin is useless when it comes to everyday things like apartment hunting. You might even think him wholly unfit to live independently, but he had actually managed to subsist all on his own before he ever met Birgit. Somehow. He fares considerably better with Birgit, though.

Anyway, I've actually been banned from the premises ever since I told Martin a week ahead of time what Birgit was getting him for his birthday. I had meant well, since Martin was about to buy *himself* a new pair of fuzzy pajamas, the kind normally only babies wear. Very warm, very fluffy, with wide cuffs at the wrists and ankles, so absolutely no cold drafts can reach his sleeping body. But Birgit had already gotten him a pair of pajamas for his birthday. Which he didn't know yet, of course. But I did. So I told him. To *help* him.

OK, I knew I was butting in when I brought it up, but Martin had pissed me off with all his usual drivel about personal space and blah blah blah. So I exacted revenge. The man just cannot lie, not even a little bit. So he looked pretty stupid on his birthday when he tried to feign surprise at all the light-blue plush-wear he pulled from the wrapping paper.

When I pull stunts like that, the only person I feel even a little bad for is Birgit. But it's on her for picking this dweeb for a boyfriend.

Now, banning me from the apartment didn't stop me from coming in. But even so, I couldn't disturb Martin at night anymore, because now he slept under a kind of anti-electrosmog netting that keeps me out. People buy such netting to keep Wi-Fi signals and whatnot at bay, but Martin had bought it first and foremost to keep *me* away. It looked like mosquito netting—in other words, totally kooky—but unfortunately it worked very well.

So, unable to wake Martin to tap his in-depth medical knowledge of comatose states in elementary-school children, I instead slipped over to my favorite sleeping spot: nestled in Birgit's fragrant clothes, which she had casually tossed onto the chair in the corner of the bedroom, and there I promptly zoned out.

We ghosts can't actually sleep, sadly.

Wednesday, 4:32 a.m.

My peace and quiet was over by around four thirty. Moldering around idly is the purest form of torture if you can't switch off your brain, and mine didn't want to rest. Those brats kept haunting me, which is why I gave up my resting phase and decided to float back through the city. I zoomed back to the scene of the accident, but I couldn't make anything out in the dark, and from there, I ambled along the road in the direction that the Kangoo had been driving. At some point on that trajectory was the destination of the teacher's road trip.

I flew relatively high to orient myself in the neighborhood. I hadn't spent much time here when I was alive, since the area wasn't exactly a preferred field of operations for a car thief who specialized in high-end rides. Half of the residents here drove tricked-out commuter bikes, often towing little trailers with orange safety pennants. They hauled around their children with hyphenated names like Leon-Pius, or cases of mineral water or whatever. The other half drove Mercedes 190Ds. (Can you believe people still drive those?)

So I didn't know my way around. But instead of gaining a geographic overview, I noticed reflections from police flashers not far away. Naturally I followed the lights and quickly reached a small, neglected cobblestone square with a tall tree and several bushes in the middle. Someone was lying under one of these bushes. And that someone was—if I interpreted the barrier tape, crime-scene squad, and photographers correctly—dead.

A woman sat trembling in a squad car with a dachshund on her lap, also trembling. Dog owners are some of the best aides to any homicide investigation, both in urban green spaces and out in flat country fields. I spared myself the stammering and stuttering of the little lady and the slobber dripping from the enthusiastic furry sausage, turning my whole attention to the victim instead. Fortunately I could get past the police barrier unnoticed by the photographer and CSI team and zoom close to the body.

I hadn't expected this type of corpse. Maybe a bum who'd boozed himself to death, I'd thought. Or some zit-faced teen, drunk on hormones, whose hot blood had landed him a stab wound instead of a date. Maybe even a junkie. But definitely not a chick whose clothes clearly identified her as neither junkie nor bum. Skinny jeans, thick boots, tight-fitting turtleneck sweater with a wide belt and a lightweight quilted jacket. And peppered all over her upper torso: slits in her sweater, each surrounded by a huge, dark bloodstain.

Something was stuck to her turtleneck that at first I took for a clump of dry, dead leaves, but that wasn't it. It was a piece of paper that someone had taped to the tip of one of her breasts. Written on the paper was a single word: *paçavra*.

The age of a body is hard to estimate. Obviously you can easily tell if a chick is younger than thirty or way past fifty, but there was no way I could even begin to guess whether our gal here was a chesty teen or a youthful thirty-year-old. She had black hair, black eyebrows, long black eyelashes, and darker skin than your average German jane.

Maybe we had an extremely unlucky schoolteacher on our hands who had first rammed into a bridge and then been stabbed to death.

Sometimes people have a really, truly shitty day.

I hung out for a while as the investigation went on. As it happened, it was being led by Martin's best friend, Gregor, who looked both seriously sleep deprived and seriously dispirited. Gregor's a cop, and he takes corpses personally, especially when they're young women. And starting now he wouldn't nap, he wouldn't eat sensibly, he wouldn't even take the time for a piss, because he would have ants in his pants until he could collar the murderer.

As soon as the CSI clowns gave the green light, Gregor snatched the piece of paper off the body's boob, slipped it into a transparent evidence bag, and trudged over to the other end of the square to the newspaper kiosk, which was just opening for the day. It was five thirty. Jeez, some people have seriously sucky work hours even without a murder investigation.

"What does this mean?" Gregor asked.

The man in the kiosk gaped, furrowed his brow, shot Gregor an angry look, and turned away.

"Do you understand what this says?" Gregor asked.

The man nodded.

"What does it mean?"

Shrug.

"Listen . . ."

"Elmas!" The man roared so loud that it almost blew me back across the square.

A woman in a greasy apron appeared out of nowhere. And along with her came the smell of fried meat with onions and garlic. Heavenly.

The old guy yelled something else, while she hesitantly approached Gregor and looked down at the paper. Then she slapped her hand over her mouth.

"What does this mean?" Gregor repeated.

She bowed her head and spoke so softly that Gregor had to bend down to hear her: "Whore."

And that's when Gregor turned into the guy who sees red.

With another thumbs-up from CSI, Gregor dug into the pockets of the dead woman's quilted jacket and pants, but all he found was a used Kleenex, which he stuck without further investigation into an evidence bag, and another wadded-up piece of paper. He unfolded the paper. A phone number was written on it. Gregor jotted it down before officially bagging, numbering, and logging the piece of paper.

"Did anyone find a phone?" he asked the increasing number of passersby standing around him, but they all just shook their heads. By now the investigators must have been pretty sure the woman's death involved some foul play. Ten or so stab wounds from a knife could still qualify as an accident if someone had been buttering bread, but a *woman* with no cell phone? Well, that just wasn't a thing.

Gregor fumbled his phone out of his pants pocket and dialed the number on the piece of paper. I snuck up close to his phone for a listen. The recorded message on the other end of the line reeled off the usual business about the nonavailability of the callee, so Gregor hung up in frustration.

Once the ambulance pulled away with the body, Gregor made his way to the office to get the bureaucratic side of the case rolling. I had easily two hours free until the plainclothes had sorted things out and got the investigation going.

So I zoomed over to Martin's. Technically I had fifteen minutes before his alarm clock was scheduled to go off, but Martin was already up when I arrived. Gregor had probably called him and asked him to do the autopsy lickety-split.

"Hey, Martin, what *is* a coma, actually?" I asked him.

Martin was in the kitchen grinding happy coffee beans from sustainably managed, old-growth-forest-friendly organic planta-tions for Birgit's espresso while his green tea from a socioeco-logically exemplary, biodiversified, grassroots, cooperative tea garden on the fog-rich slopes of some culturally and histori-cally significant Himalayan nation was steeping in the reusable infuser. Faced with so much political correctness I would nor-mally puke—most unecologically—but today I wasn't interested in the world-saving scenery because I couldn't shake the weird ghost kids out of my head. I just didn't understand how they could communicate with me despite not being dead.

"Good morning," Martin replied, distracted as usual.

Barf. This was his new scheme. It had something to do with the communal living arrangement we had going on here recently. For the three of us. With one woman. And suddenly there were tons of new social rules in force, even though Birgit couldn't hear me.

I put my best effort into an equally cordial greeting. "Good morning, my dear Martin. You look like you had a rough night's sleep. Those duds you have on could be an object lesson in history for some high-school class. And the part in your hair is getting wider and wider every day."

Another new rule we had: no more lies.

The coffee mill squealed.

"Coma!" I yelled so he could hear me over that hideous noise. "What is a coma?"

"A coma isn't a disease but a symptom that presents usually after disruptions to cerebral function, such as after alcohol poisoning, for instance—"

"Or an accident?" I barged in. "How bad is a coma after an accident?"

"It depends on the cause or whether there is an underlying condition."

"Oh for the love of God, don't make me squeeze every individual word out of you," I grumbled.

"Do you have a concrete example in mind?" he asked.

"Yep."

"Is the patient on artificial respiration? If so, then it's fairly bad. It may not even technically be a coma but a short-term blackout, circulatory collapse, I don't know. We would need to examine the patient more closely."

Terrific. This wasn't any help at all.

Martin was no doubt wondering why I was suddenly interested in comatose states. But he didn't ask. *Presumably because he was pouting about my tone,* I thought.

"Exactly," he confirmed.

I told him there had been a hit-and-run accident overnight, leaving four kids in comas. I decided not to mention anything about the kidnapping. His brain's shock lamp started flashing upon mention of the word *kids*, because even though most coroners develop a sort of thick skin over their compassion sensors, that naturally didn't apply when it came to kids.

"Tragic," Martin mumbled as he drew his tea infuser out of the teapot.

Before I had a chance to explain to him that the pesky little souls weren't buzzing around in a tragic daze but were all bright as buttons and seriously getting on my nerves, Birgit appeared at the door to the kitchen and asked, "What's tragic on such a beautiful morning as this?"

Her body was freshly showered and her hair freshly blow-dried, the long blonde strands shining like flowing gold. She wore a sleek, dark suit, and her face was beaming. But that was the only thing beaming on this dark and rainy November morning.

Martin bit his lip. Birgit actually did know that he occasionally heard voices from the beyond, kind of like a medium (hence the anti-electrosmog netting over the bed), but she didn't know anything about me specifically or my ongoing presence in Martin's life.

I left the two of them alone, because the mere sight of the silly bliss on Martin's face drove me up the wall. What had this drama queen in terry-cloth pajamas ever done to deserve that awesome woman? And why didn't he just *tell* her about me? Then she could say "Hello, Pascha. Everything going all right?" when she got home from her job at the bank, and I could feel like I really belonged somewhere.

But no . . . So instead of sticking around, I thought I might as well check in at the hospital to see if the little ones were properly ticking again.

I got on my way.

Immediately I regretted leaving Birgit. She's always cheerful, always a refreshing sight, and she always smells good. The mood at the hospital, by contrast, was abysmal, and it reeked of a mixture of disinfectants, overboiled vegetables, and human stink glands. The stench hung over the whole complex like a pall, and especially so in the intensive-care ward.

Grown-ups in various stages of distraughtness were sitting in two different rooms by the four beds of their still-motionless children. The sproutlets' souls hovered by their adults, bawling, confused, frightened, and upset because their families couldn't see them. It was loud as hell, each ghost was bubbling with snot and tears, and all four of them looked like they might explode at any second from the effort of trying to make the grown-ups see them—and from the frustration of failing.

"Calm down," I roared. If things kept on like this, I anticipated having to say that fairly often.

The sobbing slowly ebbed in the room where Edi and Joe were lying.

"Come on," I commanded them both. They were obviously struggling with what to do. They didn't want to leave their parents' sides, and they seemed totally exhausted and unable to make decisions.

"Let's head next door, pick up Bülent and Niclas, and then we'll hold a situation-room meeting and get the latest update on everyone."

They hesitantly followed me with twisty, wobbly flight paths into the next room.

"Bülent, Niclas, come with me. Situation room."

We whooshed up high and flew down the hospital corridor just under the ceiling toward the pediatric ward, where the friendly atmosphere would hopefully have a calming effect on the short shots. My guess was right. They relaxed noticeably when we arrived in the playroom full of colorful balls, stuffed animals, building blocks, and art easels. There weren't any other kids in here so early in the morning, which was just fine as far as I was concerned. I urgently needed to have a serious word with my new little friends.

"Uh . . ." Shit. What should I call them? Hello, children? Like they do at puppet shows? That wouldn't work.

"Whatever you call us, just don't call us snot-noses," Edi suddenly butted in.

Whoa. Impressive.

See, it's not that easy communicating on the spirit plane. It takes some getting used to. But Brace-Face had evidently gotten the knack of it so fast that she could hear my thoughts already.

"All right, *people.* What are you still doing up here with me instead of going back into your bodies?"

"I tried to get back in, but it didn't work," Edi reported matter-of-factly. Except she sniffled now and again. "I also tried talking to my mommy, but"—sniffle, sniffle—"that didn't work either."

The others nodded.

"What are the doctors saying?" I asked.

"Induced coma," little Joe pronounced carefully. "They say it's not that bad."

"They always say that," observed Edi, precocious as ever. "But it's not true," she whispered hesitantly.

And, lo and behold, all four kids started crying again.

"OK, OK, calm down, now, and tell me exactly how the accident happened," I ordered them. "Every detail."

"We were at the museum," Joe began. "Full of stuffed animals, you know, from the taxidermist. Barf!"

I had to grin. Taxidermied animals made me barf too. I preferred them grilled.

"Continue."

"On our way back to school, the first van broke down. We stood by the side of the road for over an hour until the new van came. It was really late, so our teacher called the school and said she would just drive us home herself. We all live pretty close to each other."

"The boys fell asleep in the back," Edi said, taking over.

To which the other three immediately protested.

"You did too!" she said. "And I got to sit in front, so I saw a big car suddenly come from the side and ram right into us, so she had to slam on the brakes and turn the wheel, and then the car hit the bridge."

OK, good. That's how I had imagined everything more or less to that point. The teacher was tired, wasn't paying attention, a car passed her, and she lost control while they were on the unlit pothole-ridden bypass street. Seen it before, you know, especially from women who don't have that much practice.

"And then the man came over from the big car and took her. He hit us with his car, took her, and drove off."

"Wait," I said. "You had lost consciousness from the accident."

"No, not at all," replied Edi. Had her physical self been before me, she would have been standing with arms akimbo and tapping her foot. But now she could only glare at me.

"She's always saying crazy things," Bülent said.

Kebab Boy didn't talk much, but when he did, he did it like a man.

"Were you still in your body when you saw the man take Ms. Acapulco?" the tall redhead, Niclas, asked.

"A-ki-ro-ğlu," Joe corrected.

"Yes," Edi said.

"And then?" I asked.

Her shoulders and head drooped. "Then I don't remember anything else."

I let them stay in the playroom for a while and zoomed back to intensive care to get a few more medical details. I couldn't explain the thing with the comas. After all, that one time Martin was lying there on the street in a coma, which was my fault because he had gotten—um, yeah, that doesn't matter. But in any case, his soul had stayed in his body during his coma. Or maybe it had left his body but was learning how to swim in the flower vase on his bedside table in the hospital. But it didn't come fuck around with *me*. So what was up with the bonsais here?

I arrived just in time for rounds. The doctor was lifting the eyelids of his little patients, shining a light into the pupils, checking all of the equipment, jotting things down in a squiggle that no human being could read, and reassuring the parents that all of the signs left him optimistic.

Edi's mother didn't look convinced, so the doctor put his hand on her shoulder, looked deep into her eyes, and said, "Please don't worry. It'll be OK."

She nodded, too exhausted to debate him about hope. The other kids had at least two people at their bedsides—Bülent actually had five—but Edi's mother was there alone. I felt sorry for her.

I zoomed back to the playroom in pediatrics only to find my mewling mob halfway back down the corridor to intensive care. Apparently they'd gotten bored in the playroom since they couldn't actually play with all the nice toys. Then Niclas had started bawling, Bülent called him a mama's boy, Edi tried to mediate until both boys together shouted her down, and then Joe managed to settle the dispute somehow and keep the crowd together. You couldn't leave this crew out of your sight for even a second. I took them back to their relatives, tried to talk some sense into them, and then headed off. I needed to find out who Gregor's latest customer was.

Martin had already started the autopsy on her. Which is his job, after all. He and I had met, ghostiforically speaking, during my own autopsy. I've observed lots of autopsies since then, but I still don't like all the rooting around inside human bodies. I even made an effort not to look too closely, but I looked away too late and saw Martin lifting a pretty shredded liver out of the body.

"Has the body been identified?" I asked.

Martin had been intensely focused on his work, as usual, so I startled him by speaking so abruptly. "No," he gasped, a bit out of breath.

"How did she die?" I asked. I asked because the obvious thing—in this case, the stabbing—isn't always the real answer, as any attentive coroner knows.

"Hemorrhagic shock."

"Hemor-what?"

"Shock caused by a sudden loss in blood volume," he muttered as he sawed a deli slice off the liver, which he would later drop into a Mason jar and set aside as a histology sample. *Histo* for short.

"Martin, express yourself clearly!"

"She bled to death. After multiple stab wounds."

Good. Was that so hard?

"How old is she?"

"Between fifteen and early twenties."

Shit, that didn't help me. OK, fine. Off to see Gregor. Maybe *he* had come up with some new information.

T W O

It wasn't even eight when I got to police headquarters. Gregor had left the body's discovery site around six and presumably driven straight to HQ. He was hunkered down, red eyed, over his computer, studying pictures his colleagues had taken.

There must have been hundreds, and he clicked so quickly past so many of them I could hardly make anything out. Then came the detailed shots of the body. The face with closed eyes, like a picture of someone sleeping peacefully. No surprise, no horror, absolutely nothing in her face or manner. Because at the moment of death, all muscles go limp, the face lacks any expression that might clue the investigator in on what the dead person was thinking, seeing, or feeling at the final instant of his, or her, life. That's all boob-tube, murder-mystery bullshit from authors who have no clue about forensic medicine and are too lazy to get informed. *So* lame.

I didn't have any idea what exactly Gregor was looking for in the photos, and since I can't read Gregor's thoughts (why does that only work with Martin?), I couldn't get to the bottom of anything.

Shit.

"Negative," a voice suddenly bellowed from the door.

I hadn't noticed the guy, and Gregor apparently hadn't either, because he winced as if someone had hot-wired his seat.

"Huh?" Gregor asked, annoyed.

"The missing persons list."

"Oh, thanks."

The doorman vanished.

"Who are you?" Gregor whispered to himself as the computer gave a *pling* signaling arriving new e-mail. Aha, Forensics had been quick—as you have to be when there's an anonymous body to identify—and sent over a photo of the body with her eyes open. Gregor was printing the picture when Jenny appeared in his doorway.

"What's up?" she asked.

"Did you bring breakfast?"

Detective Jenny Gerstenmüller, Gregor's still relatively new and young colleague whose guidance counselor in high school had undoubtedly pointed her toward a career as a lifeguard, florist, or stewardess—surely not as a female cop—entered the office holding two tall lattes and a giant paper bag. "Croissants, breakfast rolls with cheese, egg, or sausage, and chocolate muffins."

"And what are you going to eat?" Gregor attempted half a smile, which quickly slipped past his left ear and down to his collar into a frown. He was in a really shitty mood.

"You were at the location?" Jenny asked, setting her purchases on the desk and fishing the muffin out of the bag.

Gregor nodded.

"And?"

"I think the crime scene was somewhere else. Identity unknown. No hit on the missing persons list. So far we really don't have anything—"

The phone rang, and Jenny answered, listened, reached for a pen, scribbled something on a piece of paper, uttered the kind of noise that arises when there's a whole chocolate muffin stuffed into your vocal tract, and hung up again. Then with one hand she picked up the piece of paper and her latte, pointed the thumb of her other hand over her shoulder, and rushed out of the room.

"What is it?" Gregor called as he jumped up, grabbed his jacket from the back of his chair, and slid the printout of the photo into his pocket before running after her.

"The phone number you flagged," Jenny said, mumbling around what was left of her muffin, "belongs to a Sibel Akiroğlu. I've got the address."

"That's all? A name and address?"

Jenny shrugged.

I had to settle for that tiny bit of info for now, but I followed them, hoping for more soon.

They drove over the very bridge that, little did they know, had recently played a dramatic role in the life of Sibel Akiroğlu, teacher. They turned off the main road and continued past the square with the kiosk. Gregor drove a circle around it all so Jenny could have a look. The body's discovery site was still cordoned off with police tape, the outline of the victim still visible. They didn't get out.

A short time later they arrived at the address: a four-floor building with eight apartments. It was one of those exposed-aggregate concrete boxes, one of about a hundred lining the street. The roof was covered in satellite dishes whose cables ran down the façade and into the apartments.

"Akiroğlu," Jenny mumbled as her finger traced the name-plates at the front door. "Here."

"Here, and here too," Gregor added. The name was in fact listed three times. But one had the name *Akif*, and another had an *S*. So Jenny rang the bell for S. No answer. Gregor rang the bell for Akif. Same result. The third nameplate had no first name listed. Gregor rang that bell, and this time the door buzzer sounded.

They both walked up to the third floor.

The old man who opened the door was wearing greasy pants, a checked shirt with pointed collar, and a knit cardigan. He was unshaven and unkempt and blinked at his visitors with red-rimmed eyes. He didn't make a peep.

"Mr. Akiroğlu?" Jenny asked.

He nodded.

"We're looking for Sibel Akiroğlu."

"Have you found her?" he asked, suddenly more alert.

"Found? Has she been missing?" Jenny asked.

"May we come in for a moment?" Gregor said.

Mr. Akiroğlu nodded wearily, pointed at Jenny's shoes, and said, "Take off, please."

They took off their shoes, arranged them next to the worn-out men's shoes outside the apartment door, and entered.

The apartment was decorated in the Oriental den-of-thieves style with the most disturbing knickknacks and kitsch everywhere. Plates stood on end in the hutch with wild patterns of all different colors and gold trim. Überschmaltzy pictures of blue-green lakes, pictures of women in screamingly garish folk costumes squatting on the ground and rolling out flatbread, and those famous white-glazed bowls that every *döner kebab* shop throughout the world has hanging on the wall. Döner kebab being the sweet, garlicky Turkish version of gyros. The bookshelves hosted thousands of little figurines in folk costumes, a teeny-tiny plastic mosque lit from the inside, oil lamps, Turkish coffee pots, and cheap tin scimitars.

Mr. Akiroğlu gestured toward the sofa, which was covered with thick pillows. Jenny and Gregor sat down. Mr. Akiroğlu disappeared, and I followed him. He went into the kitchen, where he spoke a few words to a short, fat woman who was just wrapping a headscarf over herself. Mr. Akiroğlu returned to the living room, and the woman followed him shortly thereafter. She was holding a tray with three Turkish tea glasses and a small bowl of sugar cubes. She set everything on the coffee table and tried to leave again.

"It'd be nice if you would sit with us," Jenny said warmly. The woman looked at her husband, and only after he nodded did she sit on the front edge of the second armchair. Mr. Akiroğlu offered them the tulip-shaped glasses and gestured to the sugar cubes.

"Now then," Gregor said, clearing his throat as he stirred his tea. He usually took his coffee black, but here he took four cubes of sugar. Apparently he was aware that, without sugar, the concoction was about as palatable as battery acid. "We are looking for Sibel. She's your daughter, is that right?"

The Turks didn't say anything.

Gregor looked to Jenny, then back at the couple. "Do you know where we can find her?"

Head-shaking from the man, tears from the woman.

"Why are you crying?" Jenny asked.

Mrs. Akiroğlu was kneading her hands in her lap. Her dark skirt came down almost to her feet, and her massive upper body was stuffed into a sweater *and* a cardigan, even though they had the heat cranked up to Mediterranean-beach-resort temperature. She wasn't wearing any detectable makeup.

"Sibel not bad. Not run away."

I could read "Run away?" on both Jenny's and Gregor's faces. They'd come looking for a woman whose phone number was found on a dead body, and now out of the blue, they learn the chick had apparently bailed. Both plainclothes instantly scooted forward on the sofa, suddenly wide awake.

"When did you last see your daughter?" Gregor asked the man.

I heaved a sigh of relief. Finally a glimmer of cop-itude. Surely it wouldn't kill us to get down to some specifics. It couldn't kill *me*, anyway.

"Yesterday morning. Before school."

"Which school?" Gregor asked.

"Mathilde Franziska Anneke Elementary School."

"Sibel is teacher," the old man said, sitting up straighter. He was obviously proud of his daughter—although, for a teacher's reputation, it's not so great to crash a car that's full of schoolkids and then flee the scene.

"And when did she run away?" Gregor asked.

"Not run away," the father repeated.

My law enforcement friends eventually pieced together, with great effort and urgency, that Sibel had been involved in an accident with four kids in the car who were now lying in the hospital.

"And your daughter?"

"Not find her."

Jenny and Gregor still looked confused.

"Did your daughter get out of the van to get help?" Jenny-Bunny asked. I couldn't tell whether she was really that naïve or just wanted to avoid shocking the parents with nasty terms like *hit-and-run* and *fleeing the scene*.

"How did you find out about the accident?" Gregor asked the man, who was growing more and more upset.

"Police came, look for hit-and-run."

Aha, there was the nasty term after all. Pretty much any other explanation was unlikely, and the detectives should have known so.

"Why didn't you file a missing persons report?" Gregor asked.

"What for?" The mother shook her head. "Everyone looking. Son looking. Nephews, cousins, aunts, uncles, everyone looking. Friends. Everyone. Even police. Why file report too?"

Gregor and Jenny leaned back again into the soft pillows on the sofa. I could imagine what they were thinking. They had an anonymous corpse with a phone number and were hoping the woman whose number it was would give them information, only to find that she had disappeared. After a hit-and-run accident. So was it murder, or was it a coincidence? The whole thing was pretty unclear to me too, but at least now I knew the teacher's first name was Sibel and that she was somehow connected to the murder of the unidentified corpse via the phone number that was found in the body's pocket. But any other connections remained unexplained.

"Do you know this young woman?" Gregor asked as he held out the photo of the body for them to see. Sibel's parents looked at it and shook their heads. Gregor sighed and stuck the picture back in his jacket pocket.

"Is that your daughter?" Gregor asked, pointing at the gold-framed photo of a young woman on the bookshelf.

Mr. Akiroğlu nodded.

Gregor asked if he could take it, and the man took it out of the gold frame and handed it to him.

Jenny encouraged the parents to tell them a little bit about their daughter, and they obliged, talking about how hard she worked, how popular she was at school, how high her GPA had been when she graduated, how hard it had been for Sibel in school because her parents were never able to help her academically themselves, blah blah blah.

"Who is Akif Akiroğlu?" Gregor asked.

"Akif is son," the lord of the manor said.

"Where is he now?"

"Looking."

"Would you ask him to call me as soon as you see him?"

Nodding, standing up, saying good-bye, shoes on, out.

"What's the connection between the two women?" Gregor whispered to Jenny as they left. "Let's get some location tracking on Sibel Akiroğlu's cell phone. Can you please handle that?"

Jenny nodded. "What about you?"

"I'll drive over to the teacher's school. Maybe they know our dead body there."

I thought lightning fast: *It might make a lot of sense for the bonsais to be there when Gregor was nosing around their school. Maybe they'd notice something odd. And maybe someone would be lying, and they could detect the lie because they knew the real situation. Or . . .*

Oh, no matter. That was plenty of reasons right there. I zoomed back to hospital to pick them up.

I found them all in the two boys' room. They were hanging around Niclas's bed, where the grown-ups were also gathered. The second I whooshed in, I knew what was wrong. I was more familiar with all this shit than I wanted to be.

"Can you hear me?" shrieked the woman I took to be Niclas's mother, based on her fire-alarm-red hair color. She was almost crushing her son's hand, and her face was just a few inches from his, so every time she spoke to him, she splattered drops of spit onto his face.

Niclas zoomed to the EKG patch stuck to his chest and whooshed around it. The heart beeper thingy made a couple of extra peaks and valleys.

"See!" the mother yelled, turning to face the doctor.

The poor man was as pale as the incontinence-yellow sheets on the bed, checking all the equipment with trembling fingers.

"Niclas, get away from there right now!" I bellowed. At least I got to bellow something other than "Quiet!" for once.

"No!" Niclas cried hysterically.

Fine. If stress was what he wanted, then stress was what he'd have, I thought. So I flew over to the monitor too. Now the indicator started going crazy. The doctor's pale skin developed frantic red patches, and his hands started trembling so much he accidentally pulled a cable out of the device.

I rushed to Bülent's bed and performed the same number there. All of the grown-ups turned around to Kebab Boy on cue.

"Stop that, you jerk!" Bülent roared at me.

"Then stop with *your* nonsense. Now!" I roared back.

"I'm not doing anything," Bülent yelled.

"Quiet!" This time it was Joe, the little curly-head.

The four sproutlets retreated to the ceiling light. I joined them. The beep-beep from Bülent's bed sounded reassuringly regular again. Niclas's machine wasn't beeping anymore because the doc was holding the shaggy end of the torn cable and staring at it, horrified.

"You killed him!" Niclas's mother squawked. "Murderer! Murderer!" She tried to rush him but was held back by Bülent's mother, who had the shoulders of a wrestler.

"What's wrong with him?" Edi asked in a shaky voice.

"Niclas is perfectly fine," I said.

"But it's not beeping anymore," she whispered.

I thought for a moment. "Well, if the speedometer isn't hooked up, a car can still drive."

She blinked at me, not getting it.

"If the clock breaks, time doesn't come to a standstill."

"Oh."

Slowly, the minispirits relaxed, and on the highly polished, white-tiled plane of reality below, the grown-ups came back to something akin to their senses.

The doctor cleared his throat. "Will you all please wait outside while we check the equipment and"—he paused long enough to hide the rough-ended cable behind his back—"swap out this machine?"

Since no one knew we were there, we didn't feel that his banishment applied to us. We stayed put. I explained to the kids, briefly, what was going on below, how strong spirit emotions can affect sensitive electronic devices. I'd created similar havoc shortly after I died. Like the kiddos, I'd been emotional, noisy, and overactive and needed tons of practice with self-control. It took me a while to get used to everything and figure out what trouble an electromagnetic spirit can get up to. The short version: a *lot*.

We watched the doctor turn the equipment off and on again, manually take Niclas's pulse, and compare that to the readout on the monitors. He did the same with his blood pressure. A technician arrived and disconnected Niclas's unit, took it out of its stand, carried in a new machine, and left the remaining setup to the nurse and doctor. Finally, regular blips started sounding through the quieter room again.

"Pfff," Joe finally said. "God, Niclas, don't do that again."

"I just wanted to tell my mama I can hear her." Niclas sniffled.

"We know," Edi whispered. "We understand."

For the love of parking-lot attendants, what a pile of sentimental mush all this was. I was definitely going to have to keep these four busy to keep them from buzzing around in full crybaby mode and triggering more mechanical catastrophes like this.

"We've got work to do, girls," I said.

"I'm the only girl," Edi said, correcting me.

"If the boys are going to act like girls, that's how they'll be treated," I countered.

Edi giggled, Bülent pouted, and Niclas started crying again. Joe rolled his eyes. "What kind of work?"

"You guys are going to show me around your school, and then . . ." Actually, I didn't know what the next thing would be. We'd just have to find out.

We zoomed through the icy drizzle together, not that it bothered us. Although being a ghost is actually way cooler under blue skies.

"Here it is."

Joe and Edi had taken the lead and stopped above an empty schoolyard. You can always tell elementary schools and preschools from the layers of paper products plastered to the windows. In Germany, schools are usually single-story buildings with short names. But this one had a mile-long name and *two* floors: the Mathilde Franziska Anneke Municipal Elementary School, according to the sign at the gate in the masonry fence around the schoolyard.

"What kind of a freaky school name is that?" I asked.

"Mathilde Franziska Anneke was a very courageous woman who fought for gender equality and founded a school and ran a newspaper. She lived in Cologne in the nineteenth century, and there's a statue of her on the gothic turret of Old City Hall. But she's so high up you can't really see her from the square in front."

Aha! Our Edi-pedia had spoken. Still lame, though, giving a school a six-word name.

The school itself didn't look as bad as the name might lead you to expect—even with all the crap hanging from the windowpanes. Strange custom, taking all the dead leaves the janitor sweeps up daily from the schoolyard and sticking them onto the windows. Is that what they call environmental education nowadays?

"Those are the autumn decorations," Edi explained. "Colorful leaves and acorns and . . ."

Shit-filled birds' nests; feathers plucked from long-since-eaten songbirds; sticks of all lengths, even fat ones and those in the later stages of composting; a shriveled earthworm—God only knows how long ago the little schoolyard exterminators had pasted that one up. "You're stupid," Edi said.

But otherwise, everything looked great. The schoolyard was clean (obviously, since all the dirt and sticks and compost were glued to the windows), with a large grassy area with two soccer goals, and a little school garden where a few green stalks pretended they could thumb their noses at winter. There was also a large paved area with different hopscotch setups and other bullshit drawn in chalk.

A bell rang and seconds later hollering savages erupted out of every opening in the building. The decibels were like standing at a Formula One start line, although engine noise is a naturally awesome sound that makes your veins sizzle like happy hormones, whereas the screaming of kids is pure tympanic torture.

Gregor seemed to agree, because he clamped both hands tightly over his ears as he fought his way upstream into the schoolyard through the thronging hordes. Of all the times he could have chosen to visit a school, he had possibly chosen the worst, but like a true-blue cop, he remained inexorably focused on getting to the front entrance, pushing his way into the school building.

"That guy is Detective Sergeant Kreidler. He's a good friend of mine," I said. "Come on, follow him."

"Hey! There's Liliane and Jennifer . . ." Edi cried, swerving out of formation.

"Forget about them. We have work to do," I urged, but Edi was already cruising away, following two little girls who were schlepping horrendous pink knapsacks of obviously considerable weight on their shoulders.

"Lili! Jenny!" Edi called. "I'm here!"

"Come on, Edi," Joe called. "They can't hear you."

"But I need to ask them what homework we have," Edi whined.

"You must have floated off the wrong side of the bed this morning," Niclas said. "You should appreciate not having any homework to do. It's awesome. And no classes, either!"

"Your teacher isn't at school today, so there won't be homework anyway, right?" I said to Edi. "So, come on. We need you with us."

Edi reluctantly broke away from her corporeal friends, who plodded away into the crappy weather, holding their heads down to keep the drizzle from their faces. We followed Gregor through the now-quiet corridors to the main office and waited with him until the secretary logged him in as a guest and then escorted him into Principal Bieberstein's office. The introductions went as usual: name, name, handshake, have a seat, coffee? Yes, please. Of course, right away.

"You're doing a criminal investigation?" Bieberstein asked in a shaky voice once Gregor had taken his first sip. "Have you heard from Ms. Akiroğlu?"

"No, unfortunately not."

Bieberstein slouched, leaving him only about as tall as Shaquille O'Neal. Well, fine. That's a little exaggerated, but he really was gigantic. Bieberstein had to fold himself up just to fit into the chair behind his desk. Imagine how he'd look trying to sit in one of the kids' chairs during a parent-teacher conference. Or did principals even go to parent-teacher conferences?

"Uh-uh," Joe answered.

Oops. Now *that* pip-squeak was picking up on everything I thought too. I had to be more careful in the future.

"What do you have to hide?" asked smart-ass Edi. She bared her teeth so that the stainless-steel barbed wire in her mouth flashed in the light.

I shushed her silently.

"Why are the police interested?" Mr. Bieberstein asked softly.

"I'm getting to that," Gregor said. "Let's go through exactly what happened yesterday before Ms. Akiroğlu disappeared, step by step."

Bieberstein looked like he wanted to add something but just nodded and kept looking, wide eyed, at Gregor. "I waited here for the school bus to return. I always do that when a class has a field trip, to make sure everything is on track."

Gregor nodded.

"But then I got word that the school bus had broken down, and then Ms. Akiroğlu called again and said the replacement bus had arrived. She offered to drive the four kids home in her own van after the replacement bus dropped the others back at school."

"Why would she do that?" Gregor asked.

Bieberstein shrugged. "So that one of the fathers who was going to drive the kids home wouldn't to have to wait so long."

"Whose father was that?" Gregor and I asked at the same time.

"Mr. Doğan," Bieberstein said as Bülent whispered, "Mine."

"Why—" started Gregor.

"Mr. Doğan drives a taxi for a living," Bieberstein answered. "He often drives some children home from school for the other parents. He always has four booster seats for the taxi, as has Ms. Akiroğlu for her van."

Gregor frowned. "And those parents just let a man they don't know—"

Bieberstein nodded. "I know what you're getting at. But Ms. Akiroğlu assured the boys' and the girl's parents that Mr. Doğan is completely trustworthy. She and Mr. Doğan are related to each other somehow, if I'm not mistaken."

Joe, Edi, and Niclas stared at Bülent, who was watching the scene at Bieberstein's desk with a slightly tense face.

"Did you know—" Edi started to say as Joe shook his head.

"Turks live in big nests," Niclas mumbled. I stared at him. Had he really said that? Joe and Edi didn't seem to have heard.

"OK, continue," Gregor said.

"Mr. Doğan spoke briefly on the phone with Ms. Akiroğlu, informed me of their arrangement, and then drove away in his taxi. Later on, the replacement school bus finally arrived; the other parents all picked up their children. Ms. Akiroğlu left with the four kids to take them home, and that's the last I've heard from her."

"Was she supposed to be in touch with you again?" Gregor asked.

"Ms. Akiroğlu and I had agreed beforehand that she should call me and let me know once all the children were safely home, because as long as they're in the care of the teacher, the school is, of course, responsible for them."

He put his face in his hands again. "I've tried to reach her on her cell, but I only got her voice mail. At some point after eight o'clock, her mother called me. I told her to contact the police. And she apparently did just that."

Bieberstein again put his face into his enormous hands. His palms were seriously as big as frying-pan lids. Why hadn't he been a professional basketball player? He must have looked totally ridiculous, walking around the school surrounded by munchkins only coming up to his knee.

"Mr. Bieberstein is nice," Edi said. "People can't help how they look."

Of course, someone who looked like her would shoot her mouth off about something like that.

"How are the children?" Bieberstein asked.

Eight little ears pricked up around me.

"They've all been put into medically induced comas," Gregor said testily.

It didn't surprise me at all that Gregor had found time to check on the condition of the witnesses—nor that their current noninterrogability weighed on him. Purely because it was slowing the investigation, of course. As a person, he surely felt bad for the wee ones and their folks, but as a cop, he needed answers.

Bieberstein made the sign of the cross.

"Do you know this woman?" Gregor asked, setting the photo of the body on Bieberstein's desk. Bieberstein studied the picture carefully but then shook his head.

"Is she why the police . . . ?" he began.

Gregor nodded curtly, put the photo back into his jacket pocket, and pulled out a business card and gave his usual speech about calling him if he recalled even the smallest piece of information. Then Gregor left as Bieberstein sat at his desk, staring into space. A minute later Bieberstein still hadn't moved, so we went to catch up with Gregor, who we found with his jabber box to his ear.

"Are you done with the autopsy?" he was asking. Aha! He had called Martin. "Great," he said after a moment. "I'll be right over."

Finally we had the prospect of a few illuminating facts to look forward to. Because even though Martin is positively the cringeworthiest dweeb you could imagine, professionally, he provides regular proof that even a wearer of fuzzy pajamas can be brilliant. If there was a murder to discover, he would discover it. True, in a case involving a dozen stab wounds, it wasn't exactly rocket science, but most murderers didn't make things so easy for him.

So we zoomed off toward the Institute for Forensic Medicine. Halfway there, I suddenly realized what we were about to do, and I stopped. The short shots flew past me before they put on the brakes and turned around, uncertain.

"You kids go scram back to the hospital and your parents," I said. "I can't take you where I'm going."

"Where *are* you going?" Naturally, that question came from Edi.

"To the Institute for Forensic Medicine. That's where they slice up bodies and pull out all their insides . . ."

"Eew," Niclas said.

"Cool," Bülent said. "My uncle is a butcher. I've helped him slaughter a sheep before."

"March!" I said, pointing back toward the hospital.

Of course, no one started marching. I was going to have to escort them the whole way back to the hospital myself and hope they didn't follow me again.

I finally made it to the institute at the same time as Gregor and overheard his usual greeting blah-blahs with Martin. I tuned in to their conversation only when it got interesting.

"She is presumably between sixteen and her early twenties, but I believe I said that already. In addition, she is healthy apart from an influenza infection."

"Pregnant?"

"No."

"The piece of paper found on her said 'whore,'" Gregor reminded him. "Can you at least tell me if she was a virgin?"

"There is no medically valid means of determining virginity, Gregor. You should know that by now."

"External signs of force?"

"None—aside from the stab wounds and defensive injuries on her hands." That comment came rather close to what Martin would understand as dark humor.

Gregor didn't smile. "Tattoos, special marks, anything that will help with the identification?" he asked, tired.

Martin shook his head.

"When did she die?"

"No idea."

Gregor groaned. "Martin!"

Martin shrugged. "She wasn't killed at the discovery site. When she was put there is unknown. We don't know the temperature conditions to which the body was exposed. Was she inside at room temperature or outside in the frost? The redness of the bronchial mucosa combined with pus accumulation in the bronchi themselves indicates that she had bronchitis. If that infection was concomitant with a fever, the body may have started showing signs of decomposition faster, because the higher body temperature and greater number of bacteria trigger a sort of quick start, if I might term it that. But if the body was outside at freezing temperatures, it would have cooled quickly, and bacterial activity would have been inhibited accordingly. So you see, so long as I know nothing about the conditions to which the body was exposed postmortem, I can't tell you anything more precise."

Gregor shook his head. "OK, continue."

"The first stab was executed approximately like this," Martin said, making a motion as though he were trying to sock Gregor in the gut. "That strike hit the liver and portal vein. This was in and of itself a fatal injury, but she was far from dead yet."

"The usual problem?" Gregor asked.

Martin nodded.

For any of you who have never stabbed someone, here is a quick intro to the pros and cons of stabbing: the biggest pro is there's no pop or bang—thereby obviating any troublesome attention from neighbors, passersby, or cops. Con: the stopping power is pretty sucky. *Stopping power* is the technical term for the victim's responsiveness. If a weapon incapacitates its victim immediately (as in the case of a grenade exploding in your pants), it's called a man-stopper. But if the victim keeps merrily fighting on, there is no stopping power at all. That's where most perps screw up. The stabber thinks his victim will drop dead on the spot, but that's not usually the case. The victim will still be stand-ing around like an idiot, often with no clue that the unpleasant sensation in his stomach is more than just a strong punch. This in turn perplexes the attacker, who needs a couple of seconds to realize that the stab wound didn't incapacitate his target, and then he thinks, *Uh-oh, better go back for seconds.* Only then does he start stabbing like a fiend.

"I'm quite certain that the subsequent stab wounds were incurred in relatively quick succession," Martin continued. "The victim was transported postmortem lying on her side. The right side exhibits the corresponding pattern of *livor mortis* and some abrasions."

Livor mortis, if you didn't know, is when blood pools in the lower part of a body and turns the skin all purple.

"In the trunk of a car?"

"Possibly. The forensics technicians will be able to tell you in more detail."

Martin promised Gregor he would finish his written report on the medical findings by the next day, and he wished him good luck when he left.

I was only interested in the dead Turkish girl to the extent she was connected to our teacher, though. Because if there's one thing the police are amazingly good at figuring out, it's murders. Of the 2,300 crimes that occur every year in Germany involving a death, such as murder and manslaughter, more than 59 percent are solved. Gregor and Jenny were thus well on their way to find-ing the murderer of Martin's latest little toe-tagee.

But what about our teacher? Was anyone looking into her? Maybe only an annoyed traffic cop looking for the woman who did the hit-and-run? And what if she really had been abducted, as Edi claimed? I couldn't imagine that being true, but hypothetically speaking at least: Who was looking for her operating under *that* assumption? Who was working to *save her life?* No one. So once again, there was only one personage to take the matter in hand: I, Pascha, the coolest damned detective in Limbo. And now I even had four assistants. Well, OK. The peanut gallery wasn't actually any help, more like a ball and chain around my metaphorical ankle. Or better yet, like four itchy fleas on my ball sack. But in my situation, I can't be choosy, and I have to take what I can get. So back to University Medical Center.

I found the four of them in cozy communion all together in Room 1. Edi's mother was sitting cross-legged at the foot of the bed, reading a book aloud to her daughter. The story was apparently quite exciting—it sounded like some smart-ass of a little girl was investigating a mystery with a dog—because the shrimps were swirling around her all abuzz.

"Hey, people, I need your—"

"Sh!" They hushed me.

"It's about—"

"Sh!"

God, could you believe this? I stared agape at my assistants, who were refusing to obey me. And to think I was the one who had saved them. Without me, they'd all have been scattered to the wind by now.

"Aren't you too old to have shit like that read to you?" I asked in an admittedly spiteful tone.

"Jeez, Pascha. Don't be so judgmental," Joe whispered. "It's totally nice that Edi's mom is here, drowning out the annoying beeping of all those machines. The story won't take much longer, and then—"

"Bah!" I said, interrupting him.

The guy was a regular Gandhi or Mandela or Jesus, always blathering on about love and peace and strawberry fields. But I couldn't be lulled into submission so easily.

"That will be too late," I snarled at him as I turned and bailed.

No one had assigned me to this kindergarten crew. I, Pascha, had solved plenty of cases all on my own. Well, on occasion with a bit of help, but I definitely didn't need these comatose little baby brains to get behind the mystery of the disappearing teacher. A little observation and, boom, I'd conjure her up and out of whatever ditch she was in. So the bambini were welcome to go sleepy-bye to mommy's bedtime stories. It would be better to ditch 'em for a while anyway.

So I left the hospital and wafted around for a moment indecisively. Where to now? Hmm . . . Why not just take a peek at the teacher's apartment? That was a good idea. So I zoomed to the building where Gregor and Jenny had sipped their battery-acid tea that morning.

The apartment was easy to find because the residents' names were listed not only at the front door of the building but also on nice nameplates at each landing going up the stairs. S. Akiroğlu was on the top floor on the right.

The decor wasn't as dreadful as at mom and dad's, but still pretty plushy. The wallpaper was light blue with fairy glitter all over it; the carpets were thick and fluffy and more of a medium blue; and the sofa in the living room was dark blue with about twenty thousand pillows in white and silver. In front of the sofa was a glass table so clean the pillar candle in the middle of it looked like it was floating in midair. One whole wall was covered with books and folders on shelves over a tidy desk with a phone and laptop on it.

No TV anywhere in the whole place. *It must be in the bedroom*, I thought as I zoomed back there. There was a white bed with star-dotted sheets, two narrow wardrobes of white-varnished wood, and a bureau with a mirror on top. No TV. Everything was plushy and fluffy and heavenly white and blue.

Did I dare check out the bathroom? I was a fearless hero who cowered before nothing, so I took the plunge. I was expecting a fluffy toilet seat cover, but I was wrong. The tiles were white; the shower, toilet, and sink were white; only the faux-fur bathmats were—you guessed it—blue. There were bottles and jars everywhere, along with brushes, dishes full of hair bands and hair clips, and makeup and cotton balls all over, but everything was clean and tidy. No hair clips in the cotton balls, no cotton balls in the shower, and the toilet paper was neatly wound up.

The kitchen was just like the bathroom. Full of stuff, but super clean and super tidy. I could have flown into the fridge to see if the chick was more into Turkish yogurt or German minced pork tartare with onions, but the light is off inside a fridge when it's closed, so I couldn't see any more than anyone could.

People who commit suicide sometimes do one last grand cleanup in their apartments before they off themselves. They don't do that because it's nicer to hang yourself from a rafter in an uncluttered room; they do it because they don't want posterity to think ill of them.

Could that be why this pad was so shipshape?

I was mulling over the answer to that question when I heard a noise through the wall. Just to orient you: there was another apartment on the other side of the wall from the kitchen. So I flashed through the wall and landed in a mirror-image but otherwise-identical kitchen layout, although this one was lived in differently. Like, totally differently. Like from another galaxy.

In this kitchen, no horizontal surface was directly observable because there was crap stacked everywhere. A slice of old toast whose dry edges had started to curl upward. Bottles of beer, lying or standing. Ripped-open packages of peanuts, sunflower seeds, and pistachios. Dirty silverware. Half-empty yogurt containers. Empty pizza boxes. Aluminum foil in which, judging from the smell, döner kebabs had once been wrapped. Potato chip crumbs crunched under every step the man took as he walked to the fridge. He opened it (inside, furry, green slices of cheese peeked through some open deli paper beside a scrunched-up package of ground coffee), took out a bottle of beer, walked to the table, used the edge as a bottle opener (the trim all around the table looked like the scalloped border of a postage stamp, which made me think it regularly served as a bottle opener), and then finally shuffled over to a chair. He swept a heap of reeking, mildewed clothes off the seat and plopped down.

I felt instantly at home. This is how my places had always looked.

The black-haired, black-eyed, slightly doughy, unshaven guy kept making phone calls anytime he wasn't sucking beer out of a bottle. Unfortunately, all his conversations were in Turkish. And the only translator who could help me was off listening to story hour, courtesy of Brace-Face's mommy.

Since all the jabbering in Turkish couldn't get me any further in my investigation, I quickly checked out the other rooms. The living room was done in style with a floor mattress, clean clothes on a Dumpster-dived sofa, and dirty clothes on the floor with several boxes of various plunder—a couple of stained titty magazines, and yet more not-quite-empty food containers.

The two things that aroused my interest were located at the other end of the room: a serious-looking home safe that you could hold a blowtorch on for days and it still wouldn't open, and a flat-screen TV whose diagonal measurement had to be close to its owner's height.

This guy looked Turkish, and it occurred to me that he was probably the brother of the teacher lady. But what the heck was up with him? He lived in the same building as his mom, but he didn't have her clean his place! He literally lived knee-deep in garbage but had a safe that would have done Wile E. Coyote proud. And he ate only pseudofood from bags and nothing that had ever actually grown from the ground, yet he munched his pseudofood in front of the most awesome home-entertainment center I'd ever seen—and that includes all the fancy-schmancy electronics showrooms downtown.

This guy was a puzzle. And he never stopped chattering into his phone. Maybe he was just continually ordering pizza. Maybe he was whining to his mommy about his backstabbing new girl-friend. Maybe he was negotiating with some local sheikh over the right price for his cute-as-a-button sister.

Who knew? Not me, in any case. Which sucked.

I left the apartment annoyed, without looking in his bath-room because, even though I've never been a neat freak, seeing strangers' toenail clippings in the bottom of a sink or ball-sack hairs in a shower pretty much disgusts me. Anyway, I had a new problem: I didn't have the faintest idea how to proceed with my investigation.

THREE

I whooshed to police HQ to see if Gregor had IDed the body. Knowing who the victim is makes an investigation light-years easier because the perp is usually in the victim's immediate circle of acquaintances. But if you don't know who the victim is, you don't know what circle you're dealing with. I had learned a ton in the short time I'd known Martin and Gregor. If someone had told me a year ago that I'd be thinking like a cop now, I'd have called bullshit.

I found Gregor in the conference room that had been assigned as the situation room for the investigation. Someone had posted a piece of green construction paper on the door that said NOT IN KANSAS on it. Now, anyone who's seen an episode of *CSI* obviously knows that cops are genetically predisposed to having extraordinarily bad senses of humor, and I didn't get the joke until I looked at the bulletin board inside. A photo of the victim was pinned to it, with a sheet of paper underneath listing the case ID number: OZ-140503. Under that was her name: Yasemin Özcan. Özcan–*Oz*. Get it? Hardy har har.

So, one way or the other, Gregor had obviously IDed the body, and now he was standing with Jenny in front of the bulletin board, posting more pictures. Close-ups of the stab wounds, a wide-angle shot of the discovery site, a close-up of the piece of paper that said *paçavra*. Jenny handed him a computer print-out with all the victim's personal information. Age: 16. Parents: Mustafa and Ayşegül Özcan. Address: Blah blah blah. School: Nelson Mandela Comprehensive School.

Gregor glanced at his watch. "OK, we gotta head out. I want to be there when they identify their daughter."

Personally, I didn't want to be anywhere near that myself. When parents ID their dead children, it usually degenerates into torrents of tears, which incidentally is not always the case when it comes to identifications by *spouses*. Obviously not every fresh widow or widower was as delighted as this one guy I saw back in September who identified his wife and then shook Martin's hand saying, "Today you've brought me the best news I've heard all year." And even ignoring outliers like him, there were always a few people who displayed shockingly little grief.

But in the case of parents, it's *totally* different. I prefer to stay clear of scenes like that.

Instead, I figured I'd fly back to the hospital in the hopes that the fairy godmother had finally finished her tale and my assistants were now free to answer a couple of questions for me.

I found the always-inseparable Joe and Edi hovering over Joe's bed.

"*You* were the one who insisted he go to that school!" hissed the woman sitting to the left of the bed at the man sitting on the opposite side.

The man didn't respond. He just gently stroked Joe's right hand.

"*You* acted like you knew better than all of the rest of us. Me, my folks, Dieter, Inge . . ." the woman continued.

The man rolled his eyes.

"*Everybody* told us we should send Joe to the private school. He would have been with his intellectual peers there . . ."

"And you think bawling me out is going to help Joe's recovery?" the man asked. He sounded really tired.

"Recovery, pfff!" She stood and turned to the window with her back to the bed. "You really think Joe is ever going to wake up again? Even if he does, he'll probably be retarded. A drooling idiot like Elena's boy."

I felt my bonsais' reactions like shock waves, buzzing around me like bees.

"Who's Elena?" Edi asked.

"Our cleaning lady," Joe whispered in a tear-choked voice. "Her son is developmentally disabled. But he only drools when he's really excited."

"Yes," Joe's father said calmly. "I do indeed believe Joe will recover fully."

"Yes," Edi agreed in a low voice. "I do too."

"I'd rather be prepared for the worst-case scenario," the woman said with a shrug. "I already made an appointment with Mr. Kesselstein . . ."

"Sophie! Joe doesn't need a lawyer. What he needs are his parents."

"Please, Bernd. Be realistic. There's nothing we can do for Johannes-Marius, but at least we can sue the teacher who crashed her car into the bridge and ran off without calling for help." She snatched her bag and coat off the chair and left the room, her high heels clicking.

"What a bitch," I said without thinking, because she *was* a bitch. Her hair was a shade of blonde the good Lord had never intended; she had crazy hips and a full, round ass under a close-cut business skirt that stretched tight over her solid thighs with every step.

"Are they always like that?" Edi asked.

"Constantly," Joe muttered, rolling his eyes. "At least when they think I can't hear them."

I felt really bad for Joe. His mom might make a perfect hot blonde, but as a mother, she was horrifically miscast.

"Hey, chill out," I told him. "At least your mom's both a beauty *and* a beast. And your dad's OK," I said jokingly, trying to pep up my mourners. "Look, right now, I need all of your help with my investigation."

But the bonsais lingered at Joe's bedside, watching Joe's father awkwardly fish a book out of his briefcase with one hand and contort his body every which way to open it without letting go of Joe's arm with the other.

"Not another story hour," I moaned. "Come on, you guys!"

Joe shook his head. "I'm staying with Pa."

"Me too," Edi added.

I should have known. The limpet and the leech were inseparable. Fine, then it was Kebab Boy's turn. I whooshed to the next room and found Bülent hovering at his own bedside. Four women, three in headscarves, were cavorting around his bed. The mother (with headscarf) was sitting in the chair, holding Bülent's hand; two fifteenish chicks (with headscarves) were perched at the foot of the bed, reading some brightly colored celebrity rags; the fourth (no headscarf) was leaning against the window, staring out into the murky soup of the November fog. She was at least twenty with bright-red lipstick and black-rimmed eyes. And she was pouting. Kind of babelicious, if you overlooked her business attire, which consisted of a pinstriped suit and white, ruffled blouse.

"Who are the harem hotties?" I asked Bülent.

"Hey, what do you mean by that?" Bülent demanded.

"Nothing. I—"

"Fuck you," he snapped. "If you're trying to make fun of me, you've picked the wrong guy."

So angry . . . But I could feel him running out of steam.

"Whatever," he mumbled. "My big brother was just here. He drives me crazy. So, yeah, I guess I'm just a little mad."

"Does he do the full-on Turkish routine?" I asked.

"Mm-hmm."

With that, Bülent started sniffling and rushed to the billowing folds of his mommy's skirt.

Suddenly I felt like a third wheel. As I often do in such cases, I decided to head to Martin and Birgit's, since they were now *my* family, even though one of them didn't know it and the other didn't want it. The two of them were having a little lunch date considerably after noon, as usual.

I found them sitting in one of their regular spots, a restaurant that I would never have set foot in while I was alive. It was Asian, naturally, which is almost always what Martin eats when he eats out, since he's vegetarian. It was also super small, the tables pushed so close together that no patron would have had trouble helping himself to the rice bowl of his neighbor. And they didn't have normal silverware. Although no one seemed to miss it, either. Martin loved this place, and I wondered why a member of an industrialized, Western civilization that had invented cutlery centuries ago might be content to eat his way through a dingy Third World cantina using two plastic sticks.

Did he feel guilty for being able to eat his fill while the child laborers harvesting rice from sweltering paddies went hungry? And by the way, how can kids harvesting food even go hungry?

Wouldn't you pocket enough leftovers as you worked? They never show that on the news. Just the ones with swollen bellies with the voice-over pleading for donations.

I didn't get it. But you know what I got less? How Birgit could go along with Martin's self-mortification. Admittedly, today she didn't seem enthralled by what was on her plate. To me, their vegetarian fare generally looked more or less like cattle feed anyway, but this Asian slop looked particularly so. In any case, Martin kept munching away enthusiastically until he noticed Birgit's unhappy face. He immediately dropped his chopsticks and gently rested his fingers on Birgit's hand.

"Aren't you feeling well?" he asked.

Birgit's fine, I thought. *The food is the problem, man!*

"No, I don't know what's wrong. Before we got here I was nearly dying from hunger, but now I can't get a bite of this down."

Pure self-preservation, sweet Birgit, I called to her. *Trust your instincts!*

"You're quite pale too. Maybe an infection?"

"No ide—" Birgit started to say, but then she leaped out of her rickety chair and stormed, hand over her mouth, toward the ladies' room. Martin rushed after her. He stood outside the door with a chopstick-style *D* painted on it. For *Damen,* which means "ladies." Like everything else in this place, the door was as primitive as plastic toys from Taiwan, so at least Martin could make out enough of the sounds through the flimsy boards to form an image of what all was transpiring inside: Birgit was puking her soul out.

Martin raised his hand to knock.

"Go in there!" I ordered him.

"But what if another woman . . ." he thought back at me.

I flashed into the restroom. Birgit was kneeling over a toilet bowl, retching. Squatting in the stall next to her was a shriveled old Asian woman, picking her nose with the stall door wide open. She was ripping out some juicy ones in a most disturbing way. No wonder, what with the food in this place.

"No one else is in there. . ." I encouraged him.

Martin pushed the door in like a special-ops commando storming a terrorist cell, rushing to Birgit in two long steps and squatting beside her.

The old lady in the adjacent stall let loose a singsong shriek of crescendo and diminuendo. Martin jumped up, staring at her as though she were a fire-breathing dragon, and then slammed her stall door shut. He wasted no time in mentally chewing me out.

"No one else except for an old woman with rectal disharmony."

I interrupted his rant. "You never give me a chance to finish."

Martin flashed a look of annoyance in my direction, then he sat beside Birgit on the cracked floor tiles.

Hearing someone else spew always used to make me need to blow chunks myself, and I felt a flutter in my gut even now, though, technically, I no longer had one. I figured I'd better clear out. So I went looking for Gregor instead.

Based on past experience, Gregor would probably be talking with the parents after they IDed the body, and he would also want to see where Yasemin lived. I had made a mental note of her address. It turned out to be a multistory building with at least six apartments, which is why it took me a while to hunt through it until I found Gregor and Jenny in one of them. They were in a super tiny but extremely tidy girl's room, where no one would ever climb into the frilly bed again, where no one would pose in front of the mirror with the kitschy frame, and where no one would gaze up at the poster of the Turkish boy band hanging above the bed.

Gregor stood with his notebook and pen beside Yasemin's father in the doorway as Jenny went through the desk drawers.

". . . since Monday afternoon, you say?" Gregor asked.

"My wife says Yasemin came home from school on Monday and went out again at four."

"Did she say where to?"

"School."

"What kind of phone does your daughter have?"

"Nokia."

"Do you know what kind of Nokia?" Gregor asked.

The father shook his head.

"And her phone number?"

The father rattled off a number.

"Do you have any idea where her phone might be?"

"She always has it with her. Always."

Jenny was done looking through the desk and was now kneeling beside the bed as she lifted the bedspread to look underneath. Then she stood and opened the closet.

"Do you recognize this woman?" Gregor asked, showing the father the picture of Sibel Akiroğlu.

"I don't think so," he said.

"Please give me all of the names you remember your daughter ever mentioning," Gregor asked.

"What kind of names?"

"All names. Teachers she particularly liked or didn't like, friends from school, other friends, boyfriends . . ."

"My daughter doesn't have any boyfriends. My daughter is a good girl."

Gregor just nodded. "I'd like to speak with your son as well."

"Mehmet isn't here."

"Can you reach him?"

The father shrugged, went to the landline phone mounted on the wall in the narrow hallway, and dialed. The call didn't go through.

"When are you expecting Mehmet back?"

He shrugged again.

"But he does still live with you, right?" Gregor asked.

"Yes."

"Then will he be home this evening?"

"I don't know."

Gregor lowered his notebook and looked the father in the eyes. "What does that mean?"

"A brother looks out for his sister, but he wasn't there for her then, and he's not here now."

Gregor briefly closed his eyes. "Did you kick your son out?"

Yasemin's father put his hands into his pants pockets, looked down at his cheap house slippers, and shook his head. I had no idea whether Gregor believed him, but in any case, I didn't believe him.

"I'll need a photograph of him, his cell number, the names of his friends, and any other clue—no matter how small—as to where I can find him."

The father handed him a framed photo from the shelves in the living room, gave him Mehmet's cell phone number, and spelled the name Şükrü Bozkurt.

"How old is your son?"

"One year older than Yasemin. Seventeen."

"Did your children get along?"

Mr. Özcan nodded.

Jenny, who had finished her investigation and joined them in the hallway, raised an eyebrow. Gregor folded his notepad shut, gave Mr. Özcan his card, and left the apartment with Jenny. Yasemin's mother, who was sitting in the living room, surrounded by wailing women wearing headscarves, didn't even notice when they left.

I was pretty upset by this point. We had one dead Turkish teen with a missing brother and one missing Turkish woman with a messed-up brother, and both young women had something to do with each other. But what?

Did Edi, Joe, and the others know Yasemin too?

On the other hand, the much more important question was where the teacher, Sibel, had ended up, because it didn't seem like anyone was really interested in her. Was the teacher a witness to the murder? Had she gone into hiding out of fear? Or had she really been abducted, as Edi believed? Or . . . had the teacher killed Yasemin? Presumably, they had talked to each other on the phone, likely arranging to meet, but if that were so, then only the teacher had walked away again on her own two legs. That would have been on Monday, since Yasemin disappeared on Monday. Then the teacher slept on it for a night, accompanied her class to the museum, slammed into the bridge with a load of kids in the car, and finally fled and—despite probably having whiplash—disappeared into thin air. All right, that did sound unlikely. But what else did the two women have to do with each other?

I couldn't answer all of these questions myself, and I couldn't ask Gregor directly because, well, I can't chat with him. So I desperately needed Martin to meet up with his best friend and ask him all these questions for me. I needed to put him on the scent.

Before I headed over to pester Martin in the forensics lab, where he's always very curt and often irritates me with disgusting things—for example, slicing up loops of intestines to look for some object or other that the deceased had swallowed—I decided to take another detour to University Medical Center. Obviously in the hopes that for once it wasn't story hour. And on that point, I was in luck.

Instead, it was rounds. A whole scrum of white coats was standing in the room around Niclas and Bülent, eloquating lengthy Latin crap at each other. They weren't exactly treating the kids with kid gloves either, though, because they had pushed their pajama tops up and pajama bottoms down and were poking and tapping and listening at every possible location on them. They lifted the boys' eyelids, shined light into their eyes, massaged their entire scalps, jabbed sharp things into their toes, hammered their knees, and all kinds of other things the boys had no way to defend themselves from.

The four little souls were floating over this swarm of quacks and were getting on each other's nerves.

"Boy, you sure are fat," Niclas said to Bülent.

"Well, you've got knock-knees," Bülent retorted.

"You're nothing but rolls of blubber. You probably can't even see your own wee-wee under all that."

"That's not nice," Edi said, reprimanding Niclas as Bülent circled over his own body in a red cloud of rage and embarrassment.

"Hey, cover me up! There're girls here!" Niclas yelled, but of course, the doctors couldn't hear him.

"Like anyone wants to see that," said Edi, rolling her eyes.

"Actually, I was just saying Bülent wishes he could," Niclas pointed out.

"Chill out, man," Bülent growled. "It's not the 1950s anymore."

"I-I just thought boys and girls shouldn't . . ." Niclas stammered.

"That only matters after puberty," Edi explained.

Both boys' vapor clouds turned beet red.

"Well, *I* don't want to share a room with him. He's always got a thousand women around him, wailing and carrying on like at a Turkish bazaar," Niclas sulked. "My mom said—"

"Your mom is a stupid goat," Bülent interrupted. "His mom yelled at my mom, said she reeks of garlic!"

"She does reek," Niclas said.

"Your mother reeks worse, like that guck she sprays into her hair," Bülent replied.

"That is all *about* cleanliness!" Niclas shot back. "But you wouldn't understand what that means."

"Quiet!" I bellowed.

Niclas burst into tears, Edi pursed her lips, and Bülent fell silent in a huff.

Joe shook his head in disappointment. "It's seriously not helping anyone if we all keep arguing."

Jeez, what a scene this was. Naturally, I had hoped the bonsais would gradually come out of their shock, but I hadn't imagined anything like this. The mama's boy was turning out to be a racist prick; Brace-Face was not only a smart-ass but also smart *and* precocious; and Joe-the-referee already sounded like a school psychologist, without even having spat his first baby tooth into the toilet yet. Only our dumpling-shaped Kebab Boy seemed to possess any emotional stability. Maybe the layer of fat over his ribs protected him not only from the cold but also from psychological (and spiritual) cruelty.

"Bullshit," Bülent grumbled.

All right then. Evidently, he did not share my opinion.

JUTTA PROFIJT

"If you guys could lay off the fucking immaturity competition for *just* a second, you could help me with my investigation."

"You said a bad word!" Edi reprimanded.

"Oh, just let him," Joe whispered. "He needs to so he feels important."

"Then he's just being childish himself," Edi whispered back.

I pretended not to hear them. Otherwise we were never going to make any headway here.

After a few more rounds of mutual chiding, I'd herded all four kids together and flew them into police headquarters, directly to the bulletin board at NOT IN KANSAS.

"Oh, man," Joe whispered in shock as he saw the discovery-site photographs of Yasemin's body.

If a couple of snapshots had him all shaken up, then it was definitely better not to take them with me to Forensics to ID the chick in person. Especially since she'd be in pretty sorry shape with that giant Y-incision from her neck to her belly button and a slice across her scalp from ear to ear.

"What does this woman have to do with Ms. Akiroğlu?" Edi was apparently trying to keep it together, the way she always did, but even her voice was now quavering.

"That's what I was hoping you guys could tell me. Have you ever seen Ms. Akiroğlu and her together?"

Generalized head shaking.

"Bülent, you should know the Turks in town."

"Not all of them. Not her, at least."

"OK," I said. "The woman in the photos, Yasemin, had a slip of paper with Sibel Akiroğlu's phone number on it. That's why the detectives assume they knew each other. They may have both disappeared at the same time and been murdered. At any rate, they suspect the two cases are related somehow."

64

While I was talking, Bülent noticed the picture with the Turkish word for *whore* written clearly on it. He turned so pale he was practically transparent.

"What is it?" I asked.

"They called my sister that too."

"The pretty one in your hospital room, the one not wearing a headscarf?" I asked.

Bülent nodded.

"What does it mean?" Edi asked, surfacing from behind Bülent and now staring at the picture as well.

Bülent didn't say anything.

"Who called her that?" I probed.

"Boys from the mosque."

"Spit it out already," Joe urged. "What does it mean?"

Bülent pursed his lips.

"Show me these boys from the mosque," I told him.

"The day after tomorrow. Friday prayers. They'll all be there," he said.

I nodded, filing that away.

We searched the bulletin board for more clues but didn't find anything and were about to zoom off when Jenny walked in with the picture of Mehmet, Yasemin's brother.

She pinned it crooked underneath the picture of Yasemin and wrote, "BROTHER: MEHMET—MISSING" underneath, and then she left the room.

"That guy, he's one of the older boys from the mosque," Bülent whispered.

You don't say . . . But how did it all fit together? I was definitely going to need to ditch these kiddos for a while to do some thinking, since they couldn't keep quiet for more than a second at a time. Edi was whining because she wanted to know what the word on the piece of paper meant, Niclas was yukking it up because it looked like a bunch of stupid Turks were killing each other off, and Joe was trying to mediate. I took all four back to the hospital and made them promise they'd stay in their rooms with their bodies. Then I took off.

I hadn't had a day this stressful in ages. Evidently my ongoing request for spiritual companionship had been heard, but instead of sending me a hot babe or cool dude, the good Lord or fate (or Marlene—I wouldn't put this past her) had tacked four whiny, snot-nosed brats to my ass. This had to be some kind of punishment—I just didn't know what for. One thing I did know, though: I needed some peace and quiet. Never before had I felt such an overwhelming urge to sneak off and hide inside a basket, under some fluffy blankets, disappearing into the folds and not having to hear or see a single other thing. I could do that anywhere, obviously, but I was yearning for home. For a familiar environment, where I knew that the same incessant, monotonous routine that was Martin's personal life awaited me.

Martin and Birgit usually came home after work, cooked dinner together, ate, and then sat on the couch in the living room to read or stare at the boob tube. Or Birgit read while Martin sorted his collection of city maps. Around ten o'clock Martin would brew some bedtime tea, serve a cup to Birgit, and drink his in little sips until lights-out, no later than eleven o'clock. Stultifying—and just what I needed right now.

But I had bad luck yet again. I could hear Birgit's voice as I whooshed in through an old mullioned window straight into their living room.

"No, I will not calm down!" she was yelling at Martin.

Martin was standing in front of her, his arms limp at his sides, fighting off tears. "B-but you know Katrin is just a nice colleague. She doesn't mean anything more than that to me," he stammered.

For those who don't know who Katrin is, I should explain that she is one hot bunny—a detail that Martin has actually never noticed. I can assure you his eyes never linger on her well-formed tits or her long legs or tight ass. He also doesn't dream of running his fingers through her long, wild hair or losing himself in her dark eyes. Instead, he admires her professional expertise and collegial helpfulness. All that red-blooded business is left to Gregor, who's not only Martin's friend but also Katrin's boyfriend. Lover. Whatever you want to call it.

"No, I do not know that," Birgit bellowed. "From the moment I get home, all I hear is Katrin this and Katrin that. She did such great work, she found a tiny skin puncture, she solved the case, blah blah blah!"

Martin pursed his lips. "I apologize; I didn't mean to bore you with stories from work."

"Bore me?" Birgit bellowed again. "I'm *pissed off*, damn it!" Then she burst into tears, spun around, and ran into the bedroom, slamming the door behind her.

Martin sank feebly onto the sofa, staring into space with his eyes glazed.

Great!

"What did you do?" I asked Martin without even saying hello first.

Martin winced. "How long have you been here?"

"For the last three or four sentences, which was plenty. So?"

"Nothing. I was just telling her about work."

"About Katrin."

He nodded blankly.

"Martin, women don't like it when men rave on and on about other women."

"But I wasn't raving on and on about Katrin, I just . . ."

"I know," I said. "But it was enough."

"But I've always done that. Birgit likes Katrin. She knows perfectly well that I consider her only a colleague and—"

"And now you two are living together, and she's letting out her inner bitch," I said. "That's normal."

"No, it's not."

"How many women have you lived with?"

Silence.

My point exactly.

"Believe me, I know women," I said. Even though I had been 99.9 percent certain Birgit would *not* become a bitchy ballbuster. But there you go: when it comes to women, there are no exceptions.

Birgit was already sound asleep when Martin checked on her half an hour later. She hadn't washed her face or brushed her teeth. She had just taken off her clothes, crawled into her burrow, and conked out.

Martin couldn't sleep a wink all night, while Birgit snored beside him like a Russian who'd won a drinking contest with 160-proof moonshine. I planned to stay most of the night, but I'd cut and run before the alarm clock went off. The amount of patience I had for a chick in a pissy mood definitely had its limits.

FOUR

Thursday, 6:00 a.m.

"Martin, you absolutely have to go out drinking with Gregor tonight," I announced as he made his morning tea.

I'd accidentally stayed through the alarm, but Birgit, strangely, remained asleep. Two wake-up attempts had already failed so far. It was only six in the morning, however, and Birgit's bank job didn't start until nine. She normally got up with Martin for purely romantic reasons—and that sort of thing was apparently history now.

Martin remained focused on Birgit, his concern obvious.

"Are you listening to me? I've run out of leads in the search for that missing teacher."

"Missing teacher?"

Once again, Martin's mental acceleration was like a Kazakh gravel truck on the mountain stage of the Austrian Grand Prix.

"Car accident! Four kids in a coma! Teacher missing!" I screamed to jog his memory.

He thought for a moment, which proved tough for him, because his worries about Birgit kept taking over his brain. Plus, the man was a serious tea snob, and his morning tea ceremony required his full attention.

"That does ring a bell," he finally said, "but I can't think of any other associated details."

I laid out the whole story for him one more time, now with full details, including all the knowledge gained as of last night from my painstaking detective work.

"You can communicate with the children?" Martin asked, horrified.

"That's what I said."

"And you've been taking them along on your various expeditions and wanderings?"

"They're my assistants," I explained, making an effort to sound businessy.

"*Children?*" he repeated. "For heaven's sake!" He was so appalled he didn't properly seal the canister he kept his very expensive loose-leaf tea in. Tomorrow morning he would whine about how that negatively affected the flavor.

"And now," I continued, "we—the kids and I—need your help."

Martin braced himself with both hands on the kitchen counter. "My God, they're dead."

"Wrong," I said more angrily than intended. "They're just in some kind of coma. The doctor says they'll wake up soon, completely healthy, and they'll continue leading their lives just like they did before."

"But . . . can you see or talk to the souls of other people who are in comas?"

"Uh, no."

"I need to see this for myself," Martin decided, and I was pleased. If you can manage to pique his professional medical curiosity, he rises to peak investigative form.

Thursday, 7:00 a.m.

Thirty minutes later, we entered Edi and Joe's room. Edi's mother was sitting between both beds, reading aloud from a book. Edi and Joe were hovering over the bodies so they could comfortably watch Edi's mother as she read. The woman looked about ten years older than she had yesterday.

"Excuse me. May I interrupt you briefly?" Martin asked from the doorway.

At my suggestion he had put on his white jacket (there's no blood on the white one; blood only ever gets on the green scrubs, and those never leave the autopsy suite in Forensics), so he looked like a regular doctor.

Edi's mother raised an eyebrow at the timidity of his question and then waved him toward her daughter's bed.

"I'd just like to do a few reflex tests."

Edi's mother briefly stroked Edi's hand, hesitated, stroked Joe's hand as well, and then walked to the far corner of the room, where she wouldn't be in the way. She clasped the book she'd been reading tightly to her chest.

Martin mentally asked me, "Are the children here now?"

"Yes, the souls of the two bodies in the beds are buzzing around up here with me."

"Are you talking about us?" Edi asked, startling me. "With that guy?"

"Kids, this is Martin. Didn't I tell you about him yesterday?"

"What was that?" Martin asked.

"You can talk to him?" Joe asked in disbelief, circling Martin like a seagull around the Statue of Liberty.

"Yep."

"Awesome."

"Edi and Joe are here. They say hi," I explained to Martin.

"Hello! Can you hear me?" Edi roared into my ear. "If you can, tell my mommy that I love her loads!"

"He can't—" I started to say.

"And tell her I'm doing OK. I'm not in any pain."

"Edi, he can't—"

"And I'm sorry I complained about the whole-wheat bread. I like whole-wheat bread, really I do." She burst into tears.

Joe tried to console her, but Edi dissolved into a real crying fit. What a serious pain in the ass. How was I supposed to focus on Martin when I could barely hear my own thoughts?

"Can't you hear that racket?" I asked him.

"Why are you yelling like that?" Martin asked back.

"Because it's unbearably loud up here!" I roared.

Martin shook his head once as though shooing away a fly. *Great.*

He whipped out a flashlight, shined it into the patients' eyes, studied the displays on the medical equipment, read the notes in the files at the foot of each bed, and asked about a thousand questions while he did so. He did reflex tests on Edi, but since she was still indulging in her blubberfest, I directed him to Joe and interpreted Martin's questions and Joe's answers.

"Were you unconscious?"

"Yes."

"For how long?"

"No idea."

"Can you feel it when I touch your body?"

"Uh-uh."

"Can you hear and see?"

"Yes."

"Are you dizzy?"

"Uh-uh."

"Do you have any memory gaps?"

"Right after the crash—everything somehow got blurred."

"Do you feel normal?"

"What do you mean by normal?"

Martin was thinking in sweeping poetic categories like *heavenly/peaceful* versus *earthly/human*, but I was able to make very clear to him that these hell-spawned spooklets were not peaceful in the least. To the contrary, they were downright pissy, racist, egocentric, and annoying.

"You are *so* exaggerating!" Joe yelled over Edi's wailing.

Before I could respond, Edi's mother approached Martin. She had been watching his examination and subsequent silent contemplation with growing nervousness. (I'm assuming she read Martin's behavior as contemplation, since she couldn't hear any of our conversation.)

"How is she?" she asked.

Martin winced, turned to her, and smiled. "Oh, yes. You needn't worry."

He picked up Edi's case notes from the foot of her bed, glanced at them, and then checked her IV bag.

"The attending physician has put the children into what's called an induced, or artificial, coma to promote the healing process," Martin explained silently to me. "I would never have suspected that this would, uh, release the souls."

"Well, that is unfortunately what's happened," I said.

"Will Edi recover?" Edi's mother asked.

Rather than respond, Martin silently referred the question to me.

"We-e-ell," I said hesitantly. "I don't know from what distance a soul can still find its way back into the body."

Martin frowned. "What do you mean by that?"

"I've got a theory," I explained. "If the little twerps are on location here when the induced coma ends, they shouldn't actually have any trouble getting back into their bodies."

"If they're not . . ." Martin looked aghast.

Edi's mother had been watching Martin the whole time and noticed the change in his face. "What's wrong? Is it worse than they thought?"

"No, please be reassured," Martin quickly said. "I would like to ask you a favor, and it's really very, very important."

She nodded eagerly.

"As soon as one of the other doctors tells you that they will be lifting the coma, could you please call this number immediately and let me know? Any time, day or night, no matter what. Do you understand?"

He held out his business card to her; she looked at it and put her hand over her mouth. The terms *coroner* and *Institute for Forensic Medicine* tend to do that to people.

Quite justifiably, I might add.

"Why? What does a coroner have to do with this?"

"Uh, well, because . . ." Martin broke out in sweat.

"Oh, man. What's the matter with him?" Joe asked.

A flash of inspiration helped Martin out of his bind. "The children were injured in an accident, you see, and Forensics examines not only deceased persons but also survivors of accidents and violence. We basically look into the medicolegal side of things. The physicians here at University Medical Center work closely with us, but it may be that we would need to perform some tests again, so we need to know in advance when they plan on ending the induced coma. The attending doctor might forget this in the heat of battle, so to speak, but I know that you won't." He smiled. "Hence my card."

Nice save, Martin.

"I see." Edi's mother smiled with relief. "Sorry, I don't know how all these things work."

"Not at all," Martin said, giving her a flaccid handshake and then clearing out.

"I'll be right back, guys!" I yelled to Edi and Joe as I zoomed after Martin.

"I don't understand," he was muttering to himself again and again. "They're stable, completely and entirely alive, but their souls are free."

"Maybe shorty souls aren't as firmly tied to the body as grown-ups'," I suggested. I didn't have a clue why this separation of body and spirit worked with the bonsais, but I also didn't care. I was stuck with the brood, and I was dying to know for how long.

"Pascha, you know you have been given an enormous responsibility," Martin said melodramatically. "When the moment comes, you must ensure that the children's souls are ready to slip back into their bodies."

"Yeah, yeah. Incidentally, we could really use your help—"

"You mustn't take this lightly," Martin continued. "There is no greater responsibility in this world than taking care of a child."

"Martin, we desperately need to talk to Gregor and—"

"And there is no greater worry that parents harbor than for their children."

"So, when are you getting together with him?"

"With whom?"

Once again, the bozo hadn't been listening to me *at all*.

Thursday, 7:50 a.m.

Today was a regular school day, and—I glanced at the clock in the hospital hallway—school would start in just a few minutes. I was sure Gregor and Jenny would pop up at Yasemin's high school to ask her schoolmates and teachers some questions. Information about teenagers is always more credible when it comes from outside the family. Even though parents naturally never see it that way.

I considered whether I really needed the bonsais along and decided I didn't.

"So what are we supposed to do?" Niclas asked indignantly. "It's so boring here!"

"We're going to school," Edi said.

Niclas stared at her, momentarily puzzled, and then he laughed aloud. "I can't believe what a dumb-ass you are." Then he floated off on his own.

"Are you coming?" Edi asked Joe. He nodded. I wasn't clear whether Bülent would be joining the study group or preferred spending his day in a stupor at the hospital. Not that I cared.

Without another word, I whooshed away.

Gregor and Jenny were already walking out of the main office of the Nelson Mandela Comprehensive School when I finally made it to the street entrance of the building. God, did all schools have to have such long names nowadays? I mean, the Mathilde Francamawawa Whatsername Elementary School was ridiculous enough, but what did it say to name a school after Nelson Mandela? Thirty years of prison and torture?

The detectives were accompanied by a guy in a highly educational-looking corduroy suit with a highly educational look of shock on his face.

". . . best to ask Mrs. Wegen-Heinrich, with whom Yasemin had the most contact. If she has any idea which students, and you would like to know the classes those students are in, please just come back to the office and ask."

The corduroy-suited teacher smiled at Jenny, gestured at a door down the hallway, and then walked the other way back to the office.

"He's making goo-goo eyes at you," Gregor grumbled.

"Then he *must* be involved," Jenny replied. "At least, that's how it always is on TV."

"Come on."

They knocked on the door to the classroom the corduroy suit had directed them to, opened the door, and stepped inside. Jenny held back at the doorway to observe the teenagers at their desks. Gregor blinked, opened his eyes wide in disbelief, closed them again in horror, and finally opened them again as he approached with trepidation the two-legged riot of color sitting behind the teacher's desk. When he whispered something to her, she looked at him in alarm and stood, lapped by the undulating waves of red, orange, purple, and blue layers of wool that her clothes appeared to be made of. Both of her hands fumbled nervously with the large, heavy stone she wore at her neck on a thick leather band.

"It'll take only a moment, but it's really very important," Gregor whispered to her.

The class fell stock-still as the teenagers stared with interest at this unexpected spectacle.

Mrs. Wegen-Heinrich cleared her throat and said, "Class, please excuse me for a moment. Please exchange your notebooks with your neighbor and correct each other's homework."

I rolled my eyes at the teacher's inane instructions. Nerds always sit beside geeks, and losers always sit beside washouts, see, so when you have to work "with your neighbor," the brainiacs sit there bored with all the right answers, and the slowtards can't figure out how to spell their names no matter how much time you give them. Group work in school is one of those earthly annoyances that mankind evidently will never be rid of, like cockroaches, rats, and pubic lice.

"Yasemin? Yes, of course, I know her well. But she's not in school today."

"I know." Gregor stood in the quiet corridor, facing a tangle of wool that smelled faintly of damp sheep.

"What's the matter? Has something happened to her?"

I was surprised she didn't know—and I admired Gregor, who had apparently managed to keep the murder victim's name secret and out of the media. It's crazy-ass hard to do that, what with all the snapshot taking and rubbernecking that had increasingly made crime scenes a kind of spectator sport in recent years. Evidently, the doggie-walking woman from the morning they discovered the body hadn't been pointing her lens at the victim, otherwise Yasemin would have been a star on YouTube ages ago.

"We'd like to talk with the students who had a lot of contact with her. So, her best friend, people she ate lunch with, her boyfriend . . ."

"They aren't together anymore."

Gregor's left eyebrow twitched, just briefly. "I'll need his name and where I can find him."

"But what's happened to Yasemin?"

Jenny had closed the door to the classroom. She now took out a pad and pen and joined Gregor and the Technicolor sheep.

Gregor didn't answer the teacher's question. Not because he was impolite, but because he was investigating a murder case. He was here to get answers, not give them.

The Technicolor sheep finally understood that she was in a situation quite difficult for a teacher to grasp, namely, that she wasn't the one asking the questions. She sighed and said, "Amelie Görtz is in most of Yasemin's classes. But she's not her best friend. That's Zeynep Kaymaz. And Dominic Nolde was her boyfriend."

"How long ago did they break up?" Jenny asked and noted the answer: about ten days.

"Zeynep is in my class right now—do you want to speak with her?"

Gregor nodded.

The ball of wool looked like she wanted to ask again why Yasemin was absent, but she thought better of it, pointed to a door at the end of the hallway, and suggested the detectives meet with the students in the empty classroom, E17. Then she scurried back into her classroom. The smell of sheep disappeared with her.

A moment later, a petite Turkish girl stepped into the hallway. She made Danny DeVito look tall, but her curves, unlike his, were in all the right places, as shown off by her skintight jeans and white turtleneck. She had dark, mascara-thickened eyebrows and smoky makeup above and below her dark eyes; she had a side part in her long, dark hair, which she wore loose so it covered half her face. Her attitude was unambiguously ennui-ridden, but she followed Gregor and Jenny into the empty room.

"According to Mrs. Wegen-Heinrich, you're Yasemin's best friend?" Jenny began.

"If she says so," Zeynep mumbled through a strand of hair that had gotten stuck in her mouth.

"Do you see it differently?"

Shrug.

"What kinds of things have you and she been talking about recently?"

"Everything."

"Can you be more specific?"

"Boys, music, shoes . . ."

"Do you know why Dominic and Yasemin broke up?"

"No one knows."

"You don't either?"

"Uh-uh."

"Which of them broke it off?"

"No idea."

Wow. We were supposed to believe this was Yasemin's best friend? Didn't chicks spend all their time oversharing about their relationships? How her guy is in bed, or if he smokes afterward, or farts or falls asleep in nanoseconds?

"Has she been having any trouble with her parents?"

"Who doesn't?"

"What about with her brother?"

"He's OK," Zeynep said.

"Has he objected to his sister having a German boyfriend instead of a Turkish one?"

She laughed aloud. "Yasemin's brother is Dominic's biggest fan."

Jenny jotted down the answers, while Gregor simply observed the two of them.

"What's going on anyway?" Zeynep asked. "Nobody's seen Yasemin or her brother for days, and now the police turn up here. Did they do something wrong?"

"When exactly was the last day they were in school?" Jenny asked.

"I saw her on Monday."

"Where do you think they might be?" Jenny asked.

"Aha!" Zeynep said, a wide smile spreading across her face. "They took off or something, right? They had had enough of their old man. But, you know, I can't help with that at all."

Gregor scooted off the table he'd been sitting on, pulled a chair up close to Zeynep, and sat straddling it backward, facing her, his nose only a hand's breadth from Zeynep's. Gregor isn't a Quasimodo type, but there's no way you'd confuse him with George Clooney either. Least of all when he's pissed. Zeynep jerked back a little.

"We're not playing games here, Zeynep. They are both in serious trouble. If you have even the slightest idea where they might be, I want to hear it now."

Zeynep's smug grin dissolved into a look of uncertainty. "What kind of trouble?"

Gregor didn't say anything but kept staring urgently at her. Under his intense gaze, her uncertainty blossomed into authentic alarm.

"You mean serious trouble? Like, something really bad?"

Gregor again said nothing and kept staring.

"Uh, no. I don't know where they might be. Really, I don't."

Gregor pulled the photo of Sibel Akiroğlu from his jacket pocket and handed it to Zeynep. "Do you know her?"

"She's a teacher at the elementary school where my little sister goes."

"Do you know her apart from that?"

Zeynep snorted with disgust. She had apparently rediscovered her self-confidence. "No more than any of the other high-school students here."

"What does that mean?"

"She comes to this school all the time, giving pep talks and handing out brochures, saying immigrant kids should become leaders—teachers or cops or whatever."

She spit the word *cops* out kind of contemptuously, but Gregor didn't bat an eyelash.

"Have you ever seen her with Yasemin?"

Zeynep hesitated. "No."

"Thank you. That's all for now," Jenny said, handing the girl her business card.

"Is Yasemin in love with Dominic?" Gregor asked as Zeynep pushed down the door handle to leave.

"Sure. Why not?" she said. And then she was gone.

Terrific. So what new information did we have now? I watched Gregor and Jenny go back to the main office and show the corduroy suit the list of students they wanted to talk to, but ex-boyfriend Dominic Nolde—the only one I was interested in— was on a class trip and unavailable.

"When did the class leave?" Gregor asked, his interest piqued.

"They'll be gone all week."

"Where to?"

"They're staying at a youth hostel up in Hellenthal, in the Eifel Mountains near the Belgian border. They're doing an out-door experiential-learning unit that involves climbing a rope course at the aerial adventure park."

Gregor stared at the corduroy suit as though he had told him the class was on a sex-segregated applied apprenticeship on the

Reeperbahn. Which, if you don't know, is the famous and dangerous main drag in Hamburg's red-light district.

"It's such an important community-building exercise that builds trust and encourages taking responsibility and such," the corduroy suit preached as Jenny nodded solemnly and Gregor silently cursed.

"Give me the exact address and phone number where I can reach the teacher."

Supplied with this information, the two detectives left the school grounds and ordered two giant paper buckets of caffeine from the café across the street. They were evidently at odds over whether they should set out immediately for the Eifel Mountains together, or do it later, or do it separately, or not at all, or what. I let them hash that out and was glad when Gregor finally declared that the first thing they should do was in fact go scrounge up Yasemin's ex-boyfriend and question him. I thought that was the right call, because they needed to get to that before news of Yasemin's death leaked out. Plus, I definitely wanted to witness firsthand how trust building it was when the class clown pushed a nerd down a zip line from a platform twenty meters in the air.

It's not like I physically needed to ride in the car, but I started out doing just that because Gregor always plays awesome music in his clunker. This time he put on a headbanger band whose name I didn't know, but when Jenny protested before they even got onto the autobahn, I figured I should check in with my air platoon.

Long story short: I couldn't find them. They weren't at the hospital, although I looked for them in their rooms, in pediatrics, in the cafeteria, and at the gift shop. They had disappeared without a trace. I wasn't sure if that was a good sign or a bad one. Were they back in their bodies? I hung out for quite a while with the bodies of Edi and Joe, watching Joe's father hold his son's hand the whole time while reading one of the four *Winnetou* books about the great Apache hero of the same name. Edi's mother wasn't in the room, so I flew closer to Edi to see if I sensed anything around her. *Nada.* Same with Bülent, whose bed was once again mobbed by various harem ladies. Just my luck that he didn't seem to be related to a single belly dancer. And the same with Niclas, whose mother I found in the hallway arguing with his sister. No inkling of my brood. Either the bonsais were whole again—or they had taken off somewhere.

Oh, well. Change of plans. I turned and followed Gregor and Jenny up to Hellenthal.

The Eifel Mountains feature lots of trees, lots of nasty weather, and lots of hikers in knee breeches. This is Germany, after all. That's why I had always steered clear of this region when I was alive. So even I had to follow the signs on the autobahn to find Hellenthal. I arrived at the youth hostel at the same time as Gregor and Jenny. But I didn't follow them inside, since I'd seen from the air where things were happening. The hostel itself was a white, half-timbered building with a steeply pitched roof. It was quite old but well maintained. There were trails heading out into the woods in all directions and sports courts in front. The ropes course was opposite the hostel, nestled amid some super-tall trees, but you couldn't miss it. To my great surprise, it even had a corrugated roof, making it suitable for soft-bellied city slickers in inclement weather. There were more or less ridiculous combinations of ropes and rope ladders and trapezes and wooden platforms at various heights, all attached to a thin metal superstructure. The teens were up doing gymnastics, on everything from climbing walls and balance beams to elevated catwalks and zip lines, some quite high. All of these ridiculous-looking helmeted squirrels were secured via long safety ropes. If you can call that "secured." The end of each rope was being held by equally ridiculous-looking kids with metal trash-can lids strapped to their heads. What kind of freaky game was this? Plunge to Your Death: High School Edition?

But one guy stood out amid all these losers. He looked like he had beamed directly out of the latest *Indiana Jones* movie into the remotest area of the Eifel Mountains, and his name was Dominic Nolde. I realized it was Dominic when Gregor and Jenny finally showed up at the ropes course and introduced themselves to the teacher, who pointed them toward the star of the event. Dominic was standing tiptoed at the edge of the highest platform, about twenty meters in the air, when he slowly dropped backward into nothingness. Very, very slowly. At ground level, there was a cluster of four rope groupies handling his line, controlling the increasing weight by slowly adjusting the line as they lowered him evenly down. But the sudden appearance of cops who wanted to chat with the wannabe stuntman unsettled the line bearers, and the rope jerked and joggled briefly as Dominic nervously turned his head to look at the ground from the air.

Aha. So his nerves were not made entirely of steel.

Dominic finally returned to terra firma, his face slightly pale. He unhooked himself from the rope, and as he shook hands with Gregor, the cop introduced himself and suggested they have a friendly chat. The two walked over to join Jenny. The experiential-education specialist, a.k.a. teacher in a tin hat, looked on with curiosity but from a distance.

Gregor introduced Jenny, and Dominic practically batted his eyelashes at Jenny-Bunny, he was so enamored with her.

"Hi, Dominic," she said. "Is it OK if we use first names?"

"Fine by me, even though we're supposed to be addressed as Mr. and Ms. now that we've started high school."

That's one of those German things: little kids go by first names, big kids go by last names. Although I don't recall anyone ever calling me "mister" back in the day. I guess Dominic was all, like, *I'm a big boy now, but since you're a cop, I'll let you talk down to me.*

"We'd like to ask you a few questions about your relationship with Yasemin Özcan. How long did you date?"

"What's up with Yasemin?" Dominic asked. He looked first at Gregor and, when he didn't answer, at Jenny. She turned red.

"Please answer the question," Gregor said.

"Did something happen to her?"

"Where do you get that idea?"

God, Gregor. Dumb question. Dominic looked like he was about to say the same thing, but then he frowned instead. "What am I supposed to think when the police show up all the way out here in the woods asking questions about her?"

"Let's get back to the questions then," Gregor replied flatly. "How long did you date?"

"Almost a year."

Wow, a year! At that age, that's, like, half your life.

"Why did you break up?" Gregor asked.

Dominic blew air out his mouth like a tire with a nail problem, shoved his clenched fists into the pockets of his jeans, and looked up at the sky. "You'll need to ask her yourself."

"We're asking you."

Uh-oh. Was it just me, or was Gregor starting to sound like the "bad" cop on some TV show?

"No idea. One day she just starting bitching about stuff. It was like there was suddenly something wrong with *everything*. I really liked her, but at some point I bitched back at her, and then she was through with me."

He looked back at Jenny, who still hadn't found her poker face again. Their eyes locked for a moment, and then Jenny quickly lowered hers.

"What did she suddenly start complaining about?" Gregor asked.

"Oh, just, like, tons of stupid stuff."

Gregor glared at him to prompt a more forthcoming answer.

"Like, she suddenly went vegetarian and thought I shouldn't eat animals anymore either. Then she started hating everything I wore because brand-name clothes 'promote social injustices.' And it bugged her that my family lives in a big house. She kept going on and on about capitalism and redistribution of wealth and how our house is the 'epitome of the complacent and exploitative bourgeoisie.' She said I preached humanistic values but didn't actually want to change anything about the 'conditions of increasing social indifference.'"

Huh? Had I accidentally put on some kind of Marxist-Leninist earphones? The guy was spewing practically entire manifestos in the hyperperfect language of literary German. Jenny stared at him, fascinated, and even Gregor briefly forgot the next line of the script he'd shamelessly ripped from *CSI*. But he quickly pulled himself together.

"And is all of that true?"

"Whatever," Dominic said with a shrug and an exasperated grin on his face. "My father and I live in a big house, yeah. The rest is bullshit. My father is a starving left-wing intellectual, and we don't even own the big house we live in. We rent it."

"All of these criticisms you've just listed sound more like made-up justifications," Jenny suddenly interjected. She seemed to have found her way back to professional form. "What do you think was the real reason Yasemin started acting differently toward you?"

Dominic's shoulders slumped and he looked at the ground. "Maybe she was stressed out at home. She was getting to the age when traditional Turkish parents start thinking about picking men to marry their daughter off to."

"Did she ever make any comments along those lines?" Jenny asked with interest.

Dominic shook head. "No, she never did. But Mehmet said things like that."

"Her brother?" Gregor asked.

"Yep."

"Do you have any idea where Mehmet might have gone?" Gregor asked.

"Gone?" Dominic asked, confused.

"That's right," Gregor said. "Mehmet is missing."

They blabbed for a while about Mehmet. Turns out Dominic had no idea where he was either. But if you asked me, Dominic seemed at least as worried about Mehmet as he was about his former bed warmer. Then Gregor sent Dominic back to play Tarzan with his classmates some more.

So, to summarize, all we learned was that that Pretty Boy was a pretty serious dumb-ass. He didn't know why his girlfriend dumped him, he didn't know where her brother was, and he hadn't clued in that he had just been questioned as a witness in a murder case.

Gregor and Jenny spent a while near the ropes course watching the kids pulling their lines with more, or less, enthusiasm, and testing how stressed out various lofty heights made them feel. One thing was clear, though: Dominic was the coolest guy of them all. All the chicks kept throwing themselves at him. Literally. From twenty meters in the air. More than one teenaged girl managed to stumble her landing and conveniently fall into Dominic's strong arms—with varying degrees of success in making it seem unintentional.

What did this tell us about Yasemin, if she, the petite Turkish girl in class, was dating the hottest guy in the school? Or, who had been dating him until *she* dumped *him*? It was already established that she had been hot enough to date Mr. Cool here, after all. So the investigation was in the same place as before we had journeyed to the Eifel Mountains.

None of this bullshit was getting us any closer to the missing teacher. So I resolved to focus on Sibel Akiroğlu rather than waste more whole days tailing Gregor in his futile search for Yasemin's murderer. And that meant, back to the elementary school.

School was dismissed, it turned out, which is why I hovered around cluelessly for a while before remembering the teacher's older brother. I thought I'd go see what the slovenly Turk with the American-style fast-food habit was up to.

FIVE

Thursday, 5:10 p.m.

Akif Akiroğlu arrived at the building's main entrance at the same time I did. His hand was shaking so much it took him four tries to get his key into the lock. And it was another three full minutes before he reached his apartment door. The unlocking procedure again unfolded in slo-mo, but finally, standing inside his own door, he dropped his jacket, slid his feet out of his boots, shuffled stocking-footed into the bathroom, and puked for a good quarter hour into the toilet bowl, which was already beyond filthy. After he was done, he took off the rest of his clothes, leaving me with two shocking sensory impressions:

First of all, every single one of his pores stank to high heaven of beer, smoke (and not of legal tobacco products), cheap hard liquor, and sex. That last odor was clearly the freshest, but it was absolutely beyond me how a guy that schwacked could have talked his erectile tissue into rising to the occasion. So maybe he had had the sex first, and it was so bad it drove him to pickle his brain.

How he had ended up in his current condition wasn't as important as the issue of what conclusion I should draw from my second sensory impression, this one visual: Where was this guy coming from so fully cabbaged but with a fat handgun in his belt, a small handgun strapped to his ankle, and a switchblade strapped to his forearm? A switchblade? Wowza!

Finally Akif got a grip and shoveled spoonfuls of ground coffee into a coffee machine, filled the reservoir with water, and turned the appliance on. When he noticed he had forgotten to put a filter in, he shrugged and shook his head. Then he went into the bathroom to take a shower. His skin was practically sloughing off his body when he finally turned off the water and trudged dripping wet back into the kitchen, stirred five tablespoons of sugar into his murky coffee, and downed the first quarter liter of it, still scalding hot. Coffee grounds were stuck between his teeth and in the corners of his lips, but he didn't notice. He just stood there with his filthy coffee cup in his hand, still dripping water on the floor. The look in his eyes slowly grew a bit clearer, but he would keep staring off into space, motionless, for minutes at a time. I was starting to worry I was witnessing a case of slow-motion cardiac death with sudden-onset rigor mortis when he suddenly unleashed a scream and hurled his cup against the wall, showering the kitchen in coffee grounds and filling the room with clicks as porcelain shards ricocheted off the window. Then he collapsed to the floor and—fell asleep.

Hmm. Let's consider this for a moment. The guy has a serious drug problem. In addition, he has personal-hygiene issues and a sleep disorder but apparently not erectile dysfunction. So basically he's A-OK—well, except for the rocket launchers and cutting tools he keeps up his sleeves. How did this totally freaky guy even fit into a family like the Akiroğlus? And what did he do with, or to, his sister? Because it'd be the coincidence of the decade for a psychopath bristling with concealed weapons who tortures himself with scalding-hot unfiltered coffee to *not* be somehow involved in the sudden disappearance of his sister.

I zoomed through the apartment again, hoping to find an answer, but unfortunately he hadn't left any kind of confession lying around—not in German, at least—nor a ransom note he had forced Sibel to scratch out in her own handwriting, nor a key labeled "Sibel's Kidnapping Cell." *Nada.* Just the regular jumble of fast-food remains and high-tech multimedia gadgets with a drooling, snoring, naked Turkish man lying in the middle of it all—whose own drug-induced coma would undoubtedly last at least five hours.

I decided I'd check in on him again later.

For some reason I had the unsettling feeling that something bad was afoot on the bonsai front, so I quickly raced back to the hospital. The situation was unchanged, however: the physical shells of the kids lay still in their beds, with varying numbers of family members standing and sitting around. But no trace of the kids' souls. Instead, I sensed some distant vibrations . . . Like someone yelling from far, far away. I could tell the general direction, but I couldn't make out any of the words. I shot straight up in the air over University Medical Center to get a wider view. I was right: the flea circus was ghosting around to the north of me. I set course and zoomed off. The closer I got, the more I sped up, because it sounded like there was some serious trouble going on.

Niclas was whirling around in a glowing red cloud in the middle of an Internet café, squealing like a naked wheel rim on a brake dynamometer. I'm sure you know just the sound. Mouth-breathers were sitting in front of their computer stations, below, tearing out their hair. And at the counter, where a normally bored Turk manned the register, there were now three gel heads freaking out and bellowing at each other. Joe, Edi, and Bülent were orbiting Niclas, also bellowing (in the case of Bülent and Edi) and speaking calmly (in the case of Joe).

I studied the scene intently for a while. For those who aren't familiar with German gamer subculture, let me first explain what goes on in Internet cafés like this. Sure, there may actually be people who go to an Internet café to check the weather forecast or their e-mail. When they're done, they pay their fifty euro cents at the register and make their merry way home. But this doesn't apply to places like this, where the display windows have been painted opaque and the lighting inside is so dim you might think the owner hadn't paid his electric bill.

You have to understand that Germany routinely bans video games for being too violent, too gory, too racist, too Nazi . . . You get the idea. So in places like this, gel heads sit with their fingers all atremble, shooting each other to kingdom come, or racing cars against each other in driving simulators where more cars explode than in all the *Fast & Furious* movies put together. I'm sure there are Turkish equivalents of these games, where the enemy doesn't pop up with a head in a kaffiyeh but with the Stars and Stripes on his baseball cap, but you rarely encounter those since it's unwise to set foot in an Internet hole featuring illicit entertainment if your life is hanging in the balance.

However, in this particular hole, they actually did have some of that illegal Yankee-busting software. When you pulled your virtual trigger in here, you blew rows of Schwarzenegger clones into the infinite expanse of the universe.

And Niclas was *blocking* all the wireless connections in just such a terrorist den.

Everyone note: that kid had talent. And he had chosen a particularly extreme target. An authentic civil war was on the verge of breaking out among the hot-tempered garlic eaters, because the Wi-Fi problems had booted some geeks from the game, leaving others to attain galactic scores. And Niclas wasn't letting up.

He was being a regular poltergeist. He spun in circles, screeching and causing sparks to spray every which way, and no one and nothing could stop him. He'd have to stop at some point, though, because manipulating electronics is extremely tiring. When you run an interference play like that, the energy you otherwise use to keep yourself together just disappears. Either you stop before it's too late, or at some point you go poof, and, boom, you're gone.

At least, that's what I think happens. I've obviously never pushed it. *Duh.*

"Is that true, what you just thought?" Edi suddenly asked.

Ah, my presence had been noticed.

"Then do something," she said before I could respond. "Otherwise Niclas will be gone forever!"

"I hope he *is* gone forever," Bülent interjected loudly. "He's a bully and a bigot."

"Bülent's right," I said.

"We should all stick together," Joe said, struggling to control himself. His voice was trembling, but I couldn't tell whether from rage, anxiety, or excitement.

"He's always picking fights," Bülent growled. "He's got only himself to blame."

"We should give Niclas another chance," Edi said. "Please, Pascha. Keep him from going away forever."

Bülent shook his head and sulked off into a corner while Joe and Edi clung to me like pigeon shit on a shoe, badgering me to halt the raging vortex that was Niclas. But how? Had I been eating from the tree of knowledge or something?

"Just try," Edi urged me.

Hmm. I cautiously flew closer to Niclas. The vortex he had created tried to suck me in. It was a super-unpleasant feeling, like wind pulling out your hair.

"Niclas, cut the crap," I yelled.

"Grrr," was the only response. The vortex didn't ease up.

I flew even closer. The wind turned into a hurricane that almost tore me apart.

"Niclas, if you keep this up, you're going to end up inside that game, and those cumin connoisseurs are going to be shooting out your virtual brains every hour for the rest of eternity."

"What did Pascha just call us?" I heard Bülent demand.

The Niclas vortex slowed. "Like in *Tron*?" he asked.

I'll write our next bit of dialogue in normal sentences so you get what's going on, but at the time our words flew at one another like individual, torn-up scraps of letters.

"Yes, except without the happy ending."

"What do you mean, without the happy ending? I'm good. I could win."

"No, you jackass. Because you'll be *in* the game, not *out* of it. You know that the rules to the game are set from the outside."

I had no idea if the inside/outside thing made any sense because I'm no computer nerd. But it seemed to work.

The vortex lost velocity, slowing to the speed of a gentle breeze.

"I could do it," Niclas said, out of breath but defiant.

"Yes," Joe said. "We know that . . ."

"I could . . . I'm serious."

"We know . . . but leave the players alone now," Joe urged. "You've had your fun."

"Fun!" Bülent growled. "Very funny."

Niclas slowly stopped spinning and was finally floating in the air in front of us, exhausted, his hair amazingly, seriously tousled.

"Asswipe," said Bülent.

"Boy, you really scared me," Edi said.

"Come on, let's talk with Pascha about what we should do next," Joe said.

I'd just as soon have crammed all four of them into a sack and dumped them somewhere where they couldn't get into any more trouble, but unfortunately that doesn't work with disembodied beings. You can't lock us up. But what else could I do to keep the flea circus here under control?

"OK, kids, you should head back to the hospital now and—"

"Ugh, but it's so boring there!" Niclas groaned. "No Nintendo, no computer games, and they keep playing stupid kids' channels on TV."

"Yes, but you need a little rest, and I bet your parents are all there now reading to you—"

"We already know all those stories," Edi said.

Et tu, Edi? I hadn't expected *her* to whine.

"Then you'll listen to the stories one more time!" I roared. Goddammit, these bonsais were getting pissier than a chick who hadn't been shopping in two days.

"Let's make a compromise," Joe said. "We'll go to the hospital for now, but tonight we're coming with you into town."

The shorties' eyes gleamed at me.

"Nightlife in a city of a million people is not for dwarves who'd normally be home in bed with their blankies," I said resolutely.

"But nothing can happen to us," Edi said.

Shit, leave it to the brainy girl.

"Uh . . ."

"Awesome!" Niclas said.

"My dad is driving home from the hospital at ten. We can go out on the town then," Joe decided. "You can come along or not, Pascha. It's up to you."

Little Gandhi was seriously starting to piss me off.

Thursday, 5:55 p.m.

I had to talk to Martin. I needed his help as an interpreter because I had a ton of important questions to ask a few different people. And my investigation had been offering up only more and more questions but no answers.

So I raced over to the Institute for Forensic Medicine, where Martin can normally be found during office hours, and looked for him at his desk. No! Autopsy room? Nope. Toxicology? That was a new destination in the building for Martin lately, because at the start of the month, they had gotten this fancy new one-touch automatic tea maker up there that pours filtered water at *just* the right temperature over top-quality loose-leaf tea. So, boiling water for peppermint tea, water precisely one degree shy of boiling for black, and a perfect seventy-eight degrees Celsius for green. In addition, the machine preheated the teacup that you had to place under what's called the "shower head" before the end of the custom steep time, set in advance by the tea connoisseur. Thus, paying members of the Toxicology Department's "Tea Aficionados" group were able to prepare the finest tea, cup by cup, without having to resort to thermal carafes or teapot cozies. Teapot cozies—very few people know this, so be thankful I'm letting you in on the secret—happen to be mass murderers of the health-promoting components in green tea.

So, bingo, there Martin stood, in front of the greatest achievement of the third millennium, waiting for the steep timer to finish its countdown. *Five, four, three, two, one, beep!*

"Martin, I need your help looking for the missing teacher. I've got about twenty thousand questions, and I'll go crazy if I can't get any answers to them. So?"

Martin had removed his prewarmed cup filled with piss-yellow tea from the machine and was now carefully carrying it to a tall table three steps away.

"What questions do you have?"

"The brother of the missing teacher has been walking around with multiple handguns and a switchblade on him, and he still hasn't gotten in touch with the police . . ."

"I'm sure Gregor will call on him as soon as he considers it necessary."

"Gregor is looking for Yasemin's murderer—he's not interested in the teacher at all!"

"You have no idea what Gregor is interested in."

And this brought us back to one of my biggest problems. Martin is the only person whose thoughts I can read, and then only if he hasn't shielded them with a mental block or technical gizmos like anti-electrosmog netting. However, plenty of people talk about their thoughts; for example, Gregor discusses his investigations with Jenny.

"You know what, Martin? You're absolutely right. In fact, at this point you're the only hope for that teacher, who's undoubtedly being held in some dark, cold basement without heat, maybe even without light, without water and food—"

"Don't be melodramatic. It doesn't become you."

But melodrama became Martin quite well, since his heart was 100 percent malleable when it came to helping the weak and meek.

"I can't get involved in Gregor's investigation. First, because it would obstruct the work of Criminal Investigations and, second, because I cannot provide the least justification why I might be interested in the teacher."

"I can give a justification: Edi told me she was kidnapped."

"I don't have any way to be aware of that, as you perfectly well know."

If I could have puked, I'd have puked. Always the same problem. Martin doesn't want to admit to anyone that I exist, although Gregor and Katrin actually *do* know about me. That's a long story, but the upshot is that Gregor and Katrin just pretend I don't exist. After all, they can't admit there's a ghost haunting the Institute for Forensic Medicine or that the very same ghost helps out Criminal Investigations on cases. What would people think if they found out? So they deny what they know, which isn't hard for them since it's not like I can remind them I exist. By contrast, Martin has sworn he will never, ever tell anyone about me for fear people would think he's loopy. Well, loopi*er*. And this includes never mentioning me to Gregor and Katrin again. So that's why it's a problem every time he passes on, or otherwise uses, information he gets from me, because he can't say where he got it from.

"Fine, then I'll jet over to those little kids and tell them to write off their teacher."

Martin nodded absentmindedly because his thoughts were already back on the topic that was worrying him like no other at the moment: Birgit.

"Forget your hot girlfriend for a second, Martin! I'm trying to find a kidnapped teacher, and you're wasting time on heartache because your babe is in a pissy phase. It's normal! Get over it!"

"It's not at all normal," Martin said aloud and clearly, even though thinking would have sufficed. A young female toxicologist stepped into the break room at that moment and looked around, surprised to find no one apart from Martin. He nodded to her nervously and left the room. She watched him for a moment, confused, and then shook her head.

"You did talk to Edi's mother," I pointed out, "so if anyone asks, you could just say you got the tip about the brother from her."

"It was dumb of me to talk to her and even worse to leave her my business card," Martin lamented. "If that's discovered, I'll be in extremely big trouble with my boss and with Gregor."

"Martin, that teacher may die because you're being such a wuss!"

This was dirty pool because Martin inherently felt responsible for everything, even if it wasn't his responsibility. He moaned as he strolled down the corridor, carefully avoiding spilling his tea. The color and smell of the lukewarm liquid reminded me of a urine sample, but I decided not to mention that just now. He was totally deaf on that issue anyway.

"I'll have to think about it," he said with a sigh. "Either I'll ask Gregor how far he's gotten in his search for the teacher—"

"Or," I interrupted, "you're going to have to go pester the brother yourself."

I was eager to see how Martin would manage in the weapon-wielding geeks' cave.

I stayed on Martin, though, so he wouldn't get the idea he could procrastinate his way out of acting. I told him he had until seven to leave work for the day and then make his decision: Gregor, or Sibel's brother. At ten to seven I reminded him about his looming deadline. He pretended not to hear me. At five to seven I repeated my reminder, and at seven on the dot I unleashed a piercing whistle. Martin slammed both hands to his ears, although the sound wasn't actually coming from outside his noggin. Katrin, who was sitting kitty-corner from him in their shared office, looked up at him in alarm.

"What's wrong with you?"

"Headache," Martin moaned. "Sudden onset."

Katrin is superhot, with picture-perfect breasts and a chassis like a Ferrari, and she's damned smart to boot. She knows I exist, as I explained before, so she instantly suspected what was up. But she stuck to the unspoken agreement, blinked quickly a couple of times, and then mumbled something about offering Martin some aspirin. He refused. There was no pill to treat what was ailing him. No painkillers, at least.

"Maybe I should try some psychotropic drugs," he hissed at me in his thoughts.

"Yes, I'm sure that'd loosen you up," I replied. "And then you'll start talking about me out loud, and people will no longer be forced to doubt your sanity because they'll have conclusive *proof* that your timing belt has snapped."

Martin stopped midsentence in the report he was writing, switched off his computer, and with fake nonchalance asked Katrin if she'd heard anything from Gregor.

"No, he's swamped right now. He and Jenny drove out to the Eifel Mountains, I think, but they're not making any headway on the case."

"I could have told you that," I shared with Martin.

He let out a mental "pfff" at me and then stood up. "Where to now?"

I wanted action and I wanted fun, and the quickest way to get both was if I dispatched Martin off to the windowless weapon-junkies' lair. "To Sibel's brother."

Thursday, 6:40 p.m.

Not long after that, Martin arrived and rang Sibel's brother's doorbell at least ten times, but no one answered. I did a reconnaissance flight through the apartment and determined Akif wasn't there. How had that guy managed to be on the go again so soon? He should have been lying there delirious until the sun rose the next morning. Or the day after that, frankly. But no. For some reason, the schlub was back on tour already. It must have been something very, very important to lure him out of his well-earned drug coma. Maybe getting new drugs? Or stabbing some people? Or shooting them to death? The guns weren't anywhere to be found, in any case.

"The bird has flown the coop," I chirped to Martin, who was waiting, fidgeting in front of the door and repeatedly looking at his watch.

"Good," he replied without the least hesitation. "Then I can finally go home. I have to see how Birgit is doing."

I raced home ahead of him, because if there was anyone I really liked—apart from Martin, to whom I was connected by fate, and Katrin and Gregor—it was Birgit.

She was hunkered down on the toilet, staring at a stubby little plastic wand in her left hand. She had slapped her right hand over her mouth, bug-eyed.

At first I thought it was a thermometer, but normal people don't take their temperature sitting on the can. Then a lightbulb went off for me. I flew under her right shoulder and looked at the cross that had appeared in the little display. Birgit was pregnant.

Nooo!

What had I done to deserve this? Wasn't I already surrounded by snot-noses everywhere I looked? Yuck. Babies: terrorists of the nerves, shitters of diapers, tornados of screams, pukers of rice cereal. And everything revolves around those chubby little *bastards*. They constantly had to be fed, patted, and lugged around. Every shit earns its own commentary, every burp merits marveling, and every word-like coo is interpreted as early language development. A child in this household would make my life hell, not that I wasn't halfway there already. Papa Martin would completely ignore me; the whole apartment would be screamy. And gross. In other words: I wouldn't be able to stay here.

Now, you might not think homelessness is a critical issue for a ghost, but you'd be wrong. We ghosts need a home too. At least I do. And now that was being challenged by a tiny, gooey clump of cells. I was suddenly competing for Birgit's cozy corners before the little tyke even properly existed. And that was the nub of the matter: under no circumstances could I allow that dwarf to steal my home out from under me. But how was I going to finagle that?

"Have you talked to Gregor yet?" I asked, sailing back to Martin. He was only a few steps from his trash can on wheels— a.k.a. his ancient Citroën 2CV—which he had parked on a side street.

"No, why?"

"Since we haven't caught up with the missing teacher's brother yet, we need to meet with Gregor and hear how his investigation is going."

Martin frowned. "Um, no. That was not the arrangement we agreed to. I'm going home now. I need to see Birgit—"

"Birgit's fine. I just stopped by home myself. She's tired and heading to bed. There isn't anything you can do for her at all."

"If I could just be with her . . ."

It's hard enough putting up with Normal Martin. It's harder yet putting up with In-Love Martin. But Worried-about-His-Sweetheart Martin is a test of nerves only a real hero could rise to. I bridled my frantic urge to tell him what a pathetic wuss he was and instead tried the "you need to save the teacher" angle again.

"I know you know that every day counts when it comes to finding a kidnapping victim alive, and you're the only hope this teacher even has—because no one else has noticed she's missing."

"But Gregor . . ."

"Gregor is busy looking for a murderer."

"But I can't . . ."

"You could at least put his nose on the right trail."

Martin sighed and took his cell phone out of his pocket. He unlocked it and scrolled down to Gregor's name in his contacts. His finger hovered over the "Call" button, but then he put the phone away again. "No. I need to see Birgit."

He let down his mental wall, since all his thoughts were focused on Birgit anyway. Then he unlocked his swaying cardboard box of a car—have you seen how a 2CV handles curves?—and pottered on his way.

This was doubly unacceptable. On the one hand, I now faced a frightening future amid a young family with a caterwauling crawler about the house, and on the other hand, I was being rele-gated to mere "observer" status in the case of a murdered teenager and a missing teacher. This was no way to solve cases! I needed Martin to be my mouthpiece so I could communicate with the earthly plane. And with a baby in the picture, my mouthpiece would be out of commission indefinitely. And that wasn't going to work for me. I needed to take some kind of defensive action. Or . . .

Did I even need to?

Was the wailing wurst trying to force its way into Martin and Birgit's life even welcome? Hadn't those two ever discussed family planning? Didn't Birgit have career ambitions at the bank where she works? She definitely had the spirit to be an executive chick, after all. I hoped she wanted *that* modern lifestyle and not a pregnancy: no stomach horribly distended like a beached whale, no boobs leaking milk everywhere, no spit-up on her shoulder, no lullabies that rhyme *good night* and *bedight* (what does *bedight* even mean?), no seventeen colds a year or measles, mumps, or diarrhea, and whatever else those disgusting little bacilli sewers drag into the house on their sticky hands. Instead, Birgit could keep her rockin' body, hire a male secretary, and enjoy a fat bank account and showy office with a leather seat where that same sec-retary could occasionally join her to take dictation. Way hotter than pushing a stroller everywhere.

I passed Martin's trash-can-mobile, which was swaying its way through the streets of Cologne, the windshield semi-opaque with condensation from the cold, wet November fog of the Rhineland. Martin was listening to a classical channel on the radio, trundling along in the rightmost lane. Even the greenies on bikes were passing him, and he was getting flipped off right *and* left, because encumbering traffic in a rolling sardine can does not instill camaraderie in other users of the road. But Martin didn't notice any of this. There was only one thought in his brain: Birgit.

She was asleep when he got home. Martin stood for a solid twenty minutes next to her side of the bed, still wearing his winter coat, as he wrestled with waking her or letting her sleep.

"Let her sleep. Otherwise she'll just be all bitchy again."

"Birgit is not bitchy. She's come down with something. She's *ill.*"

His and my estimations of the situation were 100 percent identical on that point, except of course he didn't know what he was talking about, and if he had known, he'd likely have articulated himself differently.

I asked him to call Gregor again, but he waved me off.

I *ordered* him to call Gregor, but he sealed all his mental bulkheads.

Instead, Martin went to the living room and sat on the sofa to start cataloging street names on his city maps. For those who can't imagine this, let me explain briefly: by now most of you know that Martin collects city maps. More-modern city maps have a concordance of street names, but really old maps lack that. So Martin makes his own. He sits with an old city plan, neatly and meticulously writing down each street name he finds in the drawing. Then he alphabetizes everything and takes delight in the result, even though not another soul on earth knows what this shit could possibly be good for. But it relaxes him.

It drives *me* crazy watching him, though, so I bailed and zoomed off to find Gregor. In the time I had left before the bonsais planned to set out on their nighttime tour of the big, bad city, I thought I might catch wind of some news from him.

Gregor and Jenny were sitting in NOT IN KANSAS, munching on cold, greasy pizza and staring at the bulletin board.

"The brother, Mehmet, still hasn't shown up," Jenny said with her mouth full. "I talked to his friend, the one his dad gave us the number for. Uh . . ." She paused and glanced at her notes. "Şükrü Bozkurt. He says Mehmet was conspicuously quiet the last time he'd seen him, but he didn't know why. He said he didn't seem to want to talk about his sister at all, even though they got along well otherwise. Mehmet didn't want to go into detail, but his friend said there had to be *some* reason."

"What's that supposed to mean?" Gregor asked.

"Well, the delightful Mr. Bozkurt went on to tell me that Yasemin was a whore who dressed provocatively and had the wrong friends. He said Mehmet was much too lenient with her."

Gregor forgot to chew and stared agape into space for a while. It wasn't very appetizing, but Jenny didn't interrupt his meditation. She just looked away.

"Was he fucking around with you?" Gregor asked finally.

"I don't think so," Jenny said.

"OK, we'll put a missing person notice into the system internally, but we won't announce anything to the media," Gregor told Jenny. "And then let's get a location on Mehmet's cell phone."

Jenny-Bunny nodded.

"The murder will be in the papers in the morning," Gregor mumbled as he went for another slice of pizza. "We'll be fucked at that point anyway." A strand of cheese hung out of the corner of his mouth.

Jenny was always writing in her little red notebook, leaving me to wonder if she wrote shopping lists and secret poems in it too. Unfortunately she wasn't writing in regular letters but in those old-fashioned secretary swerves that no modern human can read anymore. Why did every earthling have to make my afterlife so hard?

It was nine o'clock already, and Gregor looked like he might fall asleep standing. Jenny wasn't any better off. She yawned with her mouth so wide open I was briefly tempted to fly in and check things out in there for myself. But mouths pose the same problem as refrigerators: inside is dark as an elephant's ass.

"That's enough for today," Gregor announced somewhat unclearly since he was simultaneously picking a piece of pepperoni gristle from between his teeth. "Tomorrow morning at seven, here. Sleep tight."

Oh, great. Once again I'd just been left hanging, hovering around in the air, so extraneous to everything and everyone that it seriously made me want to barf. It wasn't worth heading to the movies for an hour, nothing was on at Martin and Birgit's, and now the detectives were going home for the night.

Maybe I could kill an hour in the emergency room? I liked to hang out there because I was always hoping to run into a soul at the moment of its liberation, someone who might stay with me. Preferably a well-built babe like Angelina Jolie, except with a smaller mouth. I could never kiss Jolie; I'd be terrified of being devoured whole. Which actually doesn't matter since it's not like I can kiss anymore, but you can't just abandon certain preferences, even as a ghost.

The emergency room was relatively quiet. There were only a couple of flattened motorcycle drivers who had spent some of their evening airborne after being rammed by an Eastern European trucker. One was dead on arrival. The second separated from his earthly shell shortly after getting here.

"Hey, how's it going?" I called at the newborn soul as it escaped the twisted form on the gurney like a fart.

"Oh, shit, man. What's going on?" the guy mumbled. "Where am I?"

"Layover," I said. "Stay cool."

"And wh-who are you?"

The form on the gurney looked linebacker tall. In his leather gear, he looked a little like a seal that had eaten too much omega-3 fat, but the voice he was talking to me in was weak, meek, and close to tears.

"I'm Pascha. I've been here a while. Dead, that is. But it's cool. Don't freak out."

"No pulse," the nurse yelled as several aides dashed over briefly from their respective broken bones, axes in legs, and bitten-off ears. Electroshocker ready, leather gear cut off.

"Hey, that j-jacket cost almost a thousand euros," the soul stammered.

"You won't need it up here," I said, trying to comfort him. "It fit like shit anyway. Way too tight."

The body below us convulsed.

"I don't want to die," the soul cried.

"Too late," I explained—although I had my doubts. When they put the electroshocker on him, it briefly pulled his soul toward the body, kind of like a vacuum cleaner.

"I don't want to die!" he bellowed again as the next shock buzzed, and his soul suddenly sucked all the way back into his body.

I sighed and shrugged. We wouldn't have been good soul mates anyway.

Speaking of soul mates, the shorties were undoubtedly waiting for me by now, so I zoomed back over to University Medical Center. In Niclas and Bülent's room, the two mothers were perched on their offsprings' beds, taking pains to silently exude their mutual contempt for each other. That was my sense at least, although I couldn't peer into their heads. Niclas's mother sprayed lavender fragrance from a little bottle at regular intervals so that it would waft toward the other bed as she fanned herself with her magazine. Bülent's mother pretended not to notice anything. She wasn't reading. She wasn't fanning. She was just holding Bülent's hand. The pudgy little ghost had crept deep into the folds of her wide jacket and was resting quietly, while Niclas ran for safety every time his mother sprayed her lavender.

The scene was too pathetic and the sickly sweet fabric-softener smell too strong, so I flew over to Joe and Edi, hoping I might find more action there.

Instead, I landed smack-dab in the middle of a picture album. Edi's mother had the pages of family photos open across her lap as Joe's father sat on the edge of his chair beside her, looking at the images as she shared anecdotes from Edi's childhood. Edi was sobbing as she hovered over her mother's left shoulder, and Joe hovered over her right. He tried to calm Brace-Face down, but she kept squeaking like a poorly played viola.

". . . not that bad, Edi. That's just something that parents do."

"But I don't want other people to see," she said between sobs.

I knew what she meant once I glanced in the album. The photo featured the lovely Edi as a baby, lying on her back on her changing table in nothing but her shirt. In full color on a high-gloss print, filling the album page in extra-large portrait size.

The sight reminded me of a piggy bank, but I shouldn't have thought that—or at least been more careful—because she noticed me and came rushing at me, howling like an air-raid siren. "You don't have any business here, Pascha, and if you say something so mean like that again, then . . . then . . ." Her voice broke and she started sobbing again.

"Quiet!" I roared back. She was so shocked she briefly snapped out of it.

"I didn't *say* anything, I only *thought* it, and I can't help that because it was a spontaneous spiritual brain wave. Now, turn the sirens off, otherwise you're staying here while I zoom into town with the guys."

"I don't even want to go with you—" she began to say, but Joe instantly appeared at her side and made a reassuring shushing sound.

He circled her in slow undulations, and Edi's electrons finally stopped crackling like sparks from a New Year's Eve sparkler.

"Parents are just like that. There's nothing you can do about it," Joe said with a sigh as deep as the custom woofers in an Opel GT. The 2006 roadster, obviously. "Parents will show off everything. My mom's been showing off a picture of me as a baby on the changing table as I watch myself pee, right into the air."

Edi stared at him in horror. I, however, couldn't help but laugh.

Now Joe's father was leaning forward over a photo showing a laughing man holding Edi upside down from both ankles while she tied her shoelaces.

Edi deflated like a balloon with a hole in it.

"Your dad?" Joe asked.

Edi nodded.

"When did he die?"

"Two years ago."

Edi's mother ran her index finger over the picture, and Joe's father rested his hand on her shoulder. "I'm sorry," he said softly.

"Forward march!" I ordered before all the bonsais burst into tears. "We're going to steal some cars."

Unexpectedly, I heard no objections. Not even from Edi, although I would have expected her to cite the criminal code, the impossibility of executing such a plan, and her fundamental lack of interest in illegal vices. She was apparently in a foul mood about her father. Pity. I wouldn't have shed a single tear if my old man had kicked it when I was a kid.

"Was he a criminal too?" Joe asked.

"Yessiree," I replied. "He was a killer. A hired killer."

Shocked into silence, the four of them (Niclas and Bülent had since joined us, each making an extreme effort not to notice the other) moved slightly away from me. I wasn't about to trot out the fact that my father killed *animals* and turned them into wurst. Killing is killing, after all, as Martin says, which is why he's a vegetarian. And when Martin's right, he's right—at least when it comes to my father.

S I X

We found ourselves in a recently developed, high-end residential area. There were tons of family-style minivans, but there were also a couple of hot rides that some of the families' daddies had splurged on. For someone like me, this was a land of milk and honey—or low-viscosity oil and carnauba wax. The first target for theft that I showed the kids was an awesome whip in a discreet shark gray. Matte. With rims so pricey that each one cost more than the annual salary of the automotive technician who swapped them out to put on the winter tires for the season. The thing was fresh off the line and couldn't have been there for more than a few days, parked in a giant heated garage between a Swedish station wagon and a 1972 Porsche 911 Targa, with a four-thousand-euro aluminum pickle on two wheels parked next to that.

Niclas instantly recognized the shark-gray job. Bug-eyed, he flew around it. "Whoa, hey, an R8!"

"An R8 *GT*," I corrected him. Seeing one of the 333 limited-edition R8s in person is an indulgence extremely few earthbound beings ever enjoy.

"Aluminum chassis, 5.2-liter V-10, 560 horsepower. From zero to a hundred in 3.6 seconds. Midengine design, dry-sump lubrication, purchase price about two hundred thousand euronimos."

"My mom says driving cars isn't good for the environment," Edi shared.

"She just can't afford a car," Niclas said.

"OK, let's have some fun," I said, shifting my apprentices' attention to the project at hand.

It's important to mention that this baby had one extra piece of equipment you can't get off the assembly line: an online connection to daddy's smart phone. Barry Bourgeois had an app on his smart phone that let him link to the onboard computer on his car, see. He could tell at a glance when, where, and how fast the car had been driven, how many r.p.m.'s his crown jewel had done, how much gas it had burned, what the average speed per kilometer was, and what condition the ceramic brake discs and magnetorheological damper fluid were in. Since this particular hot rod wasn't used for the daily commute, the app on his phone would display all this information as still within the green zone—except for fuel consumption, of course. And I wanted to change that.

Pretty much any member of a Western, industrialized society can hack a computer nowadays, and that includes even dimwits who wear nighties, fur pants, and banana boats. But what few people know is that it's just as easy to hack *cars*. Cars have onboard computers. They're typically equipped with a chip with all the functions on it that the manufacturer offers, for an additional fee, in its super-exclusive trim catalogs. So even if you haven't paid for it, the computer is actually programmed for remote-control window operation, electronic seat adjustment, tire-pressure-sensor integration, and on and on. If you insert the right code at the right spot in the software, then all of the functions—even those blocked in basic models—instantly become available.

It works the other way around too.

Now, we ghosts are nothing more than electromagnetic waves, and if the onboard computer is connected to a phone app and both devices are active, then a small, ghostly electromagnetic wave can show up in between the car and phone and wreak a little havoc in the electronics. And that was precisely my plan.

I made a running start, concentrated on the interface, and whirled around in a few circles. The power locks clicked up, the hazard lights went on, and the surround-sound blasted some bass-heavy rumbling out from the garage. I hadn't released the parking brake, which was a relief because this kind of computer manipulation is kind of a, uh, gross motor skill.

"How'd you do that?" Bülent asked in amazement.

"Awesome!" Niclas said.

"I hope you didn't break anything," Joe muttered.

"That's not nice."

That last comment was from Edi. *Duh.*

And then things got popping in that household in a flash. Lights on in the dining room, lights on in the hallway, lights on in the foyer, buzzing from the automatic garage door, and there he was: the lord of the manor, wearing Birkenstock clogs, his smart phone in his hand and a megastupid expression on his face.

I locked the doors again. He unlocked them with his phone. I locked them again. He unlocked them again, and this time I let him have his way. He got inside, and I locked the doors again. And turned the engine on. This time he freaked out.

"Stop that!" said Edi.

"Keep going!" Niclas laughed.

Bülent stayed silent, clearly fascinated, and Joe withheld judgment for the moment. I got the impression the real boy in Joe thought the scene was awesome and was enjoying it, but the miniature pedagogue in him had reservations. Today I wanted the real boy to win out.

Meanwhile, the Audi jockey had dissolved into full-on panic mode. He kept pressing the buttons on his remote key, he hit every button he thought might help, but he kept forgetting one thing—namely, to turn off the Wi-Fi connection between his phone and the car. We wouldn't have had a chance if that channel hadn't been open.

I didn't want to make the car go kaput, and actually I was getting a little bored. So I stopped my intervention, and the Audi jockey calmed down a bit when he realized that the buttons on his phone and his car were back to doing what they were intended to do. He got out of his buggy with quivering knees, poured the cold sweat out of his cork footbeds, and staggered back into his living room. If I'd had time, I would have loved to hear him talking to customer service later about the evening's events. They probably wouldn't commit him after only one episode like this, so I made a mental note to stop back here on a regular basis. But for now the next stage of our evening program was on deck.

My trainees followed me more or less reluctantly, and Niclas did so only after I promised to teach him how to hack a car.

We whooshed a few blocks farther where we found a not-quite-new Porsche Cayenne Turbo, which hadn't even once left the asphalt in its lifetime. No matter, since crossovers like this were only supposed to *look* like they could go off-roading. It had been washed, clear-coated, and presumably freshly waxed, simply swallowing the light from the streetlight in its dark-black paint. Like a black hole.

"Awesome," Bülent whispered. "How do we open this one?"

But I stopped a meter away from the Cayenne as though I had flown into a wall.

"This one's a no-go," I said. "Taboo."

"Why?" Edi asked, curious. She flew to within a centimeter of the tinted windows and peered inside.

"Dangerous." I could hear my own voice shaking. "Life threatening."

"I don't get it," Joe whispered. "Why?"

"Because it belongs to a really dangerous person."

"A gangster?" Niclas asked all excited.

"A drug dealer?" Bülent suggested.

The four of them were now orbiting the car like a swarm of wasps around a hot, gooey slice of German plum tart.

"Worse," I explained in a grave voice. "You see that thing in the backseat?"

I sensed confusion.

"That's right," I said. "A child seat. The car belongs to a mother."

"I don't get it," said Niclas.

"You can steal a car that belongs to a drug kingpin or the chancellor, but you are never, ever allowed to steal a mother's baby bus. A capo is easy enough to survive. The chancellor doesn't have the time of day to worry about it. But a mother will k-i-l-l kill you."

The four of them stared at me, waiting for the punch line, but I was dead serious. I had tried one time to pinch an A-Class that was parked outside a daycare. It was an emergency, because the Ferrari that had actually been my target had gotten towed right from under my nose, and I *had* to get hold of it before it made it to the impound lot, which was under gapless video surveillance.

I nearly paid for that operation with my life. The mother came running after me like an Olympic champion, and when I was forced to brake at the arterial, she tore open the driver-side door, grabbed my hair with her right hand, and gave me two serious clips around the ears with her left.

"How am I supposed to take Lisa-Marie to ballet class if you steal her car?" she shrieked as she pushed me to the ground and perforated my kidneys with the pointy tips of her pumps. "And her piano lesson after that. And her photographer appointment at six . . ."

The rest of what she said just kind of flew past me as I crept with mortal fear between two parked cars and hoped the police would come and arrest me.

"And?" Edi asked. "Did they arrest you?"

Bülent and Joe were grinning from ear to ear, Niclas was smiling at me with disappointed contempt, and Edi was eagerly waiting to hear the end of my story.

"Not likely," I answered with pride.

Actually, the mom hadn't bothered to keep following me because she had to chauffeur Lisa-Marie to her next appointment, see, and so she left me bleeding and half-unconscious on the sidewalk. And the Ferrari was of course long gone. That was the only order that ever slipped through my fingers.

"I'd *love* to steal some really cool gangster car sometime," Niclas said.

"Sure," I said. "So let's change crime scenes."

Now, there are areas of Cologne you're better off not looking in on without an invitation. Especially with kids in tow.

And that's exactly where we were headed.

"I want to see a *really* cool car. Like, a mob boss's car. With hidden weapons and rocket launchers and a wet bar and armored panels . . ." Niclas said, pretending to fire a machine gun all around him. "He'd drive it to the Turkish neighborhood and take down Turks."

"You are such a stupid jack-off," Bülent bellowed.

"You're the jack-off!" Niclas yelled back.

"And a jack-off that smells like garlic!" Niclas yelled again.

"Neither of you even knows what a jack-off is," Edi observed.

That hit home. The cockfighters stayed quiet until Niclas ruffled his feathers again to quip, "And you do?"

"Yes," Edi said. "My mom explained it to me."

The notion of your own mother telling you what something like jacking off is shocked Niclas, Bülent, and me in equal measure. Joe smirked. Either he knew something we didn't know, or he was glad Edi had come out top dog in our crew.

"They only have mob cars like that in movies," Edi continued. "James Bond has a car like that."

Niclas had pulled himself together again. "James Bond isn't a mobster," he retorted.

"So do you want to go see gangsters or cars then?" Joe asked.

The bonsais were really worse than fleas on your sack: they kept on and on and on with their bullshit, no commas or periods. And there was no power-off button I could push. I seriously needed to get Martin to have a firm word with his white-coated colleagues and bring this brood back to life again. I wouldn't be able to take the never-ending bickering much longer.

"Wow!" That was Niclas.

We had arrived. The big boys were hanging out here with their big cars. The jiggy joint with the back room wasn't all that crowded yet. It was before midnight, after all, but there were a few rad rizzides in there already. Including a fuck-me-red 1969 Opel Rekord C, which I could tell had a nonstandard replacement engine with 259 horsepower under the hood. Niclas stopped and stared at the car, his awed face contorted like he might puke. But instead he paid a flying visit underneath and resurfaced looking like he'd been to paradise and back.

"Hey, Pascha, how do we crack *this* car?" Niclas yelled.

"We don't," I answered, distracted. "We don't steal crime lords' cars."

"Aw!" Niclas, Bülent, and Joe whined in unison.

Edi studied us as though we were six-legged insects climbing up the walls.

"Well, OK . . . if the car didn't belong to one of those mental cases inside, we could theoretically do it like this."

I zoomed over and laid out the fundamentals of car cracking for vehicles like this 1969 model, which was easy, because back in the day when this gem was first bathed in the lights of an assembly line, concepts such as *electronic antitheft system*, *motion detector*, and *driver identification system* hadn't yet been invented. Then we studied four other models, two of which featured the aforementioned electronic bells and whistles. The sproutlets caught on to my methods quickly, Niclas and Edi quickest of all. Niclas even took the time to imitate all of the physical motions he would need to know; no doubt he'd try stealing a car at some point after he'd returned to his own body.

Brace-Face had the clearest idea of what was going on but, unfortunately, the worst attitude as well. She kept getting in our faces about how it's illegal and childish and how criminals always get caught in the end.

"Nonsense," I said. "No one ever caught me."

"Or bumped off, then," she added defiantly.

Chicks always need to have the last word.

Despite our spoilsport, it was kind of cool passing on my highly exclusive expertise. Plus, you never knew when such knowledge might prove helpful to these snot-noses later in life.

After four hours of my guided tour through Cologne's nightlife, I finally took them back to their hospital rooms. They seemed tired, although I couldn't tell if that was because of their induced comas (I'm full-on dead and never get tired, but maybe still-living souls need their sleep), or if it was because of their age or sensory overload or something. They certainly had every right to be exhausted. After all, we had popped in on a strip club (where the boys' jaws had dropped to the nasty carpet and Edi had stayed surprisingly silent), a Russian disco, and—at Joe's express request—a she-male revue. Along the way, we men explained to Edi how an attractive, grown-up woman should look.

"Braces and blinkers are out," I said. "Or do you see any hot babes around here with four eyes and tinsel teeth?"

This was at the Russian disco, where babes all around us were wearing boob tubes with hot pants or miniskirts so short they might have been mistaken for belts.

Edi didn't respond. I got the impression she was sulking.

"Your hair needs to be long, so you're on the right track that way, but that vole-brown color is strictly for things that live underground. Blonde is good."

I sensed that Joe secretly thought I was right but didn't dare proclaim this aloud. Bülent perked up, bashfully, at the word blonde.

"High heels need to be at least seven centimeters . . ."

"High heels are bad for your back," Edi interjected.

"Your back doesn't interest men. There are other body parts that are more important."

Edi rolled her eyes, Joe stifled a smirk, and Niclas hadn't been paying any attention to our conversation at all because he was swirling around in the subwoofer. Bülent remained silently embarrassed while listening attentively the entire time.

"And there's lipstick," I continued.

"Lipstick is unhealthy," Edi blurted out, almost anticipating my comment. "If you wear lipstick every day, you'll ingest over three kilograms of it over the course of your life."

What does a man care what a chick eats? I thought. Especially since I didn't have the foggiest idea how many calories were in lipstick. "Don't get your panties in a knot," I said. "A woman without lipstick isn't a woman. She's a coat stand."

I rattled off several celebrity bed warmers to serve as good role models for Edi, but she couldn't follow me. I hoped her appreciation of decent clothes would blossom with her impending teenage hormones, because otherwise our little Brace-Face wasn't going to cut it in life.

On our way back we got in some subway surfing too. The pressure waves from the subway hurl you through the dark tubes, and it's an awesome feeling. For everyone except Joe. It made him sick every time. Wuss.

Friday, 2:27 a.m.

When I left the hospital, I was too restless to find a cuddly spot in Birgit's clothes, so I just zoomed chaotically through the city, my thoughts whirling equally aimlessly. Unintentionally, I found myself back at the original club with that hot set of wheels out front.

I didn't let the snot-noses in on this, and I'd never admit it, but I missed my life. Stealing cars was a freaking awesome enterprise. You get all this adrenaline rushing through your veins, and then you sit in a ride that's got a couple hundred horsepower raring to go, and then you stomp the gas pedal all the way down. Until you reach the posted speed limit, obviously, because most car thieves get caught when they attract the attention of some traffic cop.

But then the car is all yours for a couple of hours. You get to sit on the soft leather that still smells new, you tickle the engine so it moans in pleasure, and you know *you* took this sweetie pie— for yourself, all by yourself.

It wasn't the same as buying a car. Anyone could do that. No, you *took* it, and then it belonged to you more than it did to its legal owner with his fat bank account.

I floated over that awesome car a little wistfully, but then I noticed something move where there shouldn't have been any movement: in the dark shadow under the tree at the end of the parking lot. I flew in closer and stared in surprise at something that didn't have four wheels or two hooters but nonetheless commanded my full attention: Sibel's missing brother, Akif. He was hanging out with another guy in the darkest corner of the entire neighborhood, pretending he was bumming a friendly smoke off his buddy. But I had noticed a tiny movement the guy had made handing the cigarette to Akif. I couldn't tell what they had swapped at a distance, of course, but I was pretty sure it wasn't soccer-player cards or stamps. If guys like these were swapping things in dark corners like that, it meant only one thing: drugs.

The guy who was keeping Sibel's brother company looked like most guys hanging around in this area. One part gangsta, one part pimp, and a pinch of psycho. He had a Turk-fro greased with about a liter of used engine oil, golden bling around his neck, and a funky look on his face. Like I told the kids, you don't steal cars from guys like this. They'll shoot up their own cars as they drive off until they stop the thief, one way or another. And when you're drooped over the steering wheel all bloody and gurgling, they'll put a gun to your temple and say, "And this is for fucking up my car," and pull the trigger.

Well, I don't know if that's how it really goes. I've never been so dim as to try. But they make an effort to look that way, and so you keep your fingers off their cars. Works better than any electronic antitheft system.

Which of the cars in the parking lot was his? Probably one of the really big ones. Like a beat-up old Mustang that hadn't seen a detailer's chamois in twenty years, since the guy didn't seem like some big shot himself. Big shots also don't spend their time lurking in the shadows; they leave that to their water bearers. So I decided to tail the guy and memorize his license plate. If at some point I ever had the good fortune to actually contribute anything to this laughable investigation, at least I'd have a piece of information they could check out.

Two gunshots in quick succession hit me unprepared. Well, obviously they didn't literally hit me. They hit Akif, but they did surprise me. I had been scanning the parking lot, so I didn't see who'd shot who, but the answer was obvious enough since Akif was on the ground, and the gel head was standing over him, laying in some solid kicks to Akif's kidney area, and then he stuck something into the rear waistband of his pants (I naturally assumed this was his weapon). He spit on Akif and headed back out to the parking lot. I followed him, noting with pride in my talents that he got into the Mustang I had already scoped out. I memorized the license number and whooshed back over to Akif.

After swirling over so many of Martin's or Katrin's autopsies, at this point I was fairly familiar with the inner workings of the human body. I thus suspected that, with a bit of luck, the shot to Akif's abdomen might not have injured any vital organs, because Akif was pressing his hand to his side over a spot that in most people is used as storage for excess body fat. The shot to his upper thigh looked pretty nasty, by contrast, and I got the impression it also hurt more than did the hole in his spare tire. Akif pressed his left hand over his bacon hole to keep the blood from gushing out, and he braced his right hand on his knee as he crawled awkwardly on one elbow toward the street. He pulled his right leg limply behind him.

Some fat-ass loser with a hot babe at his side came out of the club at that moment, almost tromping on Akif's hand. The fat-ass didn't even blink and kept moving, but the chick screeched loudly.

"Hey!" fatty barked at the woman as he pawed her ass. "Don't you worry about him. You'll only buy yourself a headache."

He tried to push her into a Hummer, whose door some groveling brownnoser had unlocked for him all cool-like, but the woman kept up the fuss.

"He's hurt! He needs help."

Meanwhile, Akif kept his eyes straight ahead, crawling toward the street.

"He got into whatever shit he's in without you, so he can get out of it again without you."

"We can't just—"

Fat-ass stopped short, grabbed the chick's upper arm firmly with one hand, and used the other to roughly turn her head to face him. She blinked into his eyes, startled.

"If you want to help the guy, be my guest. I'm going now. But I'll come back and kill you if you mention my name. I was never here, and I didn't see anything."

Then he held the passenger-side door open for her.

"I'm coming!" she said. "But I'm going to pee my pants if I don't visit the ladies' room once more before we go."

He thought for a moment and then let go of her arm. His fingers had left five red imprints on her skin. "Your cell phone stays here," he growled, grabbing for her clutch. With a huff of frustration, she handed it to him and hightailed it back to the club.

As she teetered on platform sandals back through the front door of the club, I was torn between keeping an eye on the crawling dung beetle Akif and accompanying the stacked rack back inside, nestling myself into her knocker knoll as she shuffled her way to the bathroom. Not surprisingly I guess, I chose to travel with her. In the bathroom, she locked herself in a stall but instead of sliding the ridiculously thin, ridiculously short, ridiculously tight textile tube up and over her thighs, she leaned with one hand on the wall and reached down with her other to pull a miniature cell phone out of the platform heel of her left sandal. She dialed 110 for emergency services and whispered, "There's a man with a gunshot wound in the parking lot in front of Chilling Chili." Then she turned the phone off, hid it in her shoe, tottered back out to her doughy desperado and sped off with him.

I was speechless. What was I supposed to think about this Bond-girl routine? I'm not really that familiar with female footwear, but I was pretty sure the mini cell phone wasn't standard issue. Nor were her shoes. The chick had looked like one of those super-cheap bunnies, but then she went all guardian angel on me with her salvation sandals.

How freaky was that?

Meanwhile, nearby, Akif had almost made it to the street when the paramedics pulled up. First they had to punch him down so he'd stop resisting treatment, and then they tried to give him a sedative, but the taller of the two medics checked Akif's pupils and said, "He's got enough drugs in him for a whole boys' choir, so I'd prefer not to give him any more."

They strapped him tightly to the stretcher, lifted him into the ambulance, and took him to the ER. I followed along, but when the white coat on call finally arrived with his butcher knife, I cleared out—I can't think when blood's spraying through me.

And I had a ton to think about.

The missing teacher's brother was a drug dealer—or at least dealt with drug dealers—which explained his creepy lifestyle, the guns, and the safe. In addition, he was in trouble with someone who'd sent him a bullet as a present. Did his sister have anything to do with the trouble he was in? Maybe she had gotten wind of her brother's shady way of life and tried to rat him out. So Akif had no choice but to eliminate his own little sister? If so, was tonight's shooter avenging Sibel's murder?

None of that made sense, of course, but what *did*? If I couldn't get Martin to start asking some questions here pretty soon, I was gonna go bonkers.

Away to the apartment I went, only to find myself foiled again. Martin's alarm clock went off at six, as planned, but Birgit—who was still 99 percent in REM sleep or something—had used her 1 percent of available wakefulness to cuddle back up with Martin under the covers.

Martin put on his lamest of lame happy smiles as he closed his eyes and stayed put. He snoozed the alarm clock after a few minutes. Then he did it again. And again. And again. Each time the shrill chirps turned all my electrons inside out, so I cleared out of there—and into a freezing November morning of either slushy rain or very wet snow. Call it what you like, but I call it piss weather. There was only one thing left for me to do: time for my personal wellness routine.

First, I took off for a whorehouse on a side street, where it was quitting time for the girls. There, I kept them company in the shower by bobbing and romping through the apple-scented shampoo foam in their hair. After that I made my way to the public swimming pool, where the new lifeguard was doing preshift muscle poses naked in front of the mirror in the locker room. I could have laughed my ass off if I still had one, because the guy was flexing like he was a steroid junkie with a bruiser's body, but calling his a chicken chest would have been unkind to chickens. His ass wasn't any better, but he had a willy to compete with the best Arabian stallions. And quite the stash of high-gloss porn mags. I hate to admit it, but the lifeguard's dirty pictures turned out to be the saving grace of what had otherwise been a terrible morning.

SEVEN

I stopped in at the hospital to make sure the bonsais were still floating over their hospital beds, tired and lazy after their night of excitement, and I was reassured to find them doing exactly that. No one asked me to take them somewhere and do something, and no one followed me when I left. Edi thought about going to school, but the boys displayed no motivation whatsoever. I hoped they would continue feeling lazy for a good while longer, and I made my way to work. It's not like I didn't have anything to do, myself.

I was at the institute at eight, fairly confident Martin would show up around then. He was in the break room, waiting for the tea machine to finish its enlarged-prostate drip-drip-drip, when Katrin stormed in and breathlessly exclaimed, "God, Martin! I've been looking for you everywhere!" as she held out the screen of her smart phone for him to see.

"Huh?" Martin said, staring with utter confusion at so modern a device. A picture of Gregor was featured next to a little green text bubble, which read: *Yasemin's best friend is dead. Cause of death unclear. Coming?*

Zeynep, I thought sadly, shaking my virtual head and remembering the petite Turkish schoolgirl.

Now, you may wonder why Gregor sent this message to Katrin. Here's the deal: When someone finds a body and it's not immediately clear whether the deceased kicked the can naturally or with some help, they always call the cops. The cops then decide whether to call in a coroner as well. But the cops also do that when they're not sure themselves whether the death was ordered from on high or by another mortal.

So . . . when someone has obviously been shot to death, the cops don't have to call in the medical crew—but it's better if they do because the coroners have a special eye for evidence. For example, the pattern left behind by splattered blood and brains in the room might give them an idea whether the victim had been sitting or standing, whether he had been leaning forward or with his shoulder against the wall, whether the bullet came from above or below, and all sorts of other clever things that help criminal investigators reconstruct the sequence of events. It's important first and foremost for finding the perp and second for demonstrating later in court exactly how the murder transpired, because there isn't a court in Germany that will sentence a suspect if all the detectives know is that one guy *somehow* supposedly offed the other. German judges insist on things like *evidence*, see.

And so it's usually the most with-it cops who call in a coroner to a crime scene or discovery site. Dim cops sometimes forget (like Jenny did a couple of months ago during a killing spree that people at the Institute for Forensic Medicine . . . But that's another story).

Gregor is a good cop. I said that already, right? So he called for white-coated reinforcements, and Martin is a good coroner, so he looked up from the screen and into Katrin's eyes, then glanced wistfully back at his tea, which he had to leave behind to hurry back to his office and grab his coat. He was almost out the front door when Katrin reappeared before him, waving her phone directly in front of his face again.

"Here's another assignment," Katrin said. "But only for a doctor who's all man."

Martin cocked his head to the side and again squinted at the screen, this time at a message from one of the ER doctors at the hospital: *We have a patient here with a gunshot wound, and he's driving us up the wall. Do you think you guys maybe could take a look at him for us?*

Coroners also examine living victims of crimes, you see. If the victims don't voluntarily allow the examination—and that's exactly the scenario I suspected here, based on how the ER doc had worded his message—then they can be compelled to consent, as long as the doctor is the same sex as the patient. Martin took the phone, went through the details in the message, handed the phone back to her, and nodded. "All set. I'll handle the gunshot wound. You handle Gregor's new body."

To use slightly elevated language, this increase in body count left me *cautiously* optimistic. Because I happen to know the relevant dead-body statistics for metropolitan Cologne the way your balls know your crotch rocket. It's not every night there are ten gunshot victims in Cologne. Usually there's not even one. So it stood to reason that Martin was on his way to see Sibel's brother Akif, who had been injured in last night's drug deal. I seriously deserved a happy coincidence like this, which is why I whistled as I whooshed with Martin in his sardine-can-on-wheels toward the hospital.

And I was not disappointed: the guy who had been hurling abuse at the nurses and two uniforms in Turkish (you could tell verbal accostment in any language just from the face, gestures, and intonation) was in fact the same overtired, ghost-white, two-legged dung beetle who had crawled from the parking lot in front of the club. Martin said hello to everyone with his friendly nod and then shooed all the bystanders out. I wasn't a disinterested party, so I stayed.

"My name is Dr. Martin Gänsewein from the Institute for Forensic Medicine. I'm here to examine you, Mr.—"

"Fuck off" is what I presume Akif muttered. He said it in Turkish, but again his face gave his meaning away.

"His name is Akif Akiroğlu, the brother of Sibel, the missing teacher," I informed Martin.

He blinked twice to digest this information, cleared his throat, and then continued, "You don't have to speak to me, but if you would like to tell me anything, then it would best to say it in German, Mr. Akiroğlu."

He had him. Akif suddenly turned even paler than a ghost—and I should know—as he narrowed his eyes into vicious slits and glared at Martin. "How do you know my name?"

"I would like to examine your gunshot wounds." Martin set his briefcase on the chair next to the hospital bed and took off his coat.

"I asked you a question," Akif said.

"The doctor told me that you were picked up overnight by an ambulance and brought here. He said you're not being cooperative, you're not telling them your name, you don't have any ID on you, and you're harassing the nursing staff. I don't care about any of that. I am exclusively interested in your gunshot wounds."

"They aren't any of your business either. I didn't report anything to the police."

Martin wouldn't be dissuaded and picked up a clipboard with a form, and he started jotting the date, sex, and type of injury into the boxes on it. "A police report isn't necessary. Aggravated assault and battery—and a gunshot wound certainly counts—is a felony and is something the police always follow up on. Any gunshot wound is automatically considered a crime to be prosecuted ex officio, whether or not the injured party reports it to the police."

"You can jam the legal talk up your ass."

Martin was more than a little experienced dealing professionally with people like this guy, so he kept cool—in a way he never would in his personal life. "We have two options, Mr. Akiroğlu: we can do the examination with just the two of us here. Or the two police officers I just sent out can come back in and hold you down while I document your injuries."

"That's a violation of my right to human dignity under Article 1 of the German constitution," Akif muttered, somewhat resigned.

I was impressed he was aware we even had a constitution.

"Your injuries are evidence in a case of aggravated assault and battery with a firearm, and thus you cannot refuse to be examined under the German code of criminal procedure. Therefore, your human dignity doesn't mean shit to me at the moment."

Well, well. Martin had surprised us both. Martin, my little goose, had let the naughty *S*-word leave his lips. Even Akif did a double take at that, although he had no way to truly appreciate the historic moment he had just witnessed.

"Historic moment, nonsense," Martin growled at me in his thoughts. "The man is wasting my time, and I have the impression this is the only kind of language he comprehends."

"You're doing great," I said as Akif threw the hospital blanket off to grant Martin a glimpse of his thickly bandaged thigh.

I looked away as Martin began unwrapping the bandages and focused instead on the questions I hoped to finally get answered.

"Why hasn't Akif gotten in touch with Gregor?" I asked, and Martin passed on my question as Akif stared at him with mistrust from his pillow. But his mouth stayed shut, unfortunately.

"And where are your weapons now?" Martin continued with my assistance.

No answer.

"Do you know where your sister is?"

Silence.

"What will the police find when they take a look inside your safe?"

I couldn't read Akif's mind, of course, but I could interpret facial expressions, and based on those I'd say that question had freaked Akif out pretty bad. No doubt he was wondering: *How does this doctor with the neatly parted hair know about my name, weapons, sister, and safe?*

"Did you know that another body was found this morning—the body of a person who is indirectly related to your sister?"

Nada.

"And what did that girl and your sister—two high-school students—have to do with the teacher?" Martin asked aloud, and then silently again to me.

"If you had had two minutes of time for me the last few days, I'd have explained the whole caboodle to you long ago and we'd be that much further along in our investigation now," I said. "Yasemin, the first body, had the phone number—"

Our silent conversation was interrupted by a shriek out of Akif. It didn't have to do with what we were talking about but with the medical examination.

"Who?" Akif asked, tears in the corners of his eyes.

Martin looked up from his autopsy-like examination and regarded Akif with a cold stare: "I'm sure you know the saying from TV," he told Akif without any prompting from me. "I'm asking the questions here."

He held back a self-satisfied grin, and I had to make an effort not to puke virtually over Martin's shoulder for his abysmal job of playing cool.

"So," Martin went on, "do we need to open your safe to get a few answers, or will you talk to the police?"

"Send the cops in. I'll talk," Akif said. Then he closed his eyelids and played dead for the rest of the exam. So I left Martin and his lazy-ass dealer and visited Gregor at the discovery site of Zeynep's body.

In this case, Gregor had had no choice but to call in a coroner, because the cause of death was unclear. No bullet wound at a vital location on the body, no stab wounds, no rope around her neck, no needle in her arm. Instead, on the outside at least, an almost perfectly intact but dead teenage girl lay in her own bed. A girl who would have been a witness in Yasemin's murder case: Zeynep, Yasemin's supposed best friend.

The CSI crew was already at work, three figures in white protective gear swarming through the room, which was bigger than Yasemin's room but otherwise looked similar. There were fewer frills and no floral bedspreads but tons of knickknacks and kitschy junk everywhere. An American flag was hanging peacefully beside a Turkish one, some Turkish pop star with bedroom eyes looked out from a poster over the desk, and the unspeakably schmaltzy mug of a movie vampiress blighted all of the other walls, a vision you could escape nowadays only in the waiting room for the urologist.

Gregor's and Katrin's heads hung low as they busily processed their paperwork.

"If she knew something important, either she didn't tell me or it didn't register with me," Gregor was saying as I flew in.

"Don't blame yourself," Katrin said.

"Do you have a suspect already?" Gregor asked instead of responding to that point.

Katrin hesitated. She said, "Hmm."

"Tell me—even if there's only a one percent chance it'll pan out," Gregor asked.

"Intoxication," Katrin mumbled as she read. "Here, do you see the foam-like bubbles she's got under her nose?"

Gregor didn't look that closely at the image Katrin held up for him. I wouldn't say Gregor is squeamish, but he's never eager to study the unappetizing details up close either.

"It usually doesn't mean much," Katrin said. "It could be a clue pointing to any number of possibilities, although drowning and intoxication are classics."

"And drowning is unlikely in this case," Gregor said after scanning the room for a moment.

The room was spartan, not even a goldfish bowl.

"Did you guys hear all of that?" Gregor asked the CSI team that showed up at the door, looking like aliens in their white protective gear.

"You want everything, even the smallest detail," the taller alien said.

Gregor nodded. "Every glass, every bottle, every package of pills, every plastic bag, every snippet of aluminum foil, every envelope, every pair of jeans, every shirt with pockets, every jacket. Study every dish and every centimeter of floor for particulate matter. Take all of the bedding. Every tiny bit of paper a suicide note could be written on. And from you . . ." he said, turning to Katrin.

"I know," she said, cutting him off. "We're doing the full monty, including a complete tox. All I need from you is the order from the public prosecutor; you know this is going to cost a lot."

I left the two of them alone with the aliens. It's not much fun watching a forensic pathologist, which is what a coroner is, determine how long a corpse has been lying somewhere (or "time of death," for all of you kindergarten dropouts). I won't lay out all the details here, but it involves a long thermometer and rectal temperature. My readers with medical training will grasp something quite specific from that; everyone else can go ahead and imagine something vaguer.

Gregor left the room shortly after me, taking a seat in the living room with the mother, who was hunkered down on the sofa in tears. She was wearing Western clothes without a headscarf, she had makeup on, and despite her advanced age of at least forty, she could have passed for pretty if there weren't thick black streaks of makeup running down her face like oil spills.

"When did you determine that your daughter . . ." Gregor paused. "That something wasn't right?"

She panted out something like ". . . seven . . . woke up . . . school . . . too late . . ." in between sobs.

"Where was she last night?"

Shrug. "Back pain . . . hot-water bottle . . ."

Gregor's face clearly expressed his frustration, but he had to realize that, for the moment, he wasn't going to get any reasonable information out of this woman. "Do you have anyone you can call?" he asked. "Someone who can be with you right now?"

She nodded.

"Give me the number."

Whoa. Gregor was evidently extremely concerned, because normally he doesn't personally call in someone's pit crew.

She fumbled for her cell phone, found the number, then handed the phone to Gregor. He dialed the number, and when the woman who answered confirmed she was the best friend of Zeynep's mother, he asked her to come over immediately. Then he said good-bye to the mother, Katrin, and the cart crew who had showed up to haul the body away, and he drove downtown to his office.

"We're going to drive to the school and talk with everyone who knew Yasemin and Zeynep," he announced to Jenny from the doorway. She was sitting at her desk copying information from her notebook and from various other pieces of paper into a computer file.

I took a closer look and saw that Jenny had stayed focused on Yasemin and was now reconstructing the last day of Yasemin's life. The deceased woke, dressed, rode the bus to school, took subjects for up-and-coming smart-asses such as algebra and Spanish, but also balloon bingo subjects like social sciences and psych. German schools generally get out at one for the day, which is when she headed home for lunch. Then homework in the afternoon in her room, and at four she went out, telling her mother she was meeting up with a group of kids for a class project. And no one had seen her since.

I was waiting for Jenny to enter the name of our missing teacher for the period after four o'clock—I'd have put a question mark there as well, myself—but she didn't do that. I could only hope at some point she would remember that the dead teenager had been found with a slip of paper with Sibel's cell phone number on it, but at the moment Jenny seemed to have overlooked that important detail.

And that detail was our only link between the two women, as well as my only piece of evidence on the missing teacher, who the detectives hadn't ranked very high on their list of open questions so far.

While reading Jenny's file, I missed the detectives' departure for Yasemin and Zeynep's school, but at least I didn't have to torture myself with the chaotic traffic. I caught up with them as they were meeting the teacher in the corduroy suit. He was handing Gregor a stack of papers.

"OK, so this is the list with the names of all the teachers and students who have ever had anything directly to do with Yasemin."

Gregor took the papers and scanned the names. There were at least twenty-five.

"Now, for the list of Zeynep's contacts, I'm going to need a little more time—my God, how awful . . ."

Aha, so the pedagogue was apparently only learning of Zeynep's sudden demise now. By contrast, Yasemin's death had already been page-one news in Cologne's leading daily. The newspaper was on the corduroy suit's desk, and I had seen a copy in the main office and in the slush in the schoolyard as well. We could assume that every single person at the school now knew Yasemin had been murdered. I didn't know yet if that would prove good or bad for the investigation.

"We would like to have all of the people on this list together in one big room," Gregor said. "We'll call them individually out into a separate room to talk with them, and we need to make sure that the people we've already spoken to do not return to the big room with the others afterward."

The corduroy suit nodded as he ran his trembling fingers again and again through his somehow neatly messy haircut.

"Please get us the list of names for Zeynep as soon as possible so that we know during each interview who is connected to both of them."

It took some time to get everything ready, and I watched the chaos unfold here, there, and everywhere. The schoolkids were all bawling like banshees, and the chalk pushers tried to calm them down, with no success. Instead, some of the teachers went banshee themselves. Whole peeps of chickens were clinging together in balls, wailing and sobbing like mad. The boys were trying not to bawl, but often enough they failed. The messengers then arrived in the classrooms with the list of names to call the witnesses out for questioning. When one girl's name was called, she instantly passed out. Others acted as though they were being dispatched to a Siberian quarry for the rest of their lives. But eventually everyone, apart from the passed-out chick, was gathered in the music hall, where several teachers and emergency counselors were present to take care of the wailing witnesses.

The students and teachers were called out and questioned by Gregor and Jenny—one by one, but in an order that made no sense to me. They asked if Yasemin had been under a lot of stress lately, and when the interviewees said yes, they asked whether she had seemed different than usual recently, why she had broken up with her boyfriend, what her relationship with her brother was like, etc. The answers were quite varied. The Technicolor sheep Gregor had met during his first visit to the school thought Yasemin had seemed seriously burdened. No, she hadn't spoken with her about it because Yasemin had never been very open. But the teacher said she had sensed the vibrations.

"Vibrations?" Gregor and Jenny asked at the same time.

"Yes. You, for instance," she said, looking at Gregor sternly over the top of her half-rimmed eyeglasses, "in you, I sense anger and frustration. And fatigue. And in the young detective," she said looking at Jenny, "uncertainty. Yasemin had been exuding great worry."

Jenny blushed, and Gregor rolled his eyes.

"You should take that seriously, young man," the woolly beast scolded him.

"I do," he replied casually. "However, that's not news to us. We already know something was worrying her. We just don't know what."

"Well..." clucked the ball of wool—who increasingly smelled like a house pet—when in came a girl who seemed quite different from all the others we had questioned so far. The chicks at this school were generally generic clones of each other. They were upper-middle class, had long hair, wore abundant makeup, and were laden with jewelry. All of them apart from this specimen, who proved herself a girl and not a boy only after she opened her mouth.

"I'm Amelie Görtz."

And another difference from the other chicks: she wasn't crying.

Gregor dismissed the teacher, then turned his attention to Amelie. "More than a couple of people have mentioned your name..." Gregor began. "Do you have some special type of connection or relationship with Yasemin?"

"I've been in almost all the same classes as her since we started high school."

"That's right," Gregor said. He studied the girl for a moment with amazement. "So why haven't we spoken with you previously?"

She shrugged.

"So you knew Yasemin well?"

"No."

"But . . ."

"No one knew Yasemin well. Apart from her brother, maybe. They were thick as thieves."

"Hmm," Gregor said. "Do you know where Mehmet might be?"

"No."

This canary wasn't exactly an opera singer, and I could tell Gregor was getting impatient with her monosyllabic responses.

"What's up with Zeynep, her best friend?" Jenny asked, and Amelie stared at her with surprise.

"Friend?" She laughed hoarsely. "That's cray cray!"

Gregor and Jenny leaned forward.

"Do tell," Gregor said, considerably more alert than he was a moment ago.

Amelie closed her eyes and thought. Gregor and Jenny fidgeted impatiently in their chairs, but Little Miss Muffet was the epitome of calm. She casually slouched in her chair, her hands in the pockets of her hoodie, her jeans torn at the knees, and her cheese-grater-short hair dyed platinum blonde. Apart from a wide silver ring on her left thumb, she wasn't wearing any jewelry. A deep fold formed on her forehead as she opened her eyes.

"Yasemin and Zeynep were part of the same clique, but I don't think they were friends."

"What clique?" Gregor asked.

"At first, it was Dominic, Mehmet, Zeynep, and Mariam."

"Mariam who?" Jenny asked.

"I don't know. Some Iranian or Albanian name, no idea. She's not at the school anymore. Deported."

Jenny scribbled everything into her notebook. All of that would be quick enough to verify later.

"None of them were dating each other, although Zeynep worshipped Dominic, but he was into Yasemin, and Mehmet was his yes-man. They're all beneath her, actually."

"Who are beneath her?" Gregor asked.

"The whole school. The people here. Everyone. She thought she was better. Maybe she was. Her IQ is a hundred forty-two. And then she's stuck here in this glorified kindergarten whose only justification for existence is a student body from fifty-three nations. An experiment in hugging as pedagogy. Everyone's the same, and in case of doubt, what that means here is everybody's the same *stupid*. Yasemin belonged at an élite boarding school where she could have graduated at twelve and started her PhD by nineteen. I was always surprised she got involved with Dominic. And Zeynep of course *hated* Yasemin because she had a crush on Dominic herself."

Finally something in this school that sounded *normal*. All the fabric-softener-soft "we love each other" bullshit had seriously started to piss me off. No one believes that crap anyway. So: a bitch fight over the amateur fisherman who had hooked the hottest trout in the pond, and the lugworm hated her for it. Fishpond, school. It's all the same habitat.

"Did Dominic and Zeynep start dating after he and Yasemin broke up?"

"No one knows exactly. Apparently they haven't made any appearances together."

"Because it was embarrassing to Dominic to be seen with the second tier after dating the lovely Yasemin?" Gregor asked.

"I see you're familiar with male sensibilities," the bitch parried snidely.

Gregor gave her nothing by way of a response. "OK, thank you for your—"

"Just a second," Amelie said. "You haven't heard the best part yet."

She now had Gregor's and Jenny's full attention. And mine too.

"Tristan was totally Yasemin-crazy. My guess is he killed her because she rejected him."

"Wait. Who's Tristan?" Gregor asked, confused.

"Oh, Tristan's short for Christian. Dr. Christian Seiler. The guy in the corduroy suit."

After Amelie left the room, Gregor and Jenny agreed to quietly run a criminal history and background check on Dr. "Tristan" Seiler for anything out of the ordinary, and then come back and question him later.

I took that as my cue to go looking for Martin.

Turns out he had assisted Katrin on Zeynep's autopsy and had just set down the slaughterhouse equipment and was scrubbing his hands. Quiet moments like this when he's at the sink are when I love to sneak up on him. He's always a little worn out from the autopsy and basically has no protective wall left at all.

"What did she die of?" I asked loudly, expecting him to jump.

He didn't even twitch. Worn out, perhaps.

"Suspected intoxication," he said.

In coroner speak, that means "poisoning," not "too much beer." My Latin vocabulary had increased substantially over the past few months.

"The tox screen will show the specific substances," Martin added.

As had my familiarity with abbreviations like *tox*, which means "toxicology." So Zeynep had been poisoned to death.

"Who's writing up the report?"

"Katrin."

"Great! Then maybe today at lunch you can help out a little with searching for the missing teacher," I said with fake chipperness.

Martin shook his head. "I don't have a lot of time, I still have to—"

"Martin, that poor teacher was kidnapped more than sixty hours ago, and there isn't one freaking ass out there who's worried about that. Even her own brother is out doing drug deals and getting himself shot up instead of helping his sister."

"There is no proof that she was kidnapped . . ."

"Do you want to wait for her to show up on your slaughterhouse table instead?"

"You say such things only to manipulate me," he intoned, but I could sense that my accusation had hit home. Good.

"You and I are her only chance. If you continue to refuse to help her, you'll have to apologize to her corpse. Can you live with that?"

Martin sighed; I grinned. That sound was the sound of Martin's defeat.

"We'll meet in half an hour in the office of Principal Bieberstein, Sibel's boss at the elementary school," I told him as I took off.

High time I checked in on the kiddos.

I found them all together in Edi and Joe's room. Edi's mother and Joe's father were sitting next to each other between the beds, taking turns reading *Harry*—barf—*Potter* aloud. They seemed to be having more fun than the small souls swirling around them. I couldn't follow the story much, but I quickly got that Edi's mother was reading Harry and Joe's father was reading Hermione, the smart-ass, in falsetto. Now, I couldn't stand King of the Magical Blues Harry in any case, but I already had one Miss Smart-Ass on my hands, in ghost form, and that was plenty. So I felt no inclination to listen to that bullshit.

Niclas was going through some serious video-game withdrawal; when I called out "Action time" to him, he instantly followed me. Bülent separated himself painlessly, but Edi and Joe both totally refused. Edi seemed to be more interested in what was going on between her mother and Joe's father than in listening to the story.

Womenfolk always have the wrong priorities—big surprise.

Martin was already in the schoolyard when I arrived with Niclas and Bülent in tow. I took a short fly-around to find Principal Bieberstein. It wasn't hard, not only because he was a giant of a man and hard to miss but also because he was sitting alone in his office, staring at a photo that he'd pulled from his briefcase. The photo showed Sibel, our missing teacher, in a white dress holding a candle in her hand.

"Is that a wedding?" Bülent asked from my side.

"Where's the groom then, Einstein?" That was Niclas, obviously.

I couldn't explain what was going on in that photo; all I knew was that it had been taken in a church. The background was pretty dark and murky, but ever since I was involuntarily forced to spend hours upon hours with Marlene in her convent chapel, I could tell a prayer bunker even half-asleep in the dark. So the Turkish and presumably Muslim schoolteacher Sibel Akiroğlu was standing with a candle in her hand inside a Christian church. Weird. Very weird.

"Ask the principal why he's drooling over a photo of Sibel and what she was doing in that church," I called over to Martin, who had turned around to leave the schoolyard.

"Just a second, I think I forgot to lock my car."

"Chill, Martin. No one's going to steal that thing."

Bülent giggled.

Martin would not be dissuaded, however, and when he finally made it back into the schoolyard, the principal was already driving out of the parking lot in a sky-blue station wagon.

"After him!" I yelled, and Martin's unathletic body started jiggling as he frantically ran back to his trash can and started the pursuit.

The drive didn't last long. The station wagon wasn't particularly fast or easy to lose sight of, so Martin and the principal made it to the parking lot next to the church at almost the same time. The principal got out, opened his trunk, and lifted out a large box, which he took inside with him. Martin carefully locked his trash can and then walked after the tall man.

"So," I said to Martin. "First, you need to find out what he's doing here. Then, you need to figure out if this is the same church as in the photo with Sibel. And then you need to find out what the photo means. And—"

"To what photograph are you referring?"

I quickly broadcast a brain wave to him with my memory of the photo, and Martin spontaneously responded, "A baptism."

"For crying out loud," I said. "That wasn't a baby picture of the teacher."

"So what? People can be baptized at any time. Especially converts."

"Converts?" I asked.

"She changed religions, bozo," Niclas clarified for my benefit, rolling his eyes.

Mr. Bieberstein had since made it to the main door holding his box, and he rang the bell. A minute later the door opened, and he stepped inside. Martin lolloped behind and made it to the door just in time to get his proverbial foot in the proverbial door. The woman who opened the door asked who he was, which Martin answered with a pitiful yowl as the ancient oaken panel started squeezing his toes off.

"Sorry," she said, although he was the one who had been so stupid as to jam his sensitive footsie-wootsie into the gap.

"It's, uh, fine," Martin said between moans. "It was my own fault, but I desperately need to speak with Mr. Bieberstein." God, Martin was such a wimp.

"Of course. Please come in."

Martin limped behind the woman, who looked like a smaller edition of that old crow from English TV who solves cases in endless repeats on certain channels.

Bülent, Niclas, and I followed them in formation through a long corridor, around a corner, through another corridor, and then up a set of stairs to the first story. It smelled of food. The first room on the right was a kitchen with attached dining room, where about fifteen people had gathered. Mr. Bieberstein had set down his box and said hello to the people just as the food was being brought to the table.

Quickly glancing over the crowd, I noticed children, teenagers, and grown-ups, all of them with jet-black hair, and some of the women wore headscarves. The main dish was spaghetti with tons of tomato sauce and not much meat, with a small side of salad. Each of the kids also had a little plastic cup of Jell-O by their plates.

"Jell-O!" Bülent exclaimed.

"I only like the green flavor," Niclas said haughtily.

"Quiet!" I roared—although I had to agree with him on green. But whether green or red, the food today looked less like a meal and more like a fast, compared to the copious convent food I had seen the nuns preparing when I'd been with Marlene.

"Thomas, this gentleman would like to speak with you," the old crow said at precisely the moment everyone had folded their hands to say grace.

Bieberstein stared at Martin, stood, asked the others to begin without him, and left the dining room. Once in the hallway, he looked down—way down, he was so tall—at Martin. "Yes?" he asked, clearly confused.

I couldn't say exactly if his question expressed hope, fear, or despair, but he was evidently expecting bad news about Sibel— otherwise he wouldn't have been so eager to let his lunch get cold.

"I, uh, I would like to ask you a couple of questions about Sibel Akiroğlu," Martin said. "My name is Gänsewein."

"Are you with the police?"

"No. But I'm working as a consultant on a murder investigation, and the murder in question seems to be connected with the disappearance of Ms. Akiroğlu."

"Murder? Do you mean that girl I read about in the paper today?"

"Do you know the girl?"

Bieberstein shook his head. "Let's go downstairs. We can talk there undisturbed."

He knew his way around the church building, that was for sure. Bieberstein led Martin to a sparsely decorated room with a table, four chairs, and a cross on the wall.

They both sat, and Bieberstein nervously fidgeted on his chair as Martin gathered his thoughts. Technically, he was gathering *my* thoughts, because I was trying to remind him of the most important questions he needed to ask the principal. And my miniature companions were kind enough to keep their traps shut.

"Just a moment," Martin told me. "I don't follow you. Let's go through everything in order."

"Can you tell me if Sibel is in danger as well?" Bieberstein asked, interrupting Martin's and my silent conversation.

"Unfortunately I don't know, because we didn't previously know about the connection between Ms. Akiroğlu and the murder victim," Martin explained.

Bieberstein nodded and looked into space. Suddenly he frowned and looked at Martin with alarm. "How did you find me here, actually?"

"I wanted to speak with you and saw you pull out of the parking lot in front of the school," Martin said, truthfully.

Bieberstein relaxed.

"May we begin then?" Martin asked.

Bieberstein nodded.

"Did Ms. Akiroğlu ever mention to you that she wanted to meet Yasemin Özcan on Monday or Tuesday evening?"

Bieberstein kneaded his large hands. "What do you mean exactly?"

Alarm bells started going off everywhere in my head. The question was so straightforward that there was only one reason why he might ask another question in reply: to stall. Bieberstein had something to hide. I told Martin, who nodded mentally.

"I mean, did the two of them speak with each other? Did they meet? Did they want to meet? Any connection that might help us."

Instead of answering, Bieberstein ran his gigantic hands through his hair.

"Did Ms. Akiroğlu meet the student on Monday evening? Or had she set a time to meet her on Tuesday evening?"

Bieberstein was visibly struggling. "Monday definitely not; she had, uh, something else planned then."

Martin waited, but Bieberstein apparently didn't want to say what she'd had planned.

"Mr. Bieberstein, it's best that you tell me the whole truth now. That's the only way we can help Ms. Akiroğlu," Martin pleaded. He's pretty good with emotional crap like this.

"I don't know if it's OK to speak about it. Sibel's preference was to keep it a secret for a while yet."

With the words *keep it a secret*, Martin's own alarm bells starting going off. "She's in danger," Martin said.

Bieberstein fidgeted some more in his chair and then sat up straight once he had apparently made a decision. In a tone one normally reserves only for colossal confessions, he said, "Sibel and I were here on Monday evening."

"Aha," Martin said.

That's about all I could have said myself.

Bülent added a "So what?" while Niclas yawned.

Bieberstein's expectant face fell when the reaction he had evidently been anticipating did not materialize. "We teach here every Monday and Wednesday evening."

"Teaching? Barf!" Niclas said.

"Teaching?" Martin asked as Bieberstein fell silent again. "Whom?"

The principal pointed upward vaguely.

"Spit it out, man!" I yelled.

"What kind of institution is this?" Martin asked.

"This is the former vicarage. Now it's a, uh, well . . ."

"Martin, will you please tear it out of him already, otherwise we're going to be still sitting here in the morning," I moaned.

"What's up with him?" Bülent mumbled from beside me. "He looks like he didn't do his homework."

"Or he tossed a stink bomb into a crowd," Niclas added.

"This is a sanctuary," Bieberstein suddenly blurted out as though he couldn't keep the words in anymore. "A church asylum, technically. We protect people from deportation."

"An ass-island?" Bülent asked.

Deportation? I thought. Amelie had mentioned there was one girl in the clique who had been deported. Marion or something was her name?

"What exactly does that mean?" Martin asked. "Do these people live here?"

Bieberstein took a deep breath and sat up straight again. They were sitting on either side of a table, which normally would have looked huge, especially with Martin sitting there, since he's not exactly physically imposing. But the table seemed small, and Bieberstein seemed like a giant in his chair.

"Our sanctuary is one of many church asylums in Germany. People who are being threatened with deportation come to us, and we take them in and contact the authorities to prevent their deportation."

It was all Greek to me, or maybe Turkish in this case, but Martin nodded with encouragement.

"Legally speaking, the congregation could be charged with obstruction of justice or harboring illegal aliens, but since humanitarian assistance is allowed under German law, indictments against churches generally fizzle out, eventually. Still, the legal situation is not entirely aboveboard, which is why many of

the volunteers from the congregation who are involved in helping here prefer to remain anonymous."

"And the people who seek refuge here . . ."

"They have been living here under the aegis of the church—
some of them for months or even years. While Sibel was a student
teacher, one of the children in her class was deported, and ever
since she has been involved here. With her ability to speak several languages and her understanding of how people from other
cultures think, she has been one of our most important helpers."

"Is it normal for a Protestant church to have a Muslim
woman . . . ?" Martin asked, but he didn't finish his question
because Bieberstein practically fell apart before his eyes.

"That's not all," Bieberstein said in a ragged voice. "She
decided to be baptized and join the Protestant Church in
Germany. She and I want to be married."

"What? She can't do *that*!" Bülent yelled, although I couldn't
tell if he meant the baptism or the wedding.

"Eew," Niclas said. "He was really going to marry a Turk?"

Martin's phone rang just then—some emergency at the institute. I caught only a bit of him saying good-bye to Bieberstein
through all the yammering between Niclas and Bülent, who,
despite their many disagreements, agreed on one central point:
Sibel would have done better to remain a nice, unremarkable
Muslim Turkish schoolteacher.

EIGHT

Friday, 2:05 p.m.

We would have missed Friday prayers, but Bülent reminded me we wanted to check out the group that had called one of its members a whore, so we zoomed off.

The mosque was an inconspicuous building toward the back of an industrial-zoned property. No golden domes, no minarets, nothing unusual apart from a gathering of dark-haired men streaming out of the flat-faced building. There was a backup at the door, of course, because they all had to put their shoes back on.

"Over there. I see them," Bülent called.

He pointed at a gang of five guys who were all dressed in black. Black jeans and black leather jackets, and they had pencil-thin chin beards and thick black watches at their wrists. Their hair was plastered down on their heads like duck feathers after a tanker accident, and they were lighting horrible-smelling cigarettes with silver Zippos.

The guy I took for their leader was blabbing something in Turkish.

"What's he saying?" I asked Bülent.

"He's asking if anyone has seen Mehmet."

The oil-covered birds all shook their heads, saying words full of sibilants and ö and ü sounds.

"He says Yasemin deserved to die," Bülent translated. "And Mehmet is a hero."

"You're making that up," I said.

Bülent shook his head. He was trembling, actually. "And he wants to tell my brother he should make an example of Mehmet."

Niclas starting giggling like a madman. "They're killing *each other*. Awesome."

"Not all his spark plugs are firing," I said quickly, trying to calm Bülent. "Who is that guy anyway?"

"Şükrü Bozkurt."

That name sounded familiar. Oh, yeah. Mehmet's friend, the one Jenny had asked about Mehmet's whereabouts. A fanatic. Yasemin's brother sure had nice friends.

"His father runs a plant that makes spit-ready meat for döner kebab restaurants," Bülent said. "He's an important man. Lots of people work for him." Kebab Boy sounded close to tears. "Şükrü is in college. He's going to take over his father's company."

"We need to find out if he can lead us to Mehmet," I said. "We'll stay with him."

I had to literally shout those last few words because some kind of ruckus had broken out in front of the mosque. It seemed to involve both Yasemin's father, who stood with a few other men, and Dr. Christian "Tristan" corduroy-suit Seiler, who was making aggressive poses opposite them. Tristan swayed precariously, clearly as gassed up as a Formula One tank prior to the rule change.

Tristan was caterwauling away at Yasemin's father: ". . . wasting her life, and now she's dead," is what we heard as we neared the confrontation.

"Please go," one of the men next to Yasemin's father said. "Mr. Özcan is mourning his daughter."

Tristan spit before Mr. Özcan's feet. "There," he slurred, and I half expected him to puke a shower of schnapps onto Mr. Özcan's shoes next. "Don't make me laugh! You kept her in prison. She belonged at an élite school."

A congregant took Tristan by the arm, but the totaled teacher shook him off.

"You pre . . . pre . . . prehistoric hillbilly. A woman like Yasemin . . ."

This time two men grabbed Tristan and practically carried him off the mosque grounds. Bülent, Niclas, and I stared after them, but at that point I was interested in checking in with our oil slicks again. Despite an intensive search, however, we couldn't find them. Überlame. We had lost our lead on Mehmet, the avenger of the family's honor.

I dispatched the boys with an assignment to fly directly back to their hospital rooms and wait there for further instructions. They obeyed me without objection. Maybe it was a little too intense for bonsais that age to listen in on people talking about "honor" killings of a guy's own sister. It's not like I could have helped it: I hadn't picked the topic of conversation.

Finally alone, however, I hurried to find Martin at his office.

"You need to have someone pick Dr. Seiler up off the street and ask him a few questions," I ordered.

"Who is Dr. Seiler?" he asked, distracted.

"Yasemin's teacher, who had a crush on her."

"A teacher had a crush on her?" Martin asked, shocked.

God, what galaxy did this bozo live in?

"A classmate named Amelie thought he might have killed her, but that's not how it looks now. He just walked up in front of the mosque and chewed out Yasemin's father in front of a whole horde of witnesses, and now he's sitting on the sidewalk, drunk off his ass, crying."

Martin didn't look up from his report.

"Martin, the guy's life may be in danger, first of all, and secondly, this is all very suspicious."

"Gregor will take care of it then."

Not this again.

"Call Gregor and ask him."

I had finally pestered him enough that he had lost the thread of his report. He sighed and picked up the phone on his desk.

Finally. When would he learn to listen to me the first time?

When Gregor answered, Martin began without preamble: "I've heard that a suspect in your case just chewed out the father of the murder victim, and the man is now sitting on the sidewalk in front of the mosque crying."

Gregor asked for Tristan's name and a few more details, said thanks, and hung up. He didn't ask Martin about the origin of this information, probably because he was afraid of the answer. Whatever. The main thing was that Gregor was taking action.

Well, *he* wasn't taking action. He sent Jenny. I showed up in front of the mosque at the same time she did, and we found Dr. Seiler lying on the sidewalk where the men had left him. I recognized him from the corduroy suit, although it was now stained variously with puke, blood, and street grime. His face was all puffy and dented, there were five teeth on the sidewalk beside his cheek, and the right sleeve of his corduroy jacket was ripped clean off. He was unconscious.

Jenny called the ambulance as well as Martin, and so Tristan ended up with Martin anyway. This was the second assault and battery Martin had documented among the knotty cases we were investigating, although this patient was less forthcoming than the first one had been. Of course, you couldn't blame Tristan, since he was unconscious and all. But I was still excited to hear his story. If he remembered anything, that is.

Martin took photographs of his injuries, made a cast from the imprint that had been left in his cheek by a hand wearing a ring, and counted and cataloged his teeth. One of the knocked-out teeth was missing, but no one made any effort to cruise back by the mosque and go looking through the slush for Tooth 23 on the dental chart. Martin was packing up his things when Gregor arrived.

"Can he talk?"

Martin shook his head.

"Never to talk again?"

"No, he will. I presume he'll have a lisp due to the huge gap in his teeth now, but the ER doctor said his injuries aren't serious."

"But it *was* aggravated assault and battery, right?"

"Clearly."

"Nice."

To laypeople it may sound odd for a gumshoe to be glad about aggravated assault and battery—certainly the victim would have preferred the nonfelonious version—but under German law, the police and prosecutor can't act on a simple assault if the victim doesn't want to press charges, even if there are minor injuries. By contrast, if it's *aggravated* assault and battery, German law unleashes the dogs, and then the police can do almost anything. Given the opacity of the case, I was pretty sure Gregor was happy not about the crime but about gaining another toehold for his investigation.

"Hopefully he can talk soon because the missing teacher's brother—who I came here about, actually—was a *total waste* of time," Gregor said.

"Wait," Martin said. "When I interviewed him he promised me—"

Gregor laughed like a billy goat. "Well, it turns out your patient is a drug dealer and not exactly what I'd call a man of honor."

"Where did you—"

"If the brother of a woman involved in a murder lands in the hospital with a gunshot wound, we obviously run priors and a background check on him. So, he's done some time and apparently is less than eager to renew his acquaintanceship with the police. He played us and split."

"That's not good," Martin said.

"That's very bad!" I bellowed. "Go to his place and get all up in his grill. He can't have gotten far with a torn-up thigh like that."

"Hmm," Martin muttered. "I'm sure you can find him at home . . ."

"I sent Jenny out for him already. Maybe he'll be a bit more open with a nice young woman."

I remembered the license plate number on that car from Akif's shooting, so I ordered Martin to give Gregor the number so he could at least investigate from that angle. Martin hemmed and hawed as usual when he's supposed to pass on information he actually has "no way" of having.

"Tell him the drug dealer wrote the license number on his hand with a pen," I yelled.

Martin continued wriggling. The problem is he can't lie.

"I don't *want* to lie—in contradistinction to you," he mentally corrected me.

"That teacher's gonna die because of your so-called scruples! And then you won't have just a lie on your precious conscience but also murder."

"Say, Gregor . . ." Martin mumbled as though he had a giant lollipop in his mouth.

"Yes?" Gregor said, turning around at the door.

"That drug dealer, Akif, he, uh, had written a license plate number on his hand."

Gregor squinted at Martin.

"It, uh, might have something to do with the shooting."

"And you remembered that number from the second you examined him but didn't include it in your report," Gregor said as though Martin had confessed he had seen a grown-up fire-breathing dragon in the public restroom at the hospital.

"Um, well . . ."

"OK, so what's the number?"

Martin passed it on, and I sighed with relief. Finally my contribution to this case was being taken seriously.

"I'll go see what turns up," Gregor said. He didn't jot the number down, but it would be easy enough for him to remember *K*, for Köln or Cologne, the letters *JB*, and the numbers 001.

I saw my chance with Akif and zoomed over to his apartment. Jenny was at the door of the building, holding her finger on the buzzer. Sibel's brother was standing in his apartment with a pain-contorted face and fumbling around with the fuse box. Finally the skirl from the doorbell stopped. Akif sighed with relief and hobbled back into the kitchen, where he had prepared a top-notch pot of coffee, with filter paper and everything, and clotted his caffeine with a fair bit of sugar. He then poured the slurry into a cracked, black-edged mug and limped out into the living room. The scene on the flat screen surprised me. It showed

Jenny herself, pushing the doorbell button once again. But this time the doorbell's shrill noise didn't fill Akif's place. He had pulled the fuse for the buzzer and turned on a surveillance camera that overlooked the door. This was getting better and better.

I checked the angle of the shot on the screen one more time and then zoomed downstairs. Jenny had just started walking back down the front steps in frustration. After a moment of looking, I found it: to the upper right, hidden in the trim of the awning, hung a tiny camera. No bigger than a fly, and a fly is what it looked like. I was guessing Akif hadn't picked that up at the home improvement center or Aldi. This was professional equipment that had been professionally installed. I flew back up to the seedy attic apartment to find my next surprise.

Akif had changed channels. Now the screen was split, showing six different camera images from six different perspectives. The stars of these shots were: the front entry, the street in front of the building to the right and to the left, and three angles covering the back of the building.

Akif was either an A/V junkie or a paranoid big shot in the drug scene. If it was the latter, then this run-down pad was a great hiding spot. I had always imagined Cologne's drug lords living in crazy-luxe mansions, not this West German twin of an East German prefab building. Awesome cover.

Akif watched Jenny get in her car and take off. He dialed his phone, blathered some Turkish into it, and hung up. Then, with great effort, he stood, got a box out of the fridge, and sat down with it at the kitchen table. He opened the lid.

Inside the box was something that looked like a thickish slice of kiełbasa. But it must have been left out in the butcher's case for a long time because the outer edge on one side was curling up as though it had dried out. When I changed the angle I was looking at it from, however, I realized it wasn't wurst: it was a human ear. A left ear. Without the rest of the person attached to it. Akif was studying it very closely, and then a nasty grin spread across his face. He closed the top of the box, stuck the thing back into the fridge, and went to bed. Only seconds after his own ear had touched his pillow, he was snoring evenly and very loudly.

Friday, 5:30 p.m.

"She unambiguously died of illegal drugs, presumably an active substance from the class of beta-phenylethylamine derivatives."

"Huh?" Gregor asked.

Katrin wasn't smiling. "Amphetamines."

They were sitting together in Oz, going through the autopsy report for Zeynep Kaymaz.

"Intentional overdose or an accident?" Gregor asked.

"An overdose either way, but no interaction with other factors such as medications, heart problems, or the like. Naturally I can't say whether it was intentional or accidental."

"Was she a regular user?"

"I can't tell you that either, but the hair analysis will yield some information about it for us."

"When?"

Now Katrin sighed. "Same old story: we're always backlogged. Early next week, I hope."

Gregor's phone rang, and he answered it with a simple, surly "Yes?" Then he listened briefly, grunted, and hung up. "Yasemin and Zeynep's school is holding an 'open memorial service with spiritual support.' I think we should go check that out. Especially since the students who were on that class trip will be back for it."

I didn't feel like going to an "open memorial service," whatever that was. Presumably a place for wailing teenagers to get out of their houses and stop annoying their parents. They could wail together at school. God, that was a horrible image.

As was the ear in Akif's fridge. With renewed resolve, I made my way over to my young assistants. I was still determined to find their teacher. She had been missing since last Tuesday, and now Friday was almost past. Was it a good sign her body hadn't turned up yet, or a bad one? The bonsais had to know *something* that could help me. Maybe I simply hadn't asked the right questions yet.

I found Edi, Joe, and Bülent hovering over Bülent's bed while his mother sang. To me, she sounded like a distorted slo-mo track from a DJ on the verge of passing out, but Bülent was beaming at her.

"People," I called out, "we should find your teacher before she dies of hunger or thirst."

"Yes, later," Bülent mumbled as he tried to sing along with his mother.

"That's true!" Edi yelled. "I had totally forgotten about Ms. Akiroğlu. My God, how awful!"

"Do you have any idea where we can look for her?" Joe asked.

"No," I confessed. "That's why I need you guys."

By now it was dark outside. I had the kids follow me and then found Niclas, who was hanging out in the pediatric ward staring at a cartoon on TV, and I took them all to the scene of the accident. It was cold and windy, and what had been drizzle by day was now turning into snow. Rush hour starts and ends earlier on

Fridays, so Cologne was fairly quiet by now—more or less similar to traffic conditions the night of the accident.

"So, now all of you think really hard about what was going on last Tuesday when the accident happened."

Silence.

"We drove this way," Niclas began, "and then suddenly there was a car next to us, and then it was in front of us, and we crashed."

"Was the car black, blue, brown, or what?" I asked.

"It was definitely dark and not a light color or white," Edi said.

"Red," Niclas said.

"Hey, you were asleep. You couldn't have known that," Edi said.

"Bullshit. I wasn't asleep. I was sitting right at the window, and I saw the color perfectly."

"But in the dark, colors all look the same," Joe said.

"Red," Niclas repeated.

"OK," I said. "How big was the car?"

"About this big," Edi said, making a gesture that might describe a school bus or a big-rig semi. That was obviously wildly incorrect, but what did you expect from a girl?

"Could you guys see the roof of the other vehicle?" I asked.

"Uh-uh," Niclas said. "The roof was at least as high as the roof on Ms. Akiroğlu's car. And the tires were gigantic."

"Could you see the tires in the window?" I asked.

Niclas said yes, and then I knew he'd been dreaming, because then the vehicle would have had to be a Bigfoot 20, and people would likely have noticed a monster truck like that out and about in Cologne.

"Uh-uh," Niclas said. "It wasn't that kind of truck."

"But it was dirty," Edi added excitedly.

As though a dirty car in November was unusual.

"No," she protested. "It had a thick coat of mud all over it."

"That's true," Joe chimed in. "It looked like the car the ranger drove when we took that class trip into the mountains."

"Yeah," Bülent said. "That's right."

"So could the color have been green?" I asked.

Awkward silence.

OK. But it gave me a relatively clear idea of the vehicle. We were presumably talking about an SUV in a dark color. Still, there would be thousands of cars matching that description in the city. But maybe one of them was registered to Akif Akiroğlu. Maybe the bonsais remembered seeing a guy about as big as Akif when she was kidnapped.

"How big was the guy who kidnapped your teacher?" I asked.

"Big," Edi said. "Taller than his car."

Too bad. Not Akif.

"What else can you remember?"

She shrugged.

"Did he say anything? What was his voice like? Did he smell like smoke or grass? Like alcohol or deodorant or—"

"Yes," she interrupted. "He smelled like chalk."

Chalk? I shrugged. Clearly I was no longer getting anything useful out of them. I left the four of them to their own devices. Three immediately whooshed back to the hospital, but Niclas went off someplace on his own. I had no idea where to, but I didn't care either. The guy was a whiner as well as a racist, and if he got himself into any shit, he'd have only himself to blame.

But I had earned myself a long night at the movies, and I enjoyed it to the fullest, taking in a pair of action flicks. After the late-late show was over, I checked in at the hospital again, but I didn't find any bonsais there. Maybe they were all staring mesmerized at the TV in the pediatric ward, playing its unending loop of kids' shows where a chipper babe and star-shaped puppet on a couch would order them to bed at regular intervals. The people who make children's TV have infernal senses of humor.

Another infernal thing was the sight of Edi's mom and Joe's dad in the hospital room: they had scooted their visitors' chairs close together at the back of the room so that they could lean their heads against the wall. They were asleep—hand in hand, Edi's mother's head on Joe's father's shoulder.

Yikes, I thought. If Joe's mother saw this, that daddy would find himself in a coma lickety-split too.

NINE

Saturday, 7:30 a.m.

Saturday morning, Martin was once again the first one to wake up while Birgit blissfully snoozed on. He brewed some tea for himself and waited. He ate a bowl of müsli and waited some more. He looked at the clock and waited. He went out to get fresh breakfast rolls from the bakery around the corner, returned, and waited. At ten thirty he was half-dead with worry.

I felt obligated to reassure him. At least with regard to Birgit's condition.

"Birgit isn't sick," I explained to him. "It's worse."

"Worse?" Martin's voice cracked in panic.

"Yes, much worse. She's pregnant."

Martin froze. He blinked once. Gulped.

"Really?" he whispered.

"Yes," I said in a grave voice. "But that can be changed. Nowadays it's not at all dangerous anymore or that expensive . . ."

As I continued my discussion of family planning options, Martin stood, staggered down the dark hallway, opened the bedroom door as though he were haunting the Queen's bedchamber, snuck to the bed, and knelt beside Birgit, who was breathing fast but softly. He had completely shut me out—even though I urgently wanted to address the next step to take in this special situation. He stood beside the bed, transfixed by Birgit as she rhythmically breathed. He stroked her hair. She breathed. He pulled up the covers a bit, but she snorted and pushed the covers back down. It went on like that for five minutes, and then Birgit finally woke up.

"How are you feeling?" Martin said, bombarding her before she was properly awake. "Are you OK? Or do you feel ill again? Naturally you shouldn't be drinking coffee for the time being. Maybe orange juice instead? Oh, no. No citrus. Apple or carrot juice would be best. But we don't have any at home. I'll go right now and pick some up for you, all right?"

Birgit squinted, frowned, suddenly smiled as her whole face lit up, and then whispered, "I'm pregnant."

Martin smiled. "Yes. Wunderbar!"

Oh my God. Seriously? *Wunderbar?* Were these two high? Had they been sniffing glue?

I mean, please. They obviously weren't thinking through what our future held. Instead, they were clinging to the misapprehension that kids are like they seem in commercials, always cheerfully smiling even when they're mired up to their necks in their own shit. But life is a bitch, and so is death. And snot-noses aren't like in commercials or on zwieback packages. If you could test-drive kids like cars, humanity would have died out long ago.

Birgit pulled Martin closer to her, but Martin got stuck in his anti-electrosmog net and lurched onto the edge of the bed like a drunk.

"I'm starving," Birgit said laughing. "Breakfast!"

"How did you know she's pregnant?" Martin asked me silently in the kitchen.

"Your progeny introduced itself to me, of course," I replied.

Martin froze, midmotion, leaving the müsli to pour unabated from its glass container into the bowl, where it turned into a slag heap, eventually overflowing the bowl and falling off the counter to form a shifting dune on the floor. "Introduced itself . . . I beg your pardon?"

"Well, what do you think?" I asked. "That he can just fly into my turf up here without saying hi?"

Martin turned pale.

"He? It's a boy?"

"Unfortunately. I would have preferred a girl who takes after Birgit too. But the two of us aren't that lucky. It's the Martin 2.0 release. Spine chilling."

Conditions in Martin's brain ranged from horror to curiosity.

"Can you really—"

"Yep."

"Nonsense," he suddenly yelled. "That cannot be true. At such an early stage, it's not even possible for a consciousness to exist at all."

"You're the expert on these things now, huh?" I sensed his doubt. "What's the starting point of consciousness then?"

"The brain of an unborn child doesn't develop until the eighth week of pregnancy at the earliest. We can speak only of cerebral cells and by no means of a—"

"And what does the soul have to do with the brain?"

Aha. The meister was flabbergasted.

I let Martin ponder and sweep up müsli. I didn't answer his questions about the spiritual and/or mental state of his son, congratulating myself on my spontaneous idea. Suddenly Martin found me the most important person on earth: the one who could talk to his unborn child. *Right on.* Now he couldn't refuse any request!

For the present, however, being together with him and Birgit was unbearable. When Birgit finally made her way to the breakfast table, Martin had prepared a balanced first meal of the day consisting of müsli, fresh fruit, chamomile tea, soda crackers (with sea salt, of course, not table salt—that's unhealthy, you see), gherkins, a German breakfast roll, and jam. Birgit sipped the chamomile tea, turned pale, poured a small bowl of müsli, munched it, followed it with two gherkins and a cracker with jam, and then she whined for coffee. But Martin stayed firm. He urged her to drink the chamomile tea instead, which she did with reluctance. Then she jumped up and hurled the whole shebang into the toilet bowl.

But Birgit wouldn't be Birgit if she gave up so easily. She brushed her teeth, gargled some mouthwash, came back into the kitchen, and stuffed herself again, starting from the top. And she made herself an espresso as well. Martin stood around grumbling and citing studies saying that the unborn child would fall dead on the spot. But Birgit was unmoved, explaining that Italians would have died out long ago if that were true, which Martin countered by saying that it might have been insufficient to drive them to extinction but that it still explained a few things. Birgit paused, realizing Martin had made a joke—and a mean, racist one at that—and then laughed herself silly as she set up the moka pot to brew another espresso. Martin tried to sulk, but it didn't last long in the face of Birgit's happy fressing. With cereal still in her mouth, she started discussing baby names with him.

"Pascha!" I suggested loudly.

Martin pretended not to hear me.

"Well, Sascha, at least then?" I begged. Oh God, what was I saying? Had the baby virus caught up with me now too? I needed to pull it together.

"That would lead only to confusion," Martin shared with me before sealing off all his mental bulkheads.

My enthusiasm vaporized, the schmaltzy bliss of expectant parents merely reinforcing my looming loneliness, so I decided to go in search of Gregor instead. During a murder investigation, Saturday is a normal workday for a detective. Gregor couldn't be everywhere, of course, but I was in luck: I found him and Jenny sitting in Oz, updating their database with witness statements, suspects, alibis, time lines, and so on.

Yasemin had died at some point between Monday afternoon and Tuesday evening, and the Kangoo had rammed into the bridge around seven o'clock at night. One plausible scenario was that the women had arranged by cell phone to meet on Monday, then Sibel killed Yasemin and ran into the bridge the next day. However, that wasn't likely because, first of all, CSI had found no evidence of Yasemin in the Kangoo and, secondly, it was extremely unlikely that someone would commit suicide a full twenty-four hours after the murder—with a load of innocent children in the car.

And then, of the people in Yasemin's circle of friends and acquaintances, the ones who had been on that class trip all had watertight alibis, of course. Certain other people, however, had either uncertain alibis or none at all: Had anyone even asked where Zeynep had been between Monday and Tuesday night? No one had asked the corduroy suit the same question, and Yasemin's brother, Mehmet, was still at large. Yasemin's father had colleagues to vouch for his daytime work hours, and he and his wife had each other as alibis for evenings and nights.

Yasemin's cell phone had last been used on Monday night around seven o'clock to dial the number of our missing teacher, Sibel. And Sibel Akiroğlu's cell phone had called Yasemin's number multiple times over the course of Tuesday. Neither cell phone was still on, nor did any news came back from a stealth ping—a.k.a. silent SMS—which Gregor had had a judge authorize to secretly locate the phones. The same applied to Mehmet, whose squawk box was also under the radar. When the phones are turned off, even the most far-out technology quickly reaches its limit.

At least Gregor had since posted a new item on his bulletin board: talk to Akif Akiroğlu. A start!

My review of the situation was interrupted when Gregor stood, grabbed his coat, and said, "All right, let's get going."

I had no clue where the two of them were headed, so I was going to have to follow the dream team willy-nilly through the streets. Otherwise, I could literally have flown as the crow flies.

Gregor and Jenny eventually stopped in front of a mansion that must surely have been a good address back in the 1950s, judging from the size of the property and the architecture in the neighborhood. Most of the houses here were well maintained and equipped with modern security systems, including electric garage doors and cameras. The house that Gregor and Jenny were walking toward was not among these. It was in dire need of about six fresh layers of paint as well as new windows. The front yard looked like the testing ground for an ecological movement, and the once-imposing wooden gate now hung askew on its hinges. What used to be a gravel walkway was now solid green, covered in moss. It led to the front door and to the garage, bordered on either side by weeds, which were also growing along the base of the garage door.

A brass nameplate next to the doorbell said "Schiercks," and a sticker underneath that said "Nolde."

Gregor rang.

Dominic Nolde opened the door. The teenager was not only awake already but also sober, clean, kempt, and dressed. On a Saturday before noon. *Wow.*

"Oh, I hadn't been expecting you. Did you need to speak with me?"

No. With your gardener, you Gummi Bear.

Dominic invited Gregor and Jenny inside, leading them through a dark hallway into a living room with a bay window. "Can I offer you anything? Coffee, tea, water?"

"Water would be great," Jenny said. "Is your father here?"

"In the study. Shall I get him?"

"Please."

As the sound of Dominic's footsteps grew distant down the hallway, Jenny and Gregor looked around the living room. The walls were full of bookshelves, interrupted occasionally by these huge, pretentious old oil paintings featuring withered primroses and rotting vegetables. Nasty—you don't hang crap like that in the living room. You dispose of it in the compost bin before some eco-warriors have it declared a national park and you can't ever get rid of it again.

Items stood on all the little tables everywhere, apparently serving as upscale decoration. Vases without flowers, candlesticks with candles that had never been lit, a little sculpture of a child sitting cross-legged on a stone staring into space.

"Not exactly gemütlich," Jenny said softly.

"No one actually lives here," said the man who appeared in the doorway. He was tall, rail thin, and stood crooked like the exhaust pipe on a moped. His gray hair was going every which way, and his three-day beard didn't look fashion-forward but merely unshaven. "This used to be the parlor my wife used for visitors. She moved out eight years ago, and it's been empty ever since."

"Mr. Nolde?" Gregor asked. "I'm Detective Sergeant Gregor Kreidler, Criminal Investigations with the Cologne police. This is my colleague, Detective Jennifer Gerstenmüller. We're investigating the murder of Yasemin Özcan, and we'd like to speak with your son. Would you like to be present for that?"

Nolde shook Gregor's hand and looked at him puzzled. "Murder? Who did you say was the victim?"

Dominic was standing behind his father in the doorway with a smirk on his face.

"Yasemin Özcan, your son's ex-girlfriend."

Papa Nolde turned around to look at Dominic. "Have I met her?"

"You've seen her once," Dominic replied. "The pretty one."

Mr. Nolde didn't give the impression of recalling her. "I don't know anything about a murder, so if you'll excuse me," he said, and abruptly turned and left the room.

Jenny and Gregor stared at each other and then at Dominic.

"I apologize for my father's behavior. He's a historian. He's working on a book. He doesn't live in this world."

I knew how he felt.

"What is his book on?" Gregor asked, although I couldn't tell if it was out of politeness or authentic interest.

"No idea."

Dominic left the room again but returned with three glasses and a bottle of snoot water. He poured the effervescent glacial melt into the glasses and finally turned to the matter at hand.

"You mentioned one murder, not two," Dominic began. "So it's true that Zeynep committed suicide?"

"Who is saying that?"

Dominic shrugged again. "Rumors at school. If you exclude all the totally outrageous stories, the suicide theory is the only one left."

"How outrageous are the other stories?"

"A serial killer who kills Turkish girls who wear headscarves. A Turkish man who kills all Turkish women who have non-Turkish boyfriends. A Turkish woman who kills Turkish women without headscarves. Terrorists who kill people indiscriminately, and skinheads who think the school's goal of integration is stupid. If we ignore outside-actor theories, then we have the start of a new flu pandemic, an undiscovered brain tumor, and an extra-terrestrial killer virus."

Gregor shook his head. "We can rule out all of those causes with a relatively high degree of certainty. However, it's still not clear if we're talking about an accident, a suicide, or a murder."

"Terrible," Dominic said.

I couldn't read his face, which was behind the glass he'd started drinking from.

"How are you getting along?" Jenny asked.

He shrugged. "It's weird. Her death felt, I don't know, abstract before."

Jenny nodded.

"You know, when my mother left us, my father told me she was dead. He thought that would be the end of it, and I wouldn't pester him with questions or requests to see her. You can imagine my shock when one day I found my mother standing in the doorway to retrieve a few things." Dominic laughed. "My father didn't make a sound. His shoulders merely twitched, and then he returned to his study. I was pretty mad at him for a long time."

"Did you see your mother again after that?"

"No. She remarried and moved away. To Monaco, I think. Fortunately her new guy is filthy rich. Otherwise I'm sure she would have taken the house away from us too."

"Does it belong to your mother?"

Dominic laughed again. "Do you think my father can afford a house like this? He can't even afford the maintenance on these digs. The place is rotting away underneath us. But he doesn't notice. No, my father is the academic version of a starving artist. My mother can kick him out on the street tomorrow if she wants, and he won't have a thing to his name. He couldn't even rent an apartment on his irregular royalties and advances."

"How do you get by?" Jenny asked.

Dominic shrugged again. "I've been working part-time jobs for a few years. Life isn't that great if you have zero money."

Gregor cleared his throat. Good: the kid's blather was finally getting on *his* nerves too.

"You're the person who knew both girls the best, if I might say so." Uh-oh, he was pulling out the big guns to start. "That's why I'd like to know what you think about these deaths."

Dominic looked at the floor, Jenny flashed Gregor a reproachful look, and Gregor studied Dominic.

"Yasemin had lots of enemies and a few admirers," the kid began. "I'm not sure which group was more dangerous to her."

"Please say what you mean more clearly."

Oy. Gregor was done playing games.

"Perhaps you've already heard she could have given Einstein a run for his money?"

Gregor nodded.

"The school obviously thought it was terrific she didn't transfer to a highly gifted program elsewhere. That's good for advertising, brings in a lot of strong new-admission applications."

Gregor nodded again.

"Dr. Seiler's first consideration wasn't actually the school, however."

"He had a crush on Yasemin?" Gregor asked.

"Who told you that?" Dominic seemed surprised.

"Amelie Görtz."

Dominic thought for a moment. "I don't know if he had a crush on her. But what I do know is that he really went out of his way for Yasemin because he wanted to help her get into an élite program. He wanted her to make full use of her gifts and talents, and he made it his sacred duty to persuade her parents."

"And then?" Gregor prodded.

"Amelie was envious as hell of Yasemin. For two reasons, actually. First, she took the advanced-placement test at the same time as Yasemin, thinking she would be the best, but Yasemin was best, and Amelie came in second. And secondly, Amelie is the one who has a crush on Tristan . . . Sorry, I mean Dr. Seiler. Actually, she's seriously in love with him. I would describe it even as a compulsive fixation. So Yasemin was standing in the way of both things. At least, that's what Amelie thought. So if I had to guess who would benefit most from Yasemin's death, I'd point to Amelie Görtz."

Next the discussion turned to Zeynep, who was mentally unstable, according to Dominic. One minute she'd be as high as a kite, and the next she'd be down in the dumps. Dominic knew she idolized him, but they had never been a couple. He said he couldn't pretend to be in love when he didn't feel that way, and he had no need to get involved with a girl just to "have a girlfriend."

God, what an arrogant asshole this guy was.

"Do you think she killed herself out of lovesickness?" Jenny asked. "Because of you?"

Dominic again studied the butt-ugly pattern on the carpet, which entire generations of Persian children had undoubtedly been forced to neglect their Nintendos to weave. "I hope not," he said finally. "But I can't rule it out either."

"Assuming she took the amphetamines that killed her," Gregor said once again in his bad-cop voice, "do you have any idea where she got hold of them?"

Dominic shook his head. "I'm an athlete. I don't take stuff like that."

Saturday, 7:40 p.m.

"Ninety-six hours, Martin. Ninety-six! Of those hours, you have spent twenty-eight sleeping, and the rest of the time you have jammed two kilograms of müsli down your gullet, downed eight liters of tea, tucked back three whole meals plus one dog . . ."

"That was a soy bratwurst," Martin objected.

"It looked like dog, it smelled like dog, and I'm sure it was dog," I replied. "Meanwhile, during that same period, our missing teacher has presumably not slept, eaten or drunk anything, nor seen light. Next I suppose you'll want to watch *Who Wants to Be a Millionaire* on TV."

Naturally Martin never watched *Who Wants to Be a Millionaire*. What he watched on TV was news, documentaries about strange countries, strange religions, strange animals, or science shows. But the fact was he was using a quiet evening with his beloved and their scion in front of the glowing shit pump as an excuse to put off the search for the teacher. And that wasn't an option now. I was dying from boredom. The bonsais (except for Niclas, who remained missing in action) had spent the whole afternoon hanging out around their folks and eavesdropping on anecdotes from their childhoods, which they could have told by heart anyway. Gregor and Katrin had secretly gone off radar for a while; I assumed they were in a hotel bed somewhere screwing off their frustrations. At least, I couldn't find them at police HQ or at Forensics or at their houses. Jenny was out in a coma-like deep sleep that I doubted she would wake from until Monday morning. Martin was my only hope.

"I can't leave Birgit here alone," he said.

"Then take her along."

We had come to that suggestion already before, an hour ago. I may as well have suggested Martin cryogenically freeze Birgit for the duration of his investigation, or send her to the moon in an Orion spacecraft, because he couldn't have been more appalled. And all I was suggesting was a little visit to Chilling Chili to grill a certain Bond babe with a cell phone in her platform sandal.

"Birgit needs peace and quiet and a lot of sleep," Martin explained for the umpteenth time. "Secondhand smoke, loud music, alcohol—that is all poison to her. So that really is out of the question."

I was sure Birgit would prefer a night of clubbing in style to moldering on the couch and turning in early, but I couldn't talk to her, now could I? So I was close to capitulation, when Birgit suddenly said, "How about we go out tonight?"

I wanted to yell "Yeah!" but managed to hold back.

Martin looked at his sweetheart with a half-blissful, half-bothered smile. "Where to, then? What do you have in mind? Should I check and see if the symphony has a performance tonight? Or maybe we can see a play?"

"Oh, no," Birgit said. "How about a movie? Or some live music at a club downtown?"

The memory of the last rock performance they had taken in together blitzed through Martin's brain—he had survived only with the help of multiple layers of ear protection. Wax earplugs plus headphones. And then over that he wore his soft-shell cap with a watertight, windproof membrane. With all that gear, he weathered the noise like a sailor weathers a hailstorm. Lucky for him, men often wear caps like that during the summer, so his headgear was less conspicuous than were the ironed creases in his slacks and his tie, which he was still wearing after testifying as an expert witness in court that afternoon.

"Martin, this is our chance!" I pressed him.

But Martin remained resolute. The only concession he made was a trip to the movies. And a chick flick to top it off. No noise, no action, no thrills. Nothing that might scare the mini-Martin seedling under Birgit's taut abs.

"Nothing that might scare him?" I asked. "Martin, it's never too soon to start showing your offspring what a real hero is. You two should start watching man movies now. *Rocky, Rambo,* and stuff like that. Or if you ask me, *Terminator* or *Transformers,* or at least *Fast & Furious.* It's edifying."

Martin, however, banned Birgit from Coke, popcorn, and Gummi Bears, and instead packed a little bag of sulfur-free dried apricots and a couple of walnuts, in case Birgit suddenly fell victim to a fress flash while in the movie theater. This anticipation turned out to hit the bull's-eye, except that she didn't stuff her mouth with mushy dried apricots but with popcorn stolen from the bucket of her neighbor to the left. Martin could bitch all he wanted.

But after the movie, Birgit puked all of the popcorn into the gutter outside the theater before having Martin drive her home, and once in bed she fell dead asleep within twelve seconds of her head hitting the pillow.

"Now let's get going," I ordered him. "Birgit's sleeping. She won't notice your absence, and Chilling Chili will be opening soon."

"I'm tired too and need to go to bed," Martin whined, but I wouldn't let him shake me off. Work before pleasure.

He gave in, nerve-racked as he was.

"So she's about as tall as you with black hair," I started once we were inside the Chilling Chili. "Judging by her skin, she's a regular at the fake 'n bake, and she has tits as big and round as water balloons."

Martin's brain produced an image of a stupid, leathery, brown-toasted blonde—but with black hair—and basically that picture of our quarry was dead on. I left him alone to scan the crowd, and I did my own searching. It wasn't easy to make out anything in the club at all because strobe lights kept flashing like lightning through thunderclouds, making every movement remind me of a chicken with its head cut off.

"Her sugar daddy the night Akif got shot was a fat bastard in black clothes with a lot of gold around his neck."

"Mm-hmm," Martin intoned.

The majority of the tigers in this dive matched my description, you see.

I flew through the smoke-thick air and actually felt like I was struggling my way through a pulpy goo. Cigarette smoke and cologne and black clouds from water pipes and cigarillos and miasmas of pomade and sweat displaced just about everything a human being needs to breathe. Fortunately no one here follows the smoking ban—otherwise the combination of everything exhaled, perspired, and exuded by the bodies of the clientèle here would have been unbearable. All those heinie heads who sit in the European Parliament should spend some time thinking about issues like that before they vote to ban the disinfecting fumes of such establishments. The smell from a freshly opened body bag with a six-week-old corpse inside has nothing on the smell of a nightclub that enforces a smoking ban. Which is why a ban on nicotine has never been comprehensively implemented.

Someone jostled Martin, landing his face in the cleavage of a black woman who must have weighed two hundred kilos, and he instantly found himself in the viselike grip of a guy who had at least a hundred kilos more on the woman.

"Fuck off, asshole," the bodyguard whispered into Martin's ear and gave him a friendly shove. Martin landed on the floor four meters ahead. A stiletto heel stabbed into the wood floor right between his index and middle fingers, so Martin reflexively pulled both hands to his chest. He curled up like a hedgehog and yelled when two hands grabbed him.

His bald, muscled, half-naked rescuer was not distracted by Martin's clamor as he carefully set Martin back down on two feet, tugged his shirt back down, straightened his sweater, and then carefully patted his cheek. As the guy turned back around to his colorful drink, Martin and I could see the two firearms in his belt.

Martin lowered his head like a bull preparing to charge and trudged toward the front door. Except he had gotten his directions mixed up. The ladies primping in front of the vanity mirror in the women's bathroom froze, staring at him as though he were from Mars. Martin was just as shocked himself, stammering an apology as his face turned as red as a heat lamp and he frantically retreated out the door.

"Martin, just chill out," I suggested.

"Chill out?" Martin said, still trying to find the exit. "The types of people spending time here constitute the majority of my customers."

I was pleased Martin used the word *customers*, because actually the bodies at the institute are called *patients* or, worse yet, *subjects*. Lame. I taught him to refer to them as customers, see. It sounds way nicer. The word *customer* is also nicely suited to pleasant combinations, such as *customer-friendly, customer parking* (i.e., morgue drawers), or *customer card* (i.e., the little tag they tie on your toe when you come in with *X*s for pupils).

"You know better than anyone that people in circles like this commit murders," I reminded him. "How often does someone uninvolved in a crime show up on your table? Maybe like, once a year? So why does this come as a shock to you now?"

"Because I'm always the one asking stupid questions."

OK, that was kind of a good point, because Martin really does ask a lot of stupid questions. But he hadn't actually started asking *any* questions here yet, much to my dismay. After all, asking questions was why we were here in the first place.

Meanwhile, Martin burrowed through the crowd like a prizefighter after defeat, which is how I assume he felt. I sighed. No investigator anywhere in the world could have achieved as much as I have with an assistant like Martin. Not even Stephan Derrick, the greatest detective who has ever been on TV. And that includes Columbo.

Martin had made it back to the front door. He stretched his hand out to open it, but at that moment someone pulled it open from outside. The woman we had been looking for stepped in, along with her greasy, fat companion.

Martin's hand landed on her left boob.

"Oh, well, hello!" she said as Martin stared at her in disbelief from top to bottom. "Don't you look like a bookkeeper at a day spa." She laughed shrilly. "And your grip's like a gay masseur's."

Her fat companion hadn't noticed the fondling, fortunately, so Martin survived this encounter, although he was totally shocked and already trembling uncontrollably.

"That's her!" I yelled, since nothing seemed to be clicking with him for the moment. "Stay on her!"

Now her companion became aware of Martin, who was standing in their way, pale and droopy.

"Hey, gramps, get the fuck out of the doorway," the fat-ass growled. His fleshy hand landed on the expansive hip of his bunny, who was sporting a neon-yellow full-body stocking today. I could definitely tell from a single glance that she didn't have anything on her that didn't belong. So no cell phone, no first-aid bag, and no travel kit. She wasn't even wearing anything that *did* belong, such as underwear. Well, she had a too-tight bra on, but nothing down below. No panties, no thong, no string bikini, no boy shorts, no teddy, no bodysuit, or whatever those thingies are called.

It was heard to shift my attention from the interesting details, but I still managed to zoom down to her feet and—bingo!—she had her platform sandals on.

Martin had since snuck out the door and was now walking at a somewhat brisk pace toward the street. I caught up with him in a split second.

"Martin, I need to know what's up with this chick. You need to cozy up to her and ask a few friendly questions."

"Do I look that world-weary to you?" Martin asked.

It took quite an effort on my part not to reply with a spontaneous and loud yes. Because the opposite of world-weary would be joie de vivre, as the Frogs say, and my droopy-shouldered sad sack with a face full of worry didn't even remotely look like a happy Frenchman.

"I need to know who she is and what she has to do with Akif."

"Then watch her. If she has something to do with him, you'll find out sooner or later."

"Later may be too late for his sister, you black light. Maybe she's his accomplice and knows where Sibel's being held. If so, we need to get that out of her. I doubt she's as tough a cookie as Akif."

"She is in the company of a man with whom one surely does not trifle," Martin said. "I would like to avoid crossing his path."

"We can do that. Come on already. If you bail now, the whole operation will be for nothing, and you may as well have been in bed this whole time. Since you're here now anyway . . ."

That usually cuts it because Martin is a scientist, and therefore words such as *waste* and *efficiency* have a very special meaning to him. And that helped this time as well.

Naturally we had to find the neon demon again in the crowd of gyrating hips, but thanks to her blinding body stocking, it didn't present too great a hurdle. Except that getting Martin to go over there turned out to be not merely problematic but downright impossible: the fluorescent dog was sitting beside her fat master at a low table in the columned arcade area around the outside of the club. And they were surrounded by a band of stout boys that nobody in his right mind would mess with.

"All right, then we'll have to wait," I said casually. Because if there's one thing I know, it's that all chicks need to go the ladies' room sooner rather than later.

In this case, sooner totaled forty-five minutes, which Martin spent melting into the wall next to the bathroom door. Well, he couldn't actually melt into the wall, although he probably wished he could. It's just that he needed to maintain a distance of at least five centimeters from all surfaces apart from the floor. I had no doubt that in his pocket he already had a handkerchief or latex glove from the institute at the ready so that his skin would never have direct contact with the door handle. He's pretty paranoid about things like that, but I suppose he's right. After all, he knows the bacteria that abound on door handles by both first and last names, and he knows what they do. Personally, I prefer the casual ignorance of the club visitors. It'd look really shitty if every chick stopped to put on a yellow dishwashing glove before going into the bathroom.

Our neon vixen didn't grasp the door handle anyway because the door opened at the right time as two hefty heifers emerged, their nostrils intensely red, eventually allowing our girl to make her way in. Martin gamboled after her.

"The bookkeeper!" she said when she noticed him. "You've gone in the wrong door."

Martin shook his head.

The chick, whose yellow dress took on a pukey X-ray-green tone in the blue light inside, glared at him with cold eyes.

"Out!"

Martin shook his head again, broadcasting a call for help my way. My God, he didn't know what to say.

"I beg your pardon, ma'am, but do you have your shoe phone with you again?" he asked after I came to his aid. (The *ma'am* bit was all him, though.)

Her eyes narrowed into slits.

"You risked a lot of trouble with your companion, ma'am, to call the paramedics when Akif Akiroğlu was shot. Why?"

My original wording involved *shit* and *fat bastard*, but no matter.

"How do you know about that?" she asked so softly I wasn't sure I'd really heard it.

"I'm looking for a woman who was kidnapped. Tell me where she is, then I'll leave you alone. I only want to find that woman."

She was shocked, clearly, but quickly pulled herself together. "No idea what you're talking about, sweetie. I hope you find the woman of your dreams. A ladies' room isn't the worst place to start, I suppose."

She quickly turned and tottered back to the stalls. Martin of course fled the bathroom straight away, while I followed my neon bee to her chosen stall. She squatted over the toilet and peed while yakking into her phone at the same time.

". . . follow me under no circumstances. Or talk to me again. Get him!"

Then she provided an extremely accurate description of Martin, which included the words *chucklehead* and *candy-ass*.

I zoomed to Martin and found him already in the parking lot. The man sure could be speedy when it came to escaping.

I praised him for his efforts—I'd learned about positive rein-forcement during a dog-training segment on the morning news show—because praise increases the likelihood of compliance in the future. I decided not to tell him anything about the loom-ing threat against him that I'd overheard; that would only have made him nervous, and unnecessarily so. Instead, I kept an eye on the vicinity all around us, which is how I noticed a car pulling in that looked just as out of place as Martin's 2CV. A prehistoric Volvo station wagon with a moose sticker peeling off the tailgate. Was it family night at Cologne's coolest gangsta club? The driver proceeded through the whole parking lot, turned off the "I love alt rock and granola!" station on his blaring stereo, but didn't get out.

Martin had made it to his trash can and climbed into the tattered folding chair that serves as a driver's seat in that vehicle. As always, the noise the tin-can door made when it closed brought tears to my eyes.

"Night," I wished him before turning off. Having to put up with the swaying box for any length of time really weighs on me, which is why I left Martin to rattle his way home alone, while I checked from above to see if he was being followed. And he wasn't. The weird Volvo stayed put. Good.

I spent the next couple of hours at the side of the neon bee with the rescue sandals, but I couldn't find out why she had pulled the guardian-angel routine for Akif or what she had to do with the Volvo-driving papa in the parking lot, if anything. She was acting like a typical appendage to a sugar daddy who earned his dough in an occupation that lacked a standard industrial classification code at the tax office. The only surprising thing I found out was that Fat-Ass didn't spend his late nights at his luxurious pad putting his paws all over the sandal operator but instead in his bedroom wearing women's clothes, prancing around to Jacko's greatest hits. Unappealing—and definitely bad for business if it were to ever come out.

TEN

Sunday morning started as expected. Birgit ate her breakfast three times in a row, Martin tried to keep coffee, bad news, and cell phone radiation away from her, and I had it up to here that a clump of cells that hadn't even been born had become the gooey center of my universe. So I took off and, after flying around aimlessly, landed among my ghost gang. What had drawn me there? Surely not a sense of duty or maudlin concerns about children who are our future. Way off target. Instead, I was hoping for something that, even at the ER, I couldn't find anywhere on this quiet Sunday morning: action.

Of course what I found once again was fairy-tale hour, Turkish family reunion, and—*whoa*—Principal Bieberstein.

"Yes, yes, but that's not right," Bieberstein was saying as I arrived at Edi and Joe's room. "She did not commit a hit-and-run. Definitely not."

Edi and Joe were hovering over Edi's mother and Joe's father, while Joe's mother was facing Bieberstein, threatening him with her index finger.

"I already reported this woman to the police, and on my attorney's advice, I will also be filing suit against the school."

Bieberstein turned pale as a ghost. "I can't stop you, but I tell you once again—"

"Sophie, please . . ." Joe's father began.

"No, Bernd. Now is not the time to take others into consideration. This is about Johannes-Marius."

"No, what you're doing has nothing to do with him at all," Joe's father replied. "It doesn't serve Johannes-Marius for you to sue someone else. That doesn't help him in this situation at all."

The beautiful beast fixed her green eyes on her poor husband. I half expected to see those familiar red laser dots on his forehead, but her stinkeye was far from being that well developed.

"You're blaming me? Oh, it just gets better and better! You're the one who, without even asking me, allowed a foreigner to drive Johannes-Marius home, and more than once. And that person doesn't have anything better to do than deflect his own responsibility onto a young woman who not only caused an accident but then also cowardly ran off, leaving the children entrusted to her care in the lurch. If you hadn't ceded your duty as a father to some total stranger, none of this would have happened."

Edi's mother stood silent and then tiptoed out of the room, tears glistening in her eyes.

"Ms. Akiroğlu is not a coward. She was kidnapped," Edi complained, but the grown-ups couldn't hear her, obviously.

I was reminded of the ear in her brother's refrigerator.

"An ear?" Edi shrieked. "Ms. Akiroğlu's ear?"

Shit. That girl really caught everything I was thinking. "No idea," I said lamely, but naturally she already knew that I was assuming the ear was her teacher's.

"I can assure you that both Mr. Doğan and Ms. Akiroğlu are very reliable and trustworthy . . ." Mr. Bieberstein started to say, but he stood no chance against Joe's mother. That was confirmed by the look on Joe's father's face as well, who was shaking his head in resignation.

"Don't talk to me about reliability," said Joe's mother. "A wonder the children are even alive at all."

"I can't explain it . . ." Bieberstein repeated. "Something must have happened. She was . . ."

"And what, if I may ask, supposedly happened?" Joe's mother asked, now mockingly. "Was she abducted by aliens?"

"She was kidnapped, and now she's being dismembered!" Edi yelled. "You stupid goat. Stop picking on Ms. Akiroğlu!"

Uh-oh, I thought, waiting for Joe's reaction to his mother being called a stupid goat, but he didn't say anything. Presumably he thought Edi was right. Everyone there likely thought Edi was right.

"We need to find the kidnapper," Edi said.

Finally! Maybe we'd make some progress if the sproutlets got their asses in gear and helped me with the investigation instead of whimpering in the folds of their moms' bellies all the time.

"That's great, in theory," I said quickly. "But where do we look? I'll take any suggestions. Starting with you, Edi . . . Where should we start?"

The cloud of Edi's ghost, which had been glowing bright red in rage just a moment ago about Joe's mother, now collapsed in on itself. "I don't know either."

I sighed. Back to the beginning.

I went and got Niclas and Bülent, who gave me the impression they were sick and tired of the never-ending Sunday picnic going on in their room. They were so bored, in fact, that they had stopped fighting. All five of us met in front of the aquarium in the hospital cafeteria. We stared at the fish for a while until Edi got the idea of going swimming.

"Are you going to ride your sea horse?" I asked.

She rolled her eyes at me.

Interestingly, no one held her back as she carefully touched the surface of the water and then slowly submerged.

"What does it feel like?" Joe asked.

"Really bubbly," she explained. "But not at all wet."

Nonsense, I thought. Obviously it's wet underwater, but she was just refusing to feel it. She could go right ahead. We watched Edi paddle around behind the fish as her ghostly form, which was perfectly clear when she was out of the tank, now seemed kind of camouflaged in the water.

"What have we learned so far in our investigation?" Joe asked when he got bored with staring into the water.

I updated him on Yasemin, her missing brother, Sibel's cell phone number that Yasemin had on her, Sibel's brother who was a drug dealer and had gotten shot, and the relationship between Sibel and Bieberstein. As well as Zeynep, Yasemin's classmate, who was dead now too, and Dr. Christian Seiler a.k.a. Tristan, who had gotten beat up.

Joe puffed out his cheeks and sighed. "It's all pretty confusing, huh?"

They all mumbled and rumbled their agreement. Edi surfaced again, giggling as she got caught in the stream of bubbles from the aquarium's aerator, and then came through the glass to join us. She wasn't dripping at all.

That's what I call a dry run. Hardy har har.

"Since we don't know how these individual cases are connected, it might make sense to focus our investigation on the kidnapping of our teacher," she said, pretending to shake off like a Labrador retriever that had been chasing ducklings in a pond.

Joe smiled at Edi's game and wiped imaginary water off his face. Bülent frowned, thinking hard.

Niclas just blared out a loud "Bullshit" into the room. "Well, that won't take us long, right? We know that Ms. Akiroğlu was kidnapped, no one saw the kidnapper, and no one knows why. Now what?"

Bülent huffed in disagreement. "She was kidnapped by someone who drives a big dark car and smells of chalk," he said. "And she's been baptized Christian now. And she wanted to marry Mr. Bieberstein. And she worked for that secret church asylum group. Those are all things we didn't know before."

He thought for a moment.

"Oh, boy. I'm pretty sure my mother doesn't know anything about the baptism. Or the wedding. Or the church asylum."

"Exactly," Joe said. "Very good, Bülent."

"Great," Edi said.

Bülent turned red.

Niclas sulked.

I couldn't tell if this approach to an investigation was particularly promising, but one thing was sure: focusing on the missing teacher was the only idea we had. So there was no reason not to put that church asylum under the microscope and check it out in more detail. Because, as Bülent had made very clear to us, that was something that would have shocked Sibel's Muslim social circle: her conversion and commitment to a Christian denomination.

This time around we entered the vicarage directly through the window on the second floor. It wasn't strictly necessary since we can also whoosh through walls, but it's way more pleasant if you can see where you're flying. Otherwise you might end up in a microwave or something, and that's nasty. *Seriously.* Don't try it.

I don't know what I expected, but I definitely didn't expect to find a hardworking herd of buffalo calves sitting at the dining table studying. They had books and notepads all around them, and they were doing their homework silently, occasionally chatting with each other. But their chat wasn't about whether they would willingly be bitten by a sexy vampire. No, they were chatting exclusively about their homework. What a nauseating scene.

"What are these people doing?" Niclas asked. "They're not *seriously* all studying, are they?"

"Why not?" said Edi. Obviously.

"Because it's not cool," Niclas replied.

While Edi and Niclas fought about the joy of learning and the value of good spelling, Joe and Bülent were uncommonly quiet. My attention panned over to them and landed on Joe first. He had evidently fallen instantly in love with one chick who was helping the little kids with their homework. OK, she did look nice if you're into buffalo meat.

I mean, the hair on her face was growing from all sides in toward her nose. Maybe I noticed just because her hair was absolutely jet black. Whiskers, tufts, and ruff were growing down onto her forehead, over her temples, under her ears, and forward under her jaw. Her eyebrows formed a "natural reserve," as the tree huggers so nicely call it—by which I mean a gapless unibrow over both eyes and her nose. Her forearms, which stuck out under her short-sleeved blouse, were hairy too. I didn't care to speculate about her armpits or legs.

"She's way too old for you," I informed Joe. "She's at least sixteen."

"I'm precocious," Joe whispered.

"At that age, babes are interested in men who are several years older than them. Older, dude. Not younger. And not six years younger and a half meter shorter."

All my arguments slid off Joe-meo as though he were made of Teflon. He had lost his heart and thus his mind, and I could only hope his mind, at least, might return to us in the near future, because without Joe, the other three would tatter, batter, or splatter each other—call it what you want, but things would go badly.

Bülent was also staring at someone, but in his case it was an older boy sitting at the end of the table, painting swirls on a piece of paper. He didn't have a book or photocopied homework assignment in front him, just a pad of paper. Graph paper. Recycling gray. And he was drawing swirls all over it.

He was resting his head in his left hand as he stared down at the paper, which is why I could see only half his face. Still, he struck me as familiar. Bülent too, apparently.

"Who is that?" I asked.

"Mehmet."

Shit. Of course! Yasemin's brother, who practically the entire city of Cologne was looking for by now. And here he was in a Protestant vicarage, nice and cozy, drawing swirls. How in the hell had he made it in here?

"We need to tell his father," Bülent said.

"Mehmet's father?" I asked. "Did you miswrap your turban? That guy's a case for the cops."

"No! No police! It's a family matter."

I expected Bülent to smile at me and explain he was only joking, but he didn't.

We both looked at Mehmet, and I started brainstorming how I could lure Gregor out here, since Martin would just be difficult if I asked him again. And then I caught a wisp of what Bülent was thinking. He was wondering if he would have the courage to kill his sister if someone ordered him to.

WHAT THE FUCK?

"OK, people, that's enough for now," I roared. The still-quarreling Edi and Niclas, love-struck Joe, and brooding Bülent all winced so much that the kids sitting below us had to have felt a rush of air like a Bugatti racing by.

"You guys can do what you want, but I'm going to the police. As far as I'm concerned, you can stay here and make sure Mehmet doesn't escape."

"Mehmet?" Edi asked, surprised.

"That guy," I said pointing at him. "Keep an eye on him, Edi. Hopefully I'll be back soon."

As I left the litter alone, I could hear them start to argue again. About what, I couldn't tell, but I didn't care. I needed to find Martin. And fast.

Which was unfortunately not as easy as I had expected.

His apartment was empty. No sleeping Birgit (she had spent more hours asleep than awake the past few days). No Martin. Hmm. The minute you needed him . . . I checked all the nearby spots: the park, because Martin is a great advocate of taking walks in fresh air for at least fifteen minutes a day. The café, which offered not only various hip coffee beverages (for Birgit) but also about twenty-seven different types of organic tea and house-made, whole-food pastries (for Martin), to say nothing of eight thousand books on shelves lining the walls. The local salad slaughterhouse, whose floral burgers form the basis of Martin's life. But not a trace of Martin or Birgit anywhere. Shit. Now things were going to get really tiring.

I paused . . . If I seriously concentrate, I can make a spiritual connection with him over quite a distance. It's not insanely hard when I'm already near Martin and then fly away, but it is pretty hard if I want to establish a connection but don't know where he is. I need to get within a certain range of him and operate over the open radio channel, so to speak. With effort, and given the necessary proximity, it usually works unless he's actively trying to jam me. Since I was currently not in his immediate vicinity, Martin had no reason to be jamming me, so my chances of finding him were good, all in all. The only problem was that I needed to look for him in a city of almost a million people.

So, the digest version is this: it took me a solid hour to find him, and I would never have expected to find him where I did— at a steakhouse. There he was, sitting amid all that dead meat with Birgit, Katrin, and Gregor. Birgit's plate was overflowing with a ginormous, juicy steak that she was tackling with a razor-sharp implement and a vampire-like gaze.

Martin had stuck to an aluminum-wrapped baked potato and some green-colored organic waste. Their conversation was amazingly not about the nascent nipper but about a vacation that Katrin and Gregor were planning. Over Christmas, to Florida. Hmm, going on vacation was not at all a bad idea. And I didn't even need to book a flight or hotel. Maybe I'd follow those two and watch Gregor hunt alligators and crocodiles and Katrin beach it in a skimpy bikini.

"I dug up Mehmet for you guys while you've been sitting here with law enforcement, scarfing down dead animals."

Martin didn't take the bait on the dead animals. After relying on each other for almost ten months, Martin had started seeing through some of my tricks.

"*You* rely on *me*," he said instantly, correcting my train of thought. "The opposite, not so much."

I was in a gracious mood since I was going to have to bust up this little party abruptly, which is why I refrained from reminding him how I helped save him that time he got stabbed, or how I helped save Birgit that time he reneged on being available for emergencies, or how I helped save the temporary director of the Institute for Forensic Medicine . . .

"Only one person is responsible for the *existence* all of those life-threatening situations in the first place," Martin retorted, "and that person is you."

"Mehmet," I reminded him.

"Who is Mehmet?" Martin asked—aloud.

Whoopsie! The conversation abruptly stopped. Way embarrassing!

"Sorry?" Gregor asked after a moment of silence. Only Birgit kept stuffing her face, unmoved. That woman knows her priorities.

"Um, well, you're looking for that . . . M-mehmet," Martin stammered.

I believe I've previously mentioned how Martin keeps refusing to clue his life partner in on the fact that I exist. As well as how he refuses to acknowledge the fact that Gregor and Katrin *do* know about me. And so again and again, we end up with awkward moments like this one, where the only really innocent person is Birgit, who was busy munching her meat.

"Pascha!" Martin roared, this time only mentally. He had pulled himself together.

"What's up with Mehmet?" Gregor asked.

I couldn't tell from Gregor's question if he had ever mentioned Mehmet to him before, or maybe he was just playing it cool so that Martin, Katrin, and he—who all actually knew about me—could just pretend that they weren't talking about me at all.

"What's up with him?" Martin asked mentally.

Awesome. I should have just left him hanging at that point. I could have gone on a flight around the block, and Martin wouldn't have had a glimmer of what was up with Mehmet. Awkward!

"Who is Mehmet?" he asked me mentally again.

Wow. So Gregor really hadn't mentioned Mehmet to him at all. This was just getting better and better.

"What's wrong?" Birgit asked amid the general silence.

OK, for Birgit's sake I decided not to leave Martin hanging. Although it would have been pretty funny. "Mehmet at this moment is at the church asylum."

I could only hope Mehmet was still there, but that was a secondary consideration for the present. Now Martin just needed to find a way to say this to Gregor.

Martin's brain filled with a bustle of activity. He is the absolute worst white-liar you can possibly imagine. By now, any other man could have come up with fourteen nice little stories to explain his sudden knowledge of Mehmet's whereabouts, including the reason why it randomly occurred to him halfway through spooning tuber into his mouth. But, no, not Martin. *His* cranium drained of thoughts as it filled with air, like bloated intestines after you eat raw onions, and what came out was a verbal fart in the form of, "Uh . . ."

"Who's this Mehmet?" Birgit asked innocently. She looked around the table, and Gregor took pity on her.

"He's an important witness in a murder case. He's the victim's brother."

"That teenage girl who was stabbed to death?" Birgit asked.

"That's right," I said.

"That's right," Martin said.

"That's right," Gregor said.

"And you know something about him?" Birgit asked Martin. "Did she speak to y—"

Katrin and Gregor gave Birgit a pair of major double takes.

Birgit slammed her hand over her mouth. "Sorry," she whispered.

It was a dark and gloomy night inside Martin's head. A new moon with full cloud cover. Not a star anywhere to be seen.

"What did you want to say?" Gregor asked.

Birgit batted her eyes contritely at Martin, who slowly and hesitantly nodded. Aha, he had seen the out Birgit had inadvertently created for him.

"Martin has been a medium ever since his near-death experience."

Martin stared at the paper placemat under his plate as though he had just discovered the mathematical formula for a time warp sketched on it.

"Yes," said Birgit. "You know. A little like a psychic? Sometimes the souls of the dead share things with him. We did an experiment, and you could see them."

Gregor and Katrin had since lost control of the muscles in their lower jaws.

"That's not crazy talk," Birgit added. "There's more between heaven and earth than we can see."

Martin took her hand and squeezed it. I interpreted the look on his face as heartburn, but perhaps it was also a brave smile for his beloved.

Gregor cleared his throat. "Well, successful manhunts have come about in the most unusual ways before. There have even been murder cases that were solvable only with the help of clairvoyants. So if you can tell me anything about the whereabouts of our most important witness, Martin, please go ahead."

And that's exactly what Martin did. Everything that I told him bubbled out of him, as though he were trying to break Birgit's world record in projectile vomiting. Gregor briefly closed his eyes (I assume he was wondering how he would justify the warrant he was about to request). He asked Katrin to pay for his share of the check, gave her a kiss, and left. I would have loved to listen to how Martin or Katrin was about to steer the conversation back to safe subjects, but I clung instead to the only principle that I still followed in my world: action comes first.

Gregor called Jenny, answered her question on his source for this information with "an anonymous tip," and agreed to meet in front of the vicarage. Then he called a couple of extra badges for backup to cover the rear exit—just to show their presence, not to intervene.

He didn't want to do an official arrest; he wanted them to just keep things low-key.

Wimp.

I had already checked the situation out when Gregor and Jenny arrived at the steps of the vicarage. Mehmet was still there, although now he was lying down in one of the rooms on a bunk bed, crying. The other people inside were each doing their own thing too. A few were still sitting at the table with Joe's hirsute beauty. Others were playing on the floor under the table, while three littler ones were in bed, sound asleep. My assistants had split up. Edi and Bülent were studying spelling with the remaining nerds. Bülent kept asking how to remember this or that spelling or bit of grammar, and Edi would make up the most hair-raising mnemonics.

Like this:

Comparatives that come below
have umlauted ä, ü, and ö:

jung–jünger *young*, alt–älter *old*,
scharf–schärfer *sharp*, kalt–kälter *cold*.

And this:

The accusative is the proper case
with bis *or "till some time or place";*
with durch *and* für *and* um *"about,"*
with sonder, ohne *or "without";*
and wider *meaning "opposition,"*
and gegen *any disposition.*

Or this:

Write das, *not* dass, *with a lonely* s
when with or for a noun, no less.

My God, those two were having fun. *With grammar!* Freaky, huh?

Joe was still drooling over the governess, and Niclas was doz-ing in a corner. I tried to grab their attention, but apart from Niclas, the bonsais were not interested in my return. However, Fire Alarm eventually woke up and asked all groggy-like if the cops were finally coming to nab Mehmet.

"The cops are already outside," I said.

"Awesome," he replied, now more alert. "And . . . action!"

The action sequence unfolded differently than I had planned. But in order, at least.

Gregor rang the bell. There was wild clucking in the kitchen, where a bunch of hens were cooking together. Even though at least half of what they were saying wasn't in German and the other half was broken German at best, I still understood the deci-sive issue: Should they open the door or not? Before the cluckers could decide, one of the kids got curious enough to slide down the banisters and open the front door. Gregor asked if there were any grown-ups inside, and then the cooks came down all atwitter, and Gregor sent Jenny in. A chick to calm the hens—Gregor had a good instinct for psychology.

Jenny asked if she could talk to Mehmet, and the cluckers got all flustered like a flock of geese the night before St. Martin's Day—roast duck being the main course, if you didn't know. Before the geese could agree whether they knew a Mehmet or not and, if they did, whether they should admit it and call him or maybe just deny everything, from upstairs there came a crash, a whispered curse, the squeaking of a window opening, and children's screams.

Gregor and Jenny pushed their way past the headscarves and aprons, storming up the stairs and into the large room with the dining table. Some of the kids were sitting silently on top of the table, while others were buzzing about the window like a swarm of wasps, snot and tears everywhere. The moment Gregor and Jenny burst into the room, they saw a raven-haired head at the open window take a look down and then leap off.

Jenny pulled the children to the side. Gregor jumped onto the windowsill and plunged through the window, which elicited a sharp scream from Jenny. I followed Gregor outside and had to admit that his heroic dive into the abyss was more like a hop-scotch hop, because right outside the window, there was a flat roof forming part of a postwar addition to the church. The raven-haired figure had just jumped down from the far end of that. Gregor followed suit.

I passed Gregor and the fugitive, who had no idea there were uniforms waiting for him at the back exit of the property, which is why he was running full of hope toward the backyard gate. He ran nimbly, his ponytail swinging violently back and forth with each step.

Wait. Ponytail? Ah . . . I finally got what was bugging me about Yasemin's fleeing brother. This wasn't Mehmet. Mehmet must have remained in the house. In fact, this guy was no guy. It was Joe's beloved.

"Why is she running away?" Joe cried from beside me. I almost choked I was so startled. I hadn't noticed him until now.

"What happened up there?" I asked him.

"She listened at the door to the dining room when she could tell the women were talking with strangers downstairs. Then she suddenly stormed off, threw on her coat, ripped open the window, and jumped out."

"Halt!" Gregor yelled for the umpteenth time. "I just want to talk with you!"

No way. The girl was way faster than him—until she suddenly stopped at the little backyard gate as though she had rammed into a concrete wall. Yes indeed, a blue-light special with two friendly gentlemen in fashionable dark blue can be quite a shock. I knew the feeling, back when German cops still wore green instead of blue.

She made a break to the side, looking for another way out. The girl had real stamina. She apparently didn't even think of giving up, which convinced me that she may be Yasemin's murderer, because making a dash to escape like that had to have some pretty serious reason behind it.

"She's not a murderer!" Joe bellowed at me. "She's afraid."

"Yeah, of prison," I replied as we both watched her take a huge leap up and climb some stacked outdoor furniture, trying to jump over the fence from there. At that moment Gregor grabbed the cuff of her pants leg.

If she had only stepped backward a little, Gregor would have fallen over. His face was beet red from exertion, he was gasping for air like a marathon runner who had accidentally run the race twice, and he was holding the fabric of her jeans with just two fingers. But the sprinter froze into a pillar of salt and didn't move a millimeter more. She was also breathing faster than usual, but it didn't look like her health was her foremost concern.

"Please," Gregor gasped, and it sounded like he was begging her for a cardiac massage. "I just have a couple of questions . . ."

She took pity, nimbly hopped down from the shaky stack of furniture, and started fanning air at Gregor with her hand. He stared at her, out of breath, mouth agape, and eyes wide. Aha, *der Kommissar* had finally realized what we had known for a while now: he had not been chasing Mehmet.

"Oh, no. Now he's going to put her in jail," Joe lamented from beside me.

"You should exercise more," the chick muttered. Then she turned around and trudged with head down and hands in pockets back toward the building with Gregor in tow.

Gregor made a wheezing sound that signified his agreement, and it took him another few seconds before he could ask her name.

She didn't turn around but kept walking in silence as Gregor staggered behind her, shaking his head. Meanwhile, Jenny had opened the back door of the vicarage, ready for them.

Everyone who lived in the asylum was now gathered in the dining room—except for one person. Mehmet still had not come out of his room, as Edi immediately whispered to me when I entered the room behind Gregor. "I think he's afraid."

"Of course he is," Niclas blared into my ear. "He knows he'll get sent back to live in his camel-herder's tent."

"They have proper houses in Turkey, you bozo, just like they do here," Bülent snapped.

"Quiet!" I roared.

Gregor had gotten his breath back and was now standing at the table where the women and children had taken position. No men were present. Jenny was sitting with the sprinter at the end of the table.

"We're looking for a boy who ran away from home. His name is Mehmet Özcan," Gregor said. "He's an important witness in an investigation, and we urgently need to talk to him."

No one looked at Gregor. No one said anything.

"I know you have all had run-ins with the German authorities, but that's not why I'm here. I don't want to blow the whistle on you or have anyone deported or cause trouble for anyone in any other way."

"Mehmet is standing outside the door to this room listening in," Edi whispered to me.

Nice! Brace-Face was on top of things. I could afford to get immersed in the cop show while she kept an eye on Mehmet.

"Pfff, girls," Niclas said, waiting idly in a corner and hoping a couple of foreigners would get arrested.

"Edi is ten times smarter than you, and she's nice on top of that."

That comment came from—I could hardly believe it—Bülent. Not from Joe, no, who was orbiting his heartthrob and not paying any attention to the rest of the world.

"He's really afraid," Edi whispered into my ear. Now and again the girl came off like a true professional.

At that moment, the door to the dining room opened, and Mehmet walked in with his arms dangling at his sides.

"Please don't tell my father you found me," he said, then he held out his crossed wrists for Gregor.

Oh, God. A drama queen.

Gregor had nothing so dramatic in mind. Instead, he simply called the uniforms in their blue-light special to the front door and had Mehmet taken to police HQ.

Sunday, 4:20 p.m.

"We have to inform your parents. You're still a minor, you've been reported missing, and so I'm not allowed to question you without your guardians being present," Gregor explained.

Mehmet sat on his chair, mute and head down.

Yes, dear reader, that's right. Gregor questioned the students at Yasemin and Zeynep's school no problem, but that was just chitchat. In Mehmet's case, he was suspected of murder, so the rules were way more restrictive. Too bad for Mehmet. He shrugged as if to say nothing mattered to him anymore now. And he hadn't said another word since he'd been brought in.

Mehmet's parents arrived. His father got to him first and slapped him across the face.

"He deserved that," Niclas said with a satisfied smirk. Bülent and he were hanging out around me while Joe remained with his flame, Edi keeping him company there.

Gregor told Mehmet's father to take it easy and threatened his father with handcuffs.

"Yeah, man. That's right," Niclas opined.

Bülent was getting madder and madder.

Mehmet didn't budge as his mother wailed some gibberish or other at a shrill pitch. Jenny looked like she was expecting the supervisor on duty to appear in the doorway at any second to see what the commotion was about, but she didn't say anything all the same. She knew today wasn't the day to fuck with Gregor.

"I'd like to know where exactly you were on Monday afternoon and evening starting at four o'clock."

Mehmet didn't look up, and he didn't answer.

"Do you know who your sister was going to meet?"

Silence.

"Your sister had a telephone number on her that belonged to a teacher who is now missing. Did they know each other?"

More silence from Mehmet.

"Come on, get him to talk," Niclas said.

"How well did you know Zeynep Kaymaz? Did she do drugs regularly? Who else is doing drugs at school?"

"Torture him, torture him," Niclas chanted.

"I'm so going to kick your ass when we're normal again," Bülent bellowed.

"Quiet!" I roared.

The two mad boys were circling me in glowing clouds of rage, making it hard to follow what was going on between Gregor and Mehmet. What I did pick up, however, was not very enlightening: Gregor bombarded Mehmet with about fifty more questions, and the kid just sat there, trap shut, playing deaf and dumb. Gregor even informed him he was the prime suspect in the murder of Yasemin and would spend the coming night at the police station, but he still didn't move.

Mehmet's mother pleaded with her son to tell Gregor anything and everything that could exonerate him, which my tubby little translator was kind enough to render into German for me. His father remained silent, however, and didn't even say good-bye to his son. At long last, Mehmet's parents left Gregor's office, one saying nothing, the other wailing, and then it became quiet again.

ELEVEN

Monday, 7:15 a.m.

It wasn't even eight on Monday morning when I passed through Oz to see what Gregor and Jenny were planning for the day, only to find that they had just finished up their morning meeting and were headed out. No idea where to, so I had to follow them in the sleet through Cologne's perpetual traffic congestion. It wasn't even Advent, but some of the sleet was turning to snow, which was starting to stick on the ground. The craptastic scourge of winter, arriving early. How nice.

Turned out they were paying a visit to Dr. "Tristan" Seiler.

Oh, I'd totally forgotten about him.

The toothless teacher, who'd been in the hospital since Friday, sloppily sucking up soup through straws, greeted the gumshoes with a hearty, "Finally!"

"What's that supposed to mean?" Gregor asked.

"I want to report a crime."

"We're not responsible for taking reports."

"Oh, terrific."

Of course, the way he said it, it sounded more like "Oh, fewwifigh," since Tristan's pronunciation was afflicted about as much as his appearance.

"We have a few questions about Yasemin and Zeynep."

"But I—"

"We'll get to the assault on you as well, don't worry."

Tristan crossed his arms and gave Gregor a defiant stare, which looked even more stupid than usual with the bandage on his head, his split lip, and the iridescent, purple shiner around his eye.

"Who assaulted you?" Gregor asked.

"That clique from the mosque that Mehmet used to be a part of."

"Was Mehmet among them?"

"No."

"Do you know the other boys' names?"

"Only Fügrü Bovgurt."

Translating his pronunciation, that was Şükrü Bozkurt. Mehmet's friend. The uptight, middle-class, döner-eating ass who was going to take over his father's company after graduating from the university. The adherent of a radically traditional image of women.

"How do you know Mr. Bozkurt?"

"He attended our school."

"You were sure you recognized him despite your drunken stupor?"

Tristan nodded.

"Has he always been a radical traditionalist?"

Tristan nodded again. "He eventually made every female teacher livid with rage at some point."

"What does all of that have to do with Yasemin and Zeynep?" Gregor asked.

"That whole reactionary pack completely flips out any time a young woman wants to lead a normal, free life," Tristan said assertively, albeit with a moist lisp.

"And you think that Şükrü killed Yasemin?"

"I wouldn't put it past him."

"What reason would he have had to kill Yasemin? Was he friends with her? Or related?"

Tristan pressed his lips together.

"OK, we'll talk with him."

"You can also ask Dominic. He was friends with Şükrü."

"Do you mean Dominic Nolde?" Gregor asked, surprised.

"Yes. Yasemin's ex-boyfriend. They were both in the same grade, except Dominic had to repeat a year after going on an exchange in the United States."

The detectives didn't speak for a moment, presumably because their heads were just as roiled in confusion as mine. Dominic Nolde—model student, heartthrob, from a household with clear antiauthoritarian and academic values—was friends with Şükrü, the ultimate ultramacho dude from the döner crew?

"What exactly did you go to the mosque for?" Jenny asked. It sounded more like a casual question out of curiosity than an interrogation. Clever.

Tristan sighed. "As you know, I was drunk. That, uh, happens occasionally."

It was hard to tell, what with his dome wrapped in toilet paper and his black eye, but I think he blushed.

"Yasemin's death hit me quite hard, and I was so angry because she wouldn't be able to live out the life she had so wanted. I blamed her father for that, and I wanted to tell him so. I wanted to express all of my disdain for him. Childish, I know."

"Did you blame her father for her death as well?" Jenny asked.

Tristan shrugged. "Yes, I guess so. When a father outwardly shows that he disapproves of the way his daughter is acting, it's virtually carte blanche for everyone else to condemn her for it.

He should have stood behind her. He had every reason to be proud of her."

"Were you really concerned so much with Yasemin's talents," Jenny asked in her best just-so-I-understand voice, "or were you in love with her?"

Tristan blinked at her in surprise, then he laughed aloud, cringed, and lowered his head into his hand with a moan. "No," he said at last. "I was more interested in Dominic."

"All right then," Gregor said on their way back to the car. "Dr. Seiler has no criminal record, was never in love with Yasemin, and he was also not rejected by her. I just don't see any motive. We'll strike him from our list of suspects."

"But who's left, then?" asked Jenny.

Gregor had dispatch look up the address for Şükrü Bozkurt and drove there directly. I rushed over to University Medical Center to get Bülent, because if there was one thing I'd learned, it's that all of the Turks involved in this murder investigation could speak German perfectly well but spoke only Turkish among themselves. I found Bülent bored in front of the TV in the pediatric ward, so it wasn't hard to pull him away. On the contrary, actually. I couldn't have hoped for a more willing assistant.

A little girl opened the door to the giant Bozkurt mansion. She was startled to see strangers standing on the porch asking for Şükrü, but she agreed to go get him. We followed her inside as she skipped into a dining room, where an entire family was sitting at the breakfast table stuffing substances into their mouths that looked already eaten.

"That's tahini," Bülent said. "Super yummy."

"If you say so . . ."

The coffee steamed from deep inside individual-sized copper pots with long handles, placed on saucers at each place setting.

It oozed out like mud when it was poured into little handleless cups to drink.

"Turkish coffee," Bülent said.

"I know," I said. After all, I had spent considerable time when I was alive in a game hall run by a mud cooker. Although he had always made me a proper instant coffee when I asked, none of that sludge.

"There are some people at the door. They want to talk to Şükrü," Bülent interpreted the little girl's Turkish.

"No problem," the chieftain replied.

The old man stood up from the table and came toward the detectives at a rolling gait with his head bowed, subtly guiding them back into the foyer. He asked who wanted to speak with his son.

"Criminal Investigations with the Cologne Police Department."

"Regarding what?"

"The murder of Yasemin Özcan."

"What does my son have to do with it?"

"That's exactly what we would like to ask him."

Şükrü had since turned up, just as greasy haired as he had been on Friday in front of the mosque. His right hand was bandaged.

"Any chance one of Dr. Seiler's teeth is stuck in there?" Gregor asked, glancing at the bandage. "Because he's missing one."

Bülent held his breath, afraid of what might happen next. Even as a ghost, Kebab Boy had a healthy respect for this oilcan of a man. But he was going to have to be a lot more flexible about things if he wanted to get anywhere in life. Hopefully he dug that.

"Do you think I would risk getting alcohol poisoning from one of his teeth?" Şükrü asked.

"What were you doing last week between five o'clock Monday evening and seven o'clock Tuesday night?" Jenny asked.

Şükrü Bozkurt blinked with contempt at her. "Why are you mucking through all of this?"

Jenny blinked, not sure what the punk was getting at with that question.

"A beautiful woman like you," he continued, "should be having children and leading a safe life in the protection of her family."

Now Jenny looked like *she'd* commit murder at any moment.

Bülent was undecided whether he agreed with Şükrü or not, but he sensed that I was following his train of thought and quickly added, "Wrong answer."

Good boy.

"How about you stop obstructing justice and answer the question," Gregor said with heat.

Şükrü crossed his arms and tossed his hair. "All right. On Monday I was at the university until eight o'clock. My entire statistics class can attest to that. At eight thirty I was here, had dinner with my family, and then I studied until about one in the morning. Then I went to sleep, and I spent the whole day Tuesday at the university again."

"We will need the names of witnesses for every second of that period," Gregor said.

Şükrü unloaded a whole list of names and telephone numbers from memory. With a disgusted look still on her face, Jenny recorded the whole litany with her cell phone. Jenny-Bunny had a lot to learn about police work. For instance, how to do a poker face.

"Do you really think Yasemin Özcan deserved to die?" Gregor asked.

"Of course. She went around in public with that dandy. No upstanding man will want to marry her now. She brought shame on her father and her family."

"Weren't you and Dominic Nolde best friends?" Gregor probed. "And now you're calling him a dandy?"

"He changed a lot since he came back from America."

"How did he change?"

Şükrü thought for a moment. "He used to stand by his convictions. That made him friends as well as enemies. But today he's become wishy-washy, without hard corners and edges. He wants harmony with everyone; he no longer confronts people. That is totally sick, man."

This time he had a bit of combined sympathy from Bülent, me, and probably even Gregor.

"But by contrast you still have your convictions, for instance, when it comes to the behavior of young women, correct?"

Şükrü nodded.

"If your sister did what Yasemin did—would you kill your sister for such misconduct?" Gregor asked, again casually.

Bülent gulped.

"Obviously," Şükrü said, just as casually.

Bülent was literally torn between shock and admiration.

"That's against the law in this country," Gregor said.

"And that's exactly your problem," Şükrü replied. With that he turned around and walked back through the drapes he had just come in through.

"Do you think he has something to do with Yasemin's murder?" Jenny asked once they were outside.

Gregor thought longer than usual. "No. His family's honor is not at stake here."

"That's true," Bülent confirmed. "Şükrü has no right to intervene in the affairs of another family. Unless he were affected himself. In other words, if Yasemin had dishonored him personally. Otherwise, not."

"So we're not checking his alibis?" Jenny asked.

Gregor shook his head. "At the moment we have more urgent things to attend to. If I'm wrong, we'll come back and do that, but I think the guy belongs in a special category of major asshole, nothing more."

Back at headquarters, Gregor and Jenny were called in to see their boss. I have no idea what the guy's name is. Everyone just calls him Boss.

"I just received a very unpleasant phone call," he began once Gregor and Jenny were sitting in front of him. "From the chief of police."

Neither detective said anything from the sinners' bench.

"He was very displeased because he had received an unpleasant phone call himself."

Was this a kindergarten game of telephone or what?

"To cut to the chase: you two will immediately cease all investigations pertaining to Akif Akiroğlu."

"But the man is a convicted drug dealer whose sister is missing and may have been mur—"

"I will not repeat myself. This directive also applies to Gina Bengtsfors as well."

Gregor and Jenny looked at each other. Gregor took the lead: "Gina Bengtsfors?"

"Don't play dumb," the boss snapped.

"But I really have no idea who Gina—"

"Then there should be no problem leaving her alone, Detective Sergeant Kreidler."

I could see small sparks flash in Gregor's eyes. First of all, he hated it when the boss called him "Detective Sergeant Kreidler" instead of "Gregor." Second of all, the directive had undoubtedly aroused his curiosity. If someone was going to the trouble to order him via the chief of police to leave a—still-unknown—person alone, then that person must seriously be very interesting.

"Understood," Jenny told their boss and pulled Gregor out the door.

"Who in the hell—" she started to say once they were on their way back to their own office, but Gregor put his index finger over his mouth to keep her quiet. Once they were behind the closed door of their office, Jenny repeated her question.

"I don't have the foggiest idea," Gregor said. "But it has something to do with Akif Akiroğlu. And I've been wanting a stab at him for a long time now."

He rummaged around on his desk but couldn't find what he was looking for.

"There was that license number . . ."

Aha, I knew it was a good idea to note the license of that old Mustang.

"Here." Jenny held out a piece of paper from her desk. "This is the license number. Akiroğlu's shooter was in a delivery truck that had just been reported stolen."

Shit.

"Naturally," Gregor said. "So we'll need to talk to Mr. Akiroğlu directly."

"But we're not supposed—" Jenny said.

"Don't make assumptions," Gregor called to her as he walked out. "I'm headed over to see Katrin and find out Zeynep's autopsy results."

Jenny's shoulders sagged and she shook her head.

I felt bad for Jenny-Bunny, but I followed Gregor. Where Gregor went, that's where I expected action, and where there was action, that's where I belonged.

But he didn't find Akif at home. That was too bad for Gregor, because he kept running into that wall, again and again, during this investigation. And it was too bad for me, because once again there was no action. I felt considerably worse for myself than for Gregor, frankly. I mean, for him this is all just a job in the end, but for me it was literally boring as death. Pretty nasty if you can't even *die* to free yourself from boredom.

But at least Gregor was every bit as pissed as I was, which is why he kicked and practically dented the Dumpster on the street outside Akif's apartment. Suddenly there was some pathetic meowing coming from inside it.

Gregor froze with his kicking foot in the air, listened, stepped up next to the Dumpster, and pushed the lid up. A striped cat almost jumped out, just barely missing his face. Apparently it scared both of them, because Gregor tumbled two steps backward, and the cat dropped whatever it had in its mouth and scurried away. After swearing up a shitstorm, Gregor meant to walk back to his car, when he stopped, bent down very close to the sidewalk, and stared at the thing that had been in the cat's mouth now lying there, stinking to high heaven: it was a human ear.

Monday, 11:00 a.m.

"Zeynep died of a toxic overdose of 4-MTA."

Katrin had just taken off her ridiculous-looking white coat and was now standing before Gregor in her skintight turtleneck and equally tight jeans.

"Tell me about it," he asked, staring down at her well-rounded breasts.

"Four-methylthioamphetamine. Psychoactive. Takes effect after about one hour, and the effect lasts for about six hours. It releases serotonin and creates a soft, pleasant, warm sensation. Compared to other amphetamines such as MDMA," she continued, "it takes longer to reach its full effect, so the user thinks it's not working and thus takes more pills."

"So maybe it was an accident then."

"Finding that is your job."

Gregor nodded. "Thanks."

Katrin tipped her head in a patronizing "you're welcome" gesture. "Now it's my turn to ask some questions: What smells?"

Gregor held out the plastic baggie he had asked for at a bakery and stuck the ear into. Katrin took the bag and studied the contents. Naturally she didn't make a face. Naturally she didn't drop it. Naturally she didn't squeal or yell "Eew!" or anything like that. She studied the ear with professional interest.

"Where did you get this?"

Gregor shrugged. "Found it on the street. Outside the apartment of someone who may be involved in our case. But since my boss has forbidden me from continuing that investigation, I'm standing around with an ear in a plastic baggie not knowing what to do with it."

Katrin listened to him with a furrowed brow and then laughed aloud. "Man, you've got problems."

Gregor smirked at her. "What shall we do about it?"

"About the ear or about your problems?" Katrin asked with a sassy look.

"What you can do about my *problems*, you know perfectly well. So let's talk about the ear."

At that moment Martin walked into the office and stopped short. "What's that smell?" he asked.

I zoomed off.

Monday, 11:30 a.m.

After visiting the Bozkurts early in the day, I had rounded up my assistants and formed two teams: Joe and Niclas, and Edi and Bülent. I needed to split up Niclas and Bülent because they would end up devoting all their attention to their verbal pissing contest and thus neglect their mission. And each team's mission was critical: Team 1 would shadow Joe's crush while Team 2 shadowed Mehmet.

I checked in on Team 2 first.

"Hello, Pascha," Edi greeted me when I wandered in to Mehmet's cell.

"What's up?" I asked.

"Nothing," Bülent answered with a yawn. "It's deadly boring here. He sits there on his mattress the whole time, staring into space."

I felt bad for my two surveillants, but I hadn't expected a different report. Who was Mehmet going to talk to in here? He was alone. OK, there are a lot of people who talk to themselves, but they usually have some kind of affliction, and you never know whether to believe what they say.

"How have you two been passing the time?"

"I've been learning Turkish," Edi explained dead seriously. *"Merhaba. Benim adım Edi. Sen aptalsın."*

"Huh?" I asked.

"That means, 'Hello, my name is Edi. How are you?'"

I stared at Bülent, who was grinning.

I couldn't believe it.

"You think he's pulling my leg. But he's not," Edi said. "Right, Bülent?"

She looked at him confidently. Bülent's grin crumbled, and then he looked at the floor contritely.

"What does it mean, then?" she asked in a cutting voice.

"'Hello, my name is Edi. You're stupid,'" Bülent whispered.

"Nice greeting," I said.

"You're both stupid," Edi yelled.

"Come on, Edi, it was just a joke," Bülent said.

Edi pouted.

Great. And these two weren't even my problem team. I zoomed off, now in search of Team 1.

I had taken them to the church asylum myself and put them into position watching Joe's dream woman calming the children down after Gregor had taken Mehmet in. That's where I expected to find them now as well, but neither the dream woman nor my surveillance team were anywhere in sight. The whole reason I even set up two teams of two was not just to keep all four of them busy but also so that one of them could keep an eye on things while the other was underway as a messenger. I shot straight up in the air over the church asylum and called to Team 2.

No answer.

I sent my brain waves out with more pressure. No answer.

Great. So I was missing not only the surveillance subject but also the surveillants themselves. Now what?

"Hey, man, I'm on my way. We're at the airport," panted an out-of-breath voice from next to me.

"Niclas!" I yelled. I'd never thought I'd be so happy to see Fire Alarm.

"Mariam was picked up this morning. Deportation!"

"Mariam?" I asked blankly.

"The chick we've been shadowing. And Joe is of course totally . . ."

Mariam, Mariam. I knew that name. Oh yeah! There was a Mariam in the clique Yasemin had been part of. Amelie Görtz had told Gregor she'd been deported. She apparently hadn't, though, because as of yesterday, she was still helping the kids out with homework at the church asylum. If she was part of Yasemin and Mehmet's clique at school, Gregor definitely needed to talk to her.

"Shit!" I yelled. I needed to prevent that deportation.

I zoomed off to find Martin, who was with Katrin and Gregor at the slaughterhouse, as I like to call the autopsy section, where the three of them were standing around the ear. It lay lonely and lost in the middle of a giant stainless-steel table that normally whole people lie upon.

You couldn't help feeling sorry for the ear.

"Martin," I yelled.

He dropped his scalpel onto the stainless-steel table with a soul-jangling rattle.

Katrin and Gregor both flinched.

"Martin, that young woman who tried to run away from Gregor yesterday at the church asylum—she's being deported as I speak."

"And?" Martin asked me back mentally.

"You need to stop it!" I yelled.

"Why?" he asked. His eyes turned glassy as they often do when he speaks with me. Gregor and Katrin quickly looked at each other and then back at Martin.

"She was in Yasemin's clique at school. And she was hanging around the church asylum where Sibel Akiroğlu had been volunteering. Maybe she knows what the connection is between the murders and the kidnapping. Gregor needs to talk to her!"

Martin didn't understand anything, as usual, but that was no surprise since he had never wanted to listen to me. That's what he gets.

"I can't just . . ." Martin thought.

"God, how complicated can a person be?" I roared. "If you spend too much more time thinking about how to clue him in, that chick will be on a plane out of Germany."

Martin switched his brain into frantic-thinking mode. He was looking for a starting point for the information he was supposed to pass on to Gregor.

"Yesterday during your raid at the church asylum . . ." he began.

"Yes?" Gregor said.

"Why did that girl run away from you, actually?"

OK, good. Gregor had apparently told him about her attempted escape. But how would Martin move on from that point? If I'd had a couple of fingernails, I would have been seriously biting them now. Or I would have been sinking them into Martin's throat, holding tight, and shaking vigorously.

Gregor shrugged. "No idea. I passed her off to immigration."

Oh, great.

"Martin, tell him that the principal at the elementary school is involved with the church asylum and that the missing teacher used to help out there too. Then Gregor can either—"

"I should never have gotten involved in an ongoing investigation," Martin replied. "I'm glad nothing has come of that."

I felt like I was at the oral defense of my dissertation in the field of Applied Psychology of Uptight Fusspots. "You didn't get involved in the investigation of the murders. You were looking for the missing teacher," I explained to him. "We had no way of knowing it was all connected."

"Gregor will be mad in any case."

I needed the edge of a table to bite. "We have wholly different problems at the moment." But I was speaking into the void because Martin's thoughts had already turned from me to another question, which he asked aloud: "Now, if this Mehmet is hanging out there, I mean, uh, how did he get there? How does a Turkish boy become aware of a Protestant church asylum?"

Gregor looked pensively at Martin.

I continued to practice my ironbound self-control, although I would honestly have preferred to pick up an ax and start a massacre. "That's an interesting question," I said instead, praising Martin, "but how do we get from that issue to the airport?"

Martin was no longer paying any attention to me. He was focusing on his own thoughts. "HELLO?" I bellowed. "Earth to Martin! We've got a *problem!*"

No answer.

Couldn't the good Lord, or whoever was keeping me here in this shadow world I was stuck in, at least assign Gregor to me as my ground control? A cop and I would have made an awesome team. I could do surveillance, I could give him all the things I had figured out directly and unfiltered, and I could steer the whole investigation from my higher position. Instead, I needed to use Martin as my mouthpiece—and he was more of a yogurt cup on a string than a megaphone. Kindergarten shit. We weren't getting anywhere like this.

"How far along were they with the deportation?" I asked Niclas, but he wasn't there.

For the love of leaky turbochargers, wasn't there anyone around I could rely on anymore? Where had Fire Alarm zoomed off to now?

No matter. I didn't have time now to rack my brains about that. I needed to get to the airport. Maybe there was still something I could do to salvage the situation.

I turned toward Cologne Bonn Airport. The deporters weren't hard to find. Because when you see a group of foreigners with bowed heads standing there, crying and wringing their hands, surrounded by a bunch of cops waiting at a gate for a flight to Kurrekurredutt, the likelihood is fairly high that you've found the right group. I recognized Mariam the teenaged werewolf, which confirmed it.

"She is so afraid," Joe said sadly right into my ear.

"Why? She's flying home."

"No, Pascha. That's not true at all. She came to Germany when she was just a baby, because her father and grandfather had been murdered, and since she's a part of that family, they'll kill her too."

"Where do you know that from?" I asked.

"That's what she told the police officer."

"She wants people to feel bad for her so she's making it all up," I said. *Duh.* They all do that because they don't want to go to some shitty country without proper streets, where women are running around everywhere dressed like Dementors.

Joe was speechless. I was sorry, but the little guy needed to learn how the real world actually worked.

"When does her flight leave?"

"Any moment," he whispered and then burst into tears.

I can't stand shrieking banshees. Have I mentioned that already? So I left Joe to his bawling and sailed slowly through the concourse. I needed to disrupt Mariam's flight somehow so it couldn't take off. Easier said than done, however. As I've already mentioned, we ghosts are made of electromagnetic waves, so we are fully able to impact certain technological equipment, but that mainly works only when information is being transmitted wirelessly. So I needed to find a spot where important information was being transmitted wirelessly here at the airport and then disrupt that transmission and trigger some kind of alarm so no flights could take off for a while. Hmm . . . I tried at the nearest point: security check.

I had no idea how the technology works in the scanners that every passenger has to step through before boarding a plane, but surely there was a wireless component to them. I zoomed into one of the empty scanner gates, and lo and behold: the thing set off an alarm. Initially, the bored security guards only looked on stupidly, but when I triggered the alarm for the third time, even though no passenger was going through the security check, a frantic hustle and bustle broke out.

Success! I played the same game at all six of the open security gates and watched security personnel come and lock down all access points. That was the end of security check. No one else would be able to pass through for now.

A loudspeaker announcement dampened my enthusiasm, however, saying this was the final boarding call for passengers on Flight IR-728 to Tehran. Tehran? Was that the boarding call for Mariam's flight?

Which brain-dead troll was responsible for security in this place? Everyone who had already made it through security could still board? Even though the terrorist-detection system had apparently suffered a serious fault? To be honest, isn't it reasonable to expect all flights to be nixed if the electronic bomb sniffer has gone crazy?

I went over to look at the huge arrivals and departures board in the main concourse and watched the flashing green lights that indicated flights that were boarding. I needed to come up with something fast if I was going to prevent Mariam's plane from taking off.

I could try to interfere with the main radar lobe. Yes, it's really called a lobe. And without radar, you can't use instrument landing systems. Unfortunately I had accidentally flown into radar beams several times already, and it had almost blown me to kingdom come. And I don't know if I disrupted radar doing that. Presumably not enough to put my life, er, death on the line.

But maybe I could . . .

Suddenly, the departures display showed Flight IR-728 to Tehran as DELAYED. A second later, the second flight turned to DELAYED, and then the word *DELAYED* washed down the entire board next to each flight. Had my security-control operation had the desired effect after all? That was a stroke of luck.

I flew out to the tower to find out what they would do next and how much time I had gained from my super-secret operation. I got caught in an electron strudel up there that almost knocked me off my feet—virtually, of course. But something electromagnetic was whirling all around the control room. The vortex was spinning on its own axis as it simultaneously orbited the control room so that it was positioned in front of each air-traffic controller at regular intervals. Like a tornado slowly revolving around something. The air-traffic controllers were sitting in their sleek, comfy chairs with steam coming out of their ears and frantic expressions on their faces, and they were all jabbering excitedly into their headsets.

Of course, the headsets! Martin used a wireless headset to dictate into his computer at work, and I had frequently interfered with that. The same principle worked here. But what was causing the commotion?

I followed the electron tornado by carefully taking position behind it, and, once close enough, I recognized the fire-alarm-red tuft of hair on top. Niclas. The little bastard had totally upstaged me.

"I was going to do that," I said with emphatic casualness. "Nice of you to get started."

"Stop yapping and help me."

I started at the opposite end of the room and followed Niclas at a constant distance. The air-traffic controllers now had only a few seconds of contact with each flight crew before Niclas or I would pass in front and interfere with the headsets so all they heard was white noise.

We circled a long time like that, taking a pause now and again to get a bearing on the situation. That's how I noticed that the tower boss had already given the order to close the airport. All flight operations were suspended until further notice, and all planes remained on the ground, with all landings being diverted to other airports. Mariam was safe for the time being.

I left Niclas at the tower so he could occasionally remind the air-traffic jokers that the situation was anything but safe, and I headed over to see Joe.

"The airport is closed," I told him.

"I gathered," he replied, beaming.

"It's not a coincidence either, my little friend, but my work."

"You're so cool," Joe cheered. "Now Mariam can stay here."

I checked out Mariam's cops, who were chattering frantically into their phones, and quickly learned where Mariam would spend the hours until her flight could take off. Hmm. I didn't want to spoil things for Joe. Seeing his beloved in a predeportation holding cell was definitely not going to be romantic. But I didn't have time to waste. The pressing question now was whether Martin and Gregor had come to a decision, so I zoomed fast as lightning back to the institute.

The autopsy section was empty. Well, not empty, obviously, since seventeen corpses were moldering in seventeen morgue drawers, but Martin, Katrin, and Gregor were nowhere around. And the ear had also gone missing, leaving the stainless-steel table shiny clean.

I looked for Martin at his office, but I found no sign of anyone there. Break room, bathroom: no dice. His coat was still hanging properly on its hook, so he had to be in the building. I slowly cruised through the corridors to see if I could get a heading on him, and I finally found him in the director's office.

Martin's boss was totally all right. After all, he hadn't fired Martin or had him involuntarily committed to a high-security psychiatric hospital even though Martin occasionally acted super weird. I mean, Martin talks to himself aloud (of course, no one knows he's talking to me), he drops things whenever he is startled by something (for example, *moi*), he blurts out bizarre questions that have absolutely no relationship to his work or the general conversation at a given moment (although they relate to what I'm talking to him about). Since Martin never talked about me, never wanted to tell anyone about me and our intimate friendship, he has merely made his life that much more difficult. If he would only tell the world about the ghost of Pascha, whose body had been in a morgue drawer a few months back, he wouldn't have to put on an act all the time. But no, Martin was a scientist and thus couldn't explain how my spirit was still sprightly and constantly cavorting with him. And as long as he didn't understand the whole ghost thing, he wouldn't say a word about it.

". . . to do with the children?"

Uh-oh. I had a bad feeling about this.

Martin was perched on the edge of his chair in front of Professor Dr. Schweitzer (Germans love double titles like that, you know). Martin was twitching and wriggling like an altar boy caught secretly bingeing on the sacramental wine.

"I wanted to give the mother an opportunity to call me, and I didn't have my personal contact card with me, just my business card for the institute. Naturally that should not imply I intended to suggest to her I was there in an official—"

Head shaking from the boss's chair. "Dr. Gänsewein . . ."

"A friend of mine, Detective Sergeant Gregor Kreidler at Criminal Investigations, is investigating one murder and another unexplained fatality caused by amphetamines, and—"

"Those two young women?"

"Exactly. So, he's investigating those cases, and the children are a part of it."

"In what way?"

"Uh, they, uh, they were involved in a car accident with their teacher, who disappeared after the wreck. That teacher is connected to the high-school student who was murdered."

The boss could not have looked more irritated.

"Martin, where's Gregor?" I interjected.

Martin visibly winced.

"I have still not entirely grasped why you examined those children in the hospital and gave the mother your telephone number here at the institute," the professor said.

"Gregor? Where?" I said, reminding Martin of my very important question.

Overwhelmed, my little goose answered, "Uh, on the way to the airport . . ." Unfortunately, *aloud*.

"Airport?" the boss asked. "What does the airport have to do with it?"

I left Martin to his embarrassing little gab session and took off. I had at least a half hour before Gregor found Mariam. So I had time to check in on Edi and Bülent.

They were hovering over the heads of Mehmet, Jenny, and Mehmet's father.

"Tell the woman what you know," Bülent said, translating Mehmet's father's order.

Mehmet was silent.

"Once again, where did you find out about the church asylum?" Jenny asked.

Mehmet was silent.

"Mehmet, the murderer of your sister is on the loose, unless her murderer is you."

Mehmet's father bowed his head a bit lower.

"If you know something, then tell me. Otherwise someone else may die."

Mehmet was silent.

"What are you afraid of?" Jenny asked.

Mehmet was silent.

"Has he said anything at all?" I asked.

"No," Edi said. "Detective Gerstenmüller has been really nice to him, and his father keeps telling him and telling him to answer the questions, but he won't make a sound."

"Do you think he'll say something soon?" I asked Bülent.

"No. He'll keep his mouth shut."

"OK, I'm off again."

"*Görüşürüz!*" Edi said. "That means 'bye,' 'see you.'"

I looked at Bülent, who nodded with a grin. "Really."

I hoped the two smart-ass lovebirds would be very happy together. They sure were going to have plenty of baby umlauts to take care of.

Gregor was at the airport with Principal Bieberstein and a deportation cop.

"He says she's an important witness in a murder investigation," the cop explained into his cell phone.

Bieberstein? Where did he come from? Oh, right. Someone from the church asylum would have notified him Mariam being deported, so he called Gregor, and they both dashed over here. That was a much more likely scenario than one where Gregor—all on his own or with Martin's unqualified help—figured out in the past half hour that the sprinter he had chased at the church asylum was a girl from Yasemin's clique at school. In fact, Bieberstein must have revealed her identity in view of the emergency and offered her to Gregor as a witness to keep her in Germany.

The cop listened to his phone for a long time and then hung up and nodded at Gregor.

"You can take her. But when you're done with her, please bring her back to the detention center for immigration."

Gregor nodded back. Bieberstein tried to protest, but Gregor grabbed the bigger man's arm and squeezed hard. Bieberstein shut up.

The cop brought out Mariam, made a note on the deportation order that the deportation was deferred while the deportee was needed by Criminal Investigations as a witness, and held the form out for Gregor to sign. As Gregor wrote, Joe was crying in my ear and Bieberstein pouted as though someone had fueled his Ferrari with diesel.

I had no need to stifle my grin, because neither Bieberstein nor the deportation cop could see me. But Gregor's signature—by which I mean the one that usually flows out of his pen on interrogation logs or at the bank—didn't even slightly resemble the surrealistic scrawl he had written on Mariam Barahni's deportation order. Hand-printed or typed names are routinely left off bureaucratic paperwork in Germany, so if you can't make out a signature, you're shit out of luck. Someone was going to have a freaking awful time figuring out which detective Mariam had been signed over to.

I've said it before, and I'll say it again: Gregor's a good cop, even if deep down inside dwells the heart of a savvy anarchist.

He and Bieberstein then left with the pale girl between them. Joe circled Mariam, full of excitement.

"They can't deport her," Bieberstein whispered as soon as they were out of earshot of the cops guarding the other deportees. "Her family members are opponents of the régime and have been targeted for persecution. Her father and grandfather were murdered, and the same fate surely awaits h—"

"We'll see," Gregor interrupted.

They both lapsed into a sullen silence. Gregor didn't say anything the whole way back to police HQ, where he put Bieberstein and Mariam in a room that he locked from the outside. Then he went to get some coffee. He got Jenny out of her own torture chamber.

"Is he saying anything?" he asked in the hallway.

"Not a peep. I'm sure he knows who the murderer is, or at least suspects who it is. But either he's afraid or he feels more duty to the murderer than to his sister."

Gregor sighed. "OK. We can't prove anything on him, so we can't get an arrest warrant. We're going to have to let him go. Come over here with me. I've got Bieberstein and Mariam there."

It turned out that Mariam was a much more willing witness than Mehmet.

"Sibel came to speak at our school," she said to the cops. "She told us how she was doing everything to make her dream come true of becoming a teacher."

Mariam spoke so softly you really needed to pay close attention to understand her. But at least she spoke German.

"She tried to encourage us to go into professions that foreigners don't normally try," Mariam continued. "Not stereotypical things like hairdresser, döner cook, or mechanic. After her talk, I went up to her and thanked her. She asked what I wanted to be, and I said it didn't matter because I was about to be deported."

"That's when she gave her the address to the church asylum." Bieberstein took up the story. "Sibel always did that when she knew someone was being threatened with deportation. But not that many people came."

"Did you used to be in the same clique of friends as Yasemin, Zeynep, Mehmet, and Dominic?" Jenny asked.

Mariam nodded.

"How did five people who are so different from each other come to form a group of friends?" Gregor asked.

"The school encourages that sort of thing," Mariam said. "They set up study groups that mix up nationalities, gender, and ages as much as possible. After that we just kind of stayed together."

"Even though Zeynep and Yasemin couldn't stand each other," Gregor said.

Mariam's mouth formed what could almost be described as a smile. "Yes."

"Why?" Gregor asked.

Mariam didn't blush, but she fidgeted a bit in her chair. "It was because of Dominic. He's always so cheerful and so . . ." She paused. "Determined. Yeah, I think that's the right word. When he gets an idea in his head, he makes it happen. Whenever something bugged him, he changed it. And whenever he couldn't change it, like when it was a school rule, he would talk with all of the people who could change the rule. That really impressed me, because a lot of people only complain when something doesn't suit them." She paused. "Plus, he's always nice to everyone. He doesn't make distinctions between Germans and foreigners. He gets along with everyone. It wasn't like we were a team or something—we all just wanted to be with Dominic."

"That sounds almost too good to be true," Jenny said with a smile.

Mariam smiled as well. "Well, you know. He spent a year abroad. That experience really made an impression on him."

Şükrü Bozkurt had also noticed that change, except he interpreted it completely differently.

"But you didn't tell your group of friends that you're still in Germany? For instance, Amelie Görtz—although I know she wasn't in your clique—told us you had already been deported."

Mariam shook her head. "Once all of our petitions for asylum and suspension of deportation had been rejected, the deportation order for my family came through, and we went underground. My mother went with my younger siblings to relatives in Belgium, but they don't have enough room to take all of us. That's why I came back. I didn't want to tell anyone, because that would have caused trouble. Harboring illegal aliens is against the law." She swallowed back a couple of tears, but one managed to flow down her cheek.

Joe literally dissolved, overcome with such compassion.

"Underground," Niclas complained. "Great. The cops are stupid, huh."

Edi looked at Joe with sympathy and then at Niclas with disgust.

Bülent was evidently the only one who was trying to stay on task. Kebab Boy might even make a great police *Kommissar* one day. I mean, they even had Turkish detectives on TV now.

"Where did Yasemin and Sibel know each other from?" Jenny asked.

"Yasemin used to come and visit me at the vicarage a lot, but I don't know if they knew each other beyond that."

Yasemin had known Sibel well enough to have her phone number in her pocket the night she was murdered.

"Which of you have done drugs?" Gregor asked. "All of you?"

Bieberstein leaped up from his chair. "What kind of a question is that? There are no drugs at our asylum. That's a fundamental condition of acceptance. We take in people who are being threatened with deportation. We give them a safe space, and we help them deal with the authorities, but it's all on condition that they do nothing illegal in the church. That includes drugs, violence, theft, and other offenses."

"And?" Gregor probed. He pretended as though he hadn't heard Bieberstein.

Mariam shook her head. "Zeynep sometimes took 'smart pills' before exams, but I don't know about anything other than that."

Gregor looked as his watch. "That's enough for today," he said, and he and Jenny left the room.

Joe stayed with Mariam and Bieberstein, and Edi stayed with Joe. Niclas headed off God knows where. Only Bülent joined me to follow Gregor and Jenny.

"Katrin? It's Gregor. We need a precise tox on—"

If Gregor abruptly stops talking while on the phone, it means the other person has some seriously important information. He frowned, walked to his desk, sat down, and gestured for Jenny to sit as well. Then he put his phone on speaker.

"I've put you on speaker. Could you repeat that?"

"Hi, Jenny," Katrin said. So polite. "OK, so we already had the preliminary toxicological analysis on the drugs Zeynep died from. But Gregor also asked about a drug history, and the results from the hair analysis just came in. I'll fax the full report over to you, but the digest version is that Zeynep was downing more or less everything you might remotely define as 'smart pills,' everything from Ritalin and Adderall on up."

"We've just heard a witness statement that confirms this," Gregor said.

"Well," Katrin said. "She's not alone. In the past twelve months, we've seen an explosive increase in tox hits on this stuff."

Gregor shrugged, which Katrin naturally couldn't see, which is why she continued talking.

"Zeynep was taking methylphenidate, donepezil, and MDMA in quantities that far exceed what is therapeutically available. In Germany, the first two I mentioned are prescription only, and the last is illegal."

"What exactly are we talking about?" Gregor asked.

"Methylphenidate is the active substance in Ritalin, which is a medication used to treat attention deficit disorder. Donepezil is used to treat Alzheimer's disease, and MDMA is what makes ecstasy so popular. Zeynep took them all. You can ask her mother, but I doubt she was suffering from ADD or Alzheimer's."

Gregor didn't take that bait.

"You said there's been an increase in cases. What kind of an increase are we talking about?"

"Two hundred fifty percent over the past twelve months."

Gregor whistled.

"Is there a particular clientèle?"

"Anyone looking to boost performance. Drugs such as methylphenidate and donepezil improve cognitive and memory performance. They can be prescribed for the conditions I mentioned before, but you can also get them illegally over the Internet. They are in widespread use among people who think they aren't up to the demands of their jobs. In particular, stockbrokers, managers, and people in similar jobs. To a lesser extent, also juniors and seniors in high school or college. But the numbers we've seen over the past twelve months show a shift in consumption: some eighty-five percent of the subjects we've seen in here have been younger than twenty-one."

Now I'd have whistled myself, but I've never been able to whistle, and there are some things you just can't learn when you're a ghost. Sadly.

"A few things are starting to become clear . . ." Gregor said slowly.

"What?" Katrin asked, but Gregor had already moved on mentally. She would have to make do without a response.

TWELVE

"Drugs," Gregor said.

"Drugs," Jenny said.

Then no one said anything for a long time.

Gregor was the first to open his mouth again. "Yasemin knew something, although she didn't take drugs. Zeynep did take drugs, so she knew something, at least the name of her dealer. Both girls are dead. Sibel Akiroğlu, whose telephone number Yasemin had on her when she was killed, is missing. And Sibel's brother Akif is a convicted drug dealer."

Jenny closed her eyes and nodded. "Everything points to Akif Akiroğlu."

"Oh, man," Bülent whispered from beside me.

I'd totally forgotten about Officer Kebab.

"Man, his sister, he's not . . ." Bülent said quietly as he started to tremble.

"Do you mean Mehmet or Akif?" I asked.

Kebab Boy's trembling grew worse. I felt like he was only now realizing his beloved teacher had been slaughtered by her own brother. That every Turkish woman was a sister.

"Bülent, life isn't a game," I explained. "I was murdered myself, although I hadn't done anything to the guy who killed me. What do you expect from a brother who deals drugs and whose sister wants to blow his cover? Is he supposed to ask her to pretty please not say anything?"

Bülent started to cry.

Not again! But somehow—and I'm telling you this in total confidence—I felt bad for him. For a kid Bülent's age, it'd be a serious shock to realize that practically anyone might murder his own sister. Especially among *Kanaken*.

"D-don't call us *Kanaken*, you racist idiot," Bülent stammered between sobs.

"Hey, don't take your frustration out on me," I said. "I can't help how you treat your women."

"Asshole."

Wow. Where did respect for one's elders go? I was trying to come up with a response when I heard Gregor speaking.

". . . Dr. Seiler as well." Shit. I'd missed something. "As a teacher, he has access to lots of students, which is an ideal position for a dealer."

Jenny nodded, but her face showed she didn't agree. "You shouldn't go there alone . . ."

"You can't come along, Jenny. You haven't been in the department long enough. If the boss has to kick my ass for not following orders, it's not that bad. But with a rookie like you, it would devastate your career." And with that our hero left the office.

Bülent had taken off in the meantime, so I accompanied Gregor all alone and in peace. We enjoyed our drive together, listening to roaring, loud music in Gregor's car. The guy needed moments like this.

It wasn't until after Gregor parked the car that I noticed Bülent had followed us after all. The little roly-poly had more persistence than I'd have thought. I pretended not to notice him.

He had called me an asshole, after all. He was rambling along, a few meters behind me.

I was right: Gregor was driving to Akif's. And this time he got him. But let me tell that whole story from the top, otherwise no one will believe me. Gregor buzzed, and Akif—who looked like he had just gotten up (at eight thirty on a Monday night) and who was walking naked through the kitchen, drinking coffee—came out into the living room and watched Gregor on his home-entertainment center before turning the buzzer off. Same as before. Gregor kept buzzing. Akif swore in Turkish at his flat screen.

I stifled my irritation with my assistant and asked Bülent what Akif was saying, but when I turned around, Bülent's face had turned so red I thought I could pretty much assume the contents.

While Gregor kept pushing the dead button, Akif pretended not to be interested in the guy downstairs anymore and went to take a shower. After his shower, Akif dripped through the apartment, saw Gregor still on his flat screen, and flew into a rage. He finally buzzed the door open.

"Who the fuck are you, ass face, that you're pestering me in the middle of the night for hours on end?" Akif yelled in accented German when Gregor appeared at the top of the stairs. Akif was still naked, apart from the thick gauze bandages still covering his gunshot wounds, which he had artfully made watertight for his shower by taping rectangular strips from Aldi grocery bags over them.

"Gregor Kreidler, Criminal Investigations, Cologne PD."

"Fuck off."

Gregor nodded. "Later. First, I have a few questions for you."

"I'm not the field information service."

"May I come in?"

"No."

Gregor nodded, stepped back, and then suddenly sprinted. He pushed Akif out of the way as he took three long strides into the apartment. Akif regained his balance and raced, roaring, after him. Gregor was now standing in the middle of the living room with disbelief on his face as he looked at the flat-screen TV, the camera shot from the building's front door still up. Then he looked over at the safe and the mess in the rest of the room. Akif stood behind him, boiling in fury, but he didn't make a move to strangle Gregor and instead grimly folded his arms across his chest.

Gregor turned around to face him. "I want to know why the chief of police stopped me from pursuing an investigation of a witness in a murder case who has priors in drug trafficking."

Akif didn't say anything.

"You may know that Yasemin Özcan had your sister's phone number on her when she was stabbed to death."

Akif didn't say anything.

"Did they know each other personally?"

Akif didn't say anything.

"In addition, we have a second death. Zeynep Kaymaz. She attended the same school as Yasemin."

"Was she stabbed as well?"

Those little sparks Gregor gets in his eyes appeared. "No. She died from a drug overdose. But we still don't know if it was suicide or—"

"No."

The two men stood facing each other like Stone Age hunters, except one looked like a caveman (Akif, naked, jaw pushed forward, ready to pounce) and the other was only acting like one

(Gregor, in a suit, his gun under his left armpit, and adrenaline surging through him to the roots of his hair).

"I beg your pardon?"

"You're assuming it wasn't suicide."

"OK. What was it then?"

The two men lay in wait for each other, like Tom and Jerry. I couldn't tell if Gregor had noticed the change in Akif's expression, but he's not stupid, so he must have noticed that the Stone Age diction like "ass face" and "fuck off" had receded in favor of an unaccented, fluid, and complete German sentence including the Latinate term "suicide."

"Well?" Gregor pressed.

"We're on the trail of a big shot. New guy, hard to pigeonhole, no contact with the old guard, hasn't been on our radar before, not connected with the usual suspects. We're getting close to him, and you're messing it up."

Gregor managed to maintain a completely motionless poker face as he squinted to study Akif, who had since grown more relaxed, although his arms were still crossed in front of him.

"Who is 'we'?" Gregor asked.

"I can't say more. Now, Detective, please leave my apartment."

"Is Gina Bengtsfors the second half of 'we'?"

Without warning, Akif took a quick step inside Gregor's reach and then spun him around to hold both of his hands behind his back. In a jiffy, he'd forced Gregor to his knees, and all this before I could even have said "Watch out."

Gregor couldn't have heard me anyway.

"How do you know that name?" Akif growled.

Oh, shit, I thought to myself. When Akif bellowed, it was unpleasant enough. But when he growled, he was way scarier.

"From my boss at police HQ, and presumably he has it from his boss," Gregor said. From the way Akif had twisted his arms, his shoulder joints must have been in a lot of pain, but he was putting on a brave face.

"That fucking idiot!" Akif roared, pushing Gregor forward until he fell. The naked meat-mountain grabbed the closest beer bottle from the table and smashed it against the wall. Shards sprayed the entire room. Akif looked at his bare feet, then the floor around them, and rolled his eyes at himself.

"OK, colleague . . ." Gregor started after wiping some blood from his lip and eyebrow.

"Nix the colleague talk," Akif said before swearing in Turkish.

I was going to have Bülent translate, but from the look on his face, I could see he didn't know the translation of most of the words Akif was saying. And if he did, he'd never actually say them aloud.

Gregor struggled back to his feet and looked at the broken glass everywhere. Then he shrugged and went into the kitchen. Glass crunched under his shoes.

"Listen to your boss and get lost," Akif yelled after him.

Gregor didn't respond. He headed straight for the refrigerator and opened the bottom freezer. He found a cooling gel compress, which he took out. I tried desperately to keep both brainiacs in sight at the same time, but I suspected what was about to happen. Finally, Akif's brain had associated the noise of the refrigerator with the box he had inside it. He turned around to storm into the kitchen but got held up: sharp bottle glass everywhere.

"Get out now!" he said, covering his rage with difficulty. Or was it fear?

Gregor had put the cold compress over his eye to stanch the bleeding. He rummaged deeper into the freezer and found some microwave pizzas and döners. But then he stopped and made a face. He sniffed. He went through the freezer once more, but didn't find anything suspicious. Then he stood up to look into the main compartment of the refrigerator. There were a few items in there, including undefinable foodstuffs, soap (?), and old deli wrappers, as well as a half-empty and lidless bottle of ketchup, a half-full jar of Kalamata olives, and two bottles of beer. I guess cans were too classy even for this guy. Next to them was the box that stank to high heaven. Akif took a cautious step toward the kitchen and stretched his neck forward.

Gregor picked up the box.

"Hands off!" Akif yelled.

"Or else what?" Gregor muttered. His full attention was on the box with the dark-red stain on the bottom right corner.

Akif took another step but paused and swore. A shard of glass had dug deep into the ball of his foot.

Gregor opened the box. Inside lay an ear, apparently the counterpart to the one that Gregor had already fished from the Dumpster.

"Shit," Gregor whispered.

"Oh, shit," Bülent roared into my ear. "I'm going to puke!"

"The ear is a joke," Akif yelled from the living room.

"Do you have a nose, fingertips, or perhaps a heart to go with the set?" Gregor asked.

Bülent was hyperventilating.

"It's not what it looks like. Close the fridge and get lost." Strangely, Akif suddenly sounded casual, a bit tired, even cordial.

"You've got two minutes to get dressed, and then I'm taking you downtown to HQ with me," said Gregor, who sounded much more tense.

"Bullshit," Akif replied. "One call from me, and you'll be put on leave through Easter."

"Then I want to hear the whole story," Gregor said.

"OK, fine." Akif sighed. "Pass a kitchen chair this way, and then please get my tweezers from the bathroom cabinet, along with my slippers."

Meanwhile, what was I going to do with a hyperventilating ghost? Breathing into a paper bag wouldn't work. Shaking him wouldn't either. So I left Bülent trying to gasp for breath while I focused on the discussion between the men below.

Gregor retrieved the requested equipment, and Akif pulled the glass splinter from his foot, slid on the slippers, limped into the bathroom, put on some clothes, and finally returned to the kitchen to slump into the second chair. Gregor remained standing.

"We're with the drug squad. Undercover. I grew up here, though, so everyone knows me in this neighborhood, which is why I don't need a fake identity, just a fake résumé. I went to university abroad, but the story here is that I was in prison. That also got added to your official database to make it credible. That's why I have a good reputation here: anyone who's done time is trustworthy."

Gregor nodded.

"For Gina it's different. Even I don't know her real name. It's especially important that *her* cover not be blown."

"Why did my boss ban me from bothering Gina, even though I've never seen her before in my life?" Gregor asked.

"Apparently there was an accountant type who was asking her stupid questions last Saturday night at Chilling Chili," Akif said. "Isn't he one of yours?"

It took about three seconds for the stoplight in Gregor's brain to turn green, but he decided not to answer. Instead he asked, "And your sister?"

Akif sighed, clearly worried. "She wants to save the world. And if the world is out of reach, she at least wants to save every young woman who wants to become the fully actualized person she is meant to be but is prevented from being by society, a man, prevailing mind-sets, traditions, or even bad weather. She's known far and wide in the Turkish community for helping women solve problems. All kinds of problems. For any woman with a problem, Sibel is all ears."

Akif stopped short on the word *ears*, and then Gregor and he both smirked.

"Sibel called me on Monday. A student had told her that morning that she suspected a person she knew was dealing drugs."

Bingo!

Gregor couldn't hide his excitement.

"But at that point, Sibel was, uh . . ." Akif blinked, looked at his feet, and hesitated.

"At the church asylum," Gregor said, completing his sentence.

"Oh, you know about that? Yeah, exactly. She told the student to meet her there, but the girl said it was too far because she needed to be home on time. They agreed to talk on the phone on Tuesday and arrange a place to meet late that afternoon."

"But in all likelihood Yasemin was already dead then," Gregor said.

Akif nodded. "I waited for Sibel to come on Tuesday night and tell me about her meeting with the student, but she never came home. Instead, the phone at my parents' house started ringing off the hook because everyone in the whole world was looking for Sibel. And then the police came with some nonsense about a hit-and-run. So that's when I started getting worried."

"When does the ear come into it?" Gregor asked.

"That came on Thursday. I had a hunch, and I took off to shove a guy's head in his ass . . ."

Bülent got hiccups.

". . . but he didn't know anything about it."

Aha, so that's why Akif was out all cool-like with his guns and knife on Thursday.

"So those are that poor guy's ears?" Gregor asked, incredulous.

Akif shook his head. "I wish. No, the first ear was waiting for me when I got home—along with a friendly reminder that Sibel could still cover the missing ear with an asymmetrical haircut. They said a second ear would follow if I didn't go on an extended vacation."

Gregor turned pale.

"That second one came the day before yesterday. Along with Sibel's glasses and a note saying her glasses wouldn't stay on anymore."

Bülent's condition deteriorated. In addition to hiccups, he started trembling so badly I could really make him out only as a blur.

Akif flashed a brief, worried smile. "However, one thing was clear to me: those elephant ears are *not* Sibel's. She has very delicate little ears. Like a child. This one, *blech* . . ."

Gregor opened the box again gingerly. Akif was right. That ear was enormous, with a long floppy earlobe and hair along the outside.

"But how did they even know that you were on the drug squad . . ."

Akif sighed again. "My parents think I'm really the junkie I pretend to be. It's hard on me deceiving them, but it's necessary. Sibel had been trying to convert me for years now. Every single day. One day I couldn't stand it anymore, so I told her the truth. I'm sure she'd never tell anyone my secret—unless she were being threatened with death."

Gregor nodded.

Akif sighed. "I assume my career is over now. I really can't blame her, as much as I'd like to."

Bülent exhaled a squall of hot air mixed with incomprehension, amazement, and doubt.

No one said anything for a moment.

"Where are the messages that came with the ears?" Gregor asked.

"You're not getting those." The collegial tone had vanished. "From now on, you need to stay clear of me. And Gina. And you can't try to do anything about my sister, either. Otherwise you'll do more harm than I can avenge in one lifetime."

Bülent gasped and coughed as though he were suffocating. Apparently he didn't grasp the rapid transition from understanding and brotherly love to prehistoric vendetta. But I wasn't worried about him. It's not like we ghosts can suffocate, drown, or burn . . . I assume that list goes on indefinitely.

"I need to examine those messages for prints and handwriting analysis and any other evidence," Gregor said.

"And I need to make sure my sister comes back to us alive."

They stared at each other again, as though their gazes might mutually annihilate one another.

"Fuck it," Gregor said after a while. "And your gunshot wounds?"

Akif looked at Gregor pensively for a long time. Then he sighed and nodded. "OK, I'll clue you in so you can rest easy: that doesn't have anything to do with this case. I ran into someone during my investigation. I can't say anything else, and it doesn't concern you further. Except you shouldn't waste your time on that shit."

Then Akif flipped on his stubborn switch and didn't say one more word. Gregor left the apartment with a heavy dose of frustration and a well-aged ear in a cardboard box.

Tuesday, 8:10 a.m.

"These are definitely a man's ears," Katrin said.

Gregor and she were standing at the stainless-steel table again, the two ears lying between them.

Bülent had recovered well overnight, which he had spent at his bedside, but seeing the hairy, long-lobed ear, he turned pale again.

"Both are from one and the same person. That person was dead when the ears were cut off."

"Gross," Bülent whispered.

"The ears were, how shall we say . . . not well looked after."

"A homeless person?"

"That was my first thought. We haven't had anyone come in missing in two years, but you might make some calls to police departments of cities downriver along the Rhine to see if anyone has turned up. With the recent flooding, it would be easy to get rid of a body."

"Well?" Jenny asked when Gregor returned to police headquarters. "Did you bring in Akif Akiroğlu?"

Gregor dropped onto his chair and put his head in his hands. "He's an undercover investigator for the Cologne PD drug unit."

Jenny stared him agape.

"But his sister was definitely kidnapped. The kidnapper sent him the ears, but they turned out not to be from her but from a dead man, presumably a bum or something."

One of the reasons I think Gregor's so cool is that he uses politically incorrect terms like *bum* when he's speaking off the record.

He updated Jenny on his conversation with Akif. "We aren't getting the kidnappers' messages because Undercover Akif doesn't want us to ruin his case or his sister's chances of survival," he concluded. "So now we're pretty much fucked. What have you found out in the meantime?"

"I ran some checks on Dr. Christian Seiler, a.k.a. Tristan, like you wanted. We already knew he didn't have any priors. But he also hasn't been a suspect or party of interest in any other recent case, and his name doesn't get mentioned in any other case or investigation. He doesn't even have a single point on his driver's license."

"Where did you check?" Gregor asked.

"I checked the databases for all of Cologne's police squads, and I also inquired with the North Rhine–Westphalia State Police in Düsseldorf, the Federal Police in Wiesbaden, Customs and Immigration in Dresden, and the Office for Tax Investigations in Berlin."

Gregor thought for a moment. "Fine. But that doesn't mean anything. Akif said he was on the trail of a new player. Someone new to the scene. Someone new to the drug business. So it's possible that person wouldn't have any priors."

"Then we should check out Dr. Seiler's alibis as soon as possible, right?"

Gregor nodded. "Let's go visit him at the hospital in a little while. But first, we'll go and check if we have any statistical data about this recent spate of drug-related cases. Katrin already said to look at the age of the victims. But I also want to know what school or university those victims went to, where they live, or whatever else you can find out about them. Maybe that will give us a clue what direction to look in next."

"What are you going to do in the meantime?" Jenny asked.

"I'm going to go have another chat with my special friend Amelie Görtz."

Since Jenny was going to be hunched over computer screens crunching data, and since I found Gregor cooler anyway, I decided to go with him. He found Amelie Görtz at school, where he pulled her away from a dead frog.

Bülent gagged anew.

"If you want to be a cool cop someday," I said to him, "you need to start getting used to seeing flayed bodies, severed ears, and frog guts."

Bülent nodded bravely.

"Did you know Zeynep did drugs?" Gregor asked Amelie.

Wow. Way to cut to the chase.

Amelie studied Gregor silently for a while, thinking. She was wearing the same jeans she wore the other day, and she again had on a baggy, shapeless jacket. But something was different about her. Her hair—that was it. Today her hair was orangey red. Blonde suited her better.

"What do you mean by drugs?" she finally asked.

"Uppers, downers, ecstasy, speed, crystal, GHB, hash, coke . . . pills, whatever!"

"So illegal drugs, you mean."

Gregor rolled his eyes. "Exactly."

"The teacher whose class you just pulled me out of is an alcoholic. Some days she can barely stand on two legs, but every day she drives to work and back home again. Why aren't you interested in that?"

"What k-kind of teacher is that?" Bülent stammered, his worldview being shaken.

"Totally average," I replied.

Gregor sighed. "I don't disagree with you one bit, Amelie, but . . ." He leaned forward with a stern frown. "I don't have time for this bullshit. I'm looking for a murderer. Maybe even a double murderer. I'd be happy to discuss the fine distinctions between legal and illegal drugs another time."

Amelie didn't pout. She was a strange bird, actually, in that Gregor had snubbed her, but she didn't instantly stand up and run out slamming the door like other women might.

"Fine," she said. "Zeynep was definitely taking some kind of pills. I'll fill you in on something: my mom died on shit like that, and that's why I don't touch them. I don't even take over-the-counter painkillers for a headache, even though I could really use them some days when school gets out. But Zeynep—yeah, definitely. And over time, actually, lots and lots of other kids."

"How do you know that?" Gregor asked.

"I'm not stupid, all right? I notice things like that. With my mom, I always had to check first and see what condition she was in before I knew how to deal with her. So I learned to spot the signs."

"And you think a lot of the other kids are doing various drugs?"

"Yep."

"Why?"

"Jeez . . . because life overwhelms people. Walk around the school and listen, and you'll know what I mean. Nowadays if you want to amount to anything, whatever it is doesn't matter, you still have to be the best. At the university, there are whole majors nowadays where you need a 1.0 to even get admitted. And our graduating class will be one of the first where there are two applications for each university spot in the country; when the government got rid of the draft, they didn't increase funding to the universities anywhere near enough to make room for all the kids who would be going to college instead."

Maybe I should explain a little something about German academics. First, 1.0 is the best, and not the worst, grade you can get. I only know that indirectly, since I never actually earned that grade myself, not being a nerd and all. Second, graduating senior boys used to have to do two years of military service or disaster-relief-type volunteer work before getting a job or going to college, but a while ago the government nixed that requirement, so all the nerds try to pile into college at the same time now.

At that point, Amelie paused, took a deep breath, and then continued in a hoarse voice. "Even if you don't want to go to college, you still need top grades—including in subjects like deportment—to even get an interview as an apprentice janitor. For most people, that pressure is just too much. So all the pretty, colorful pills arrive just at the right time."

I could see Gregor was hard at thought. I only wished I knew what about.

"Most parents aren't any help with that pressure," she continued. "They just make it worse, even when they don't mean to. My dad tells me he loves me no matter what. But then he sends me to take an IQ test because my grades were dropping. He couldn't believe I was as stupid as my grades said I was, because a man like him doesn't beget idiots. But here's the punch line: it turns out I'm supposedly brighter than Einstein, and now my proud papa is telling everyone I'll either be a doctor or lawyer or nuclear physicist. At the same time, he has me take a drug test every month so I don't ruin my future. What he means is *his* future, however, because he no more wants a junkie for a daughter than an idiot."

This story sounded familiar to me, except for the high-IQ bit.

"But you knew before you took the IQ test you weren't stupid, right?"

Amelie nodded.

"So why didn't you just mark the wrong answers on the test then?"

Amelie made a tortured laugh. "I wonder that myself. But in the end there's only one reason: vanity. Pure, stupid vanity."

God, women. They're all the same.

Gregor smirked. "What would you prefer to become instead of a nuclear physicist?"

"A horticulturalist," she mumbled.

"Sounds good to me," Gregor said. "So tell me, who's dealing the drugs at this school?"

Thank God he's getting back on topic, I thought. I was worried he was about to start chatting with Amelie about what her favorite flowers were next.

Amelie looked at her feet and shrugged. "I don't know. Honestly. I've wondered myself, but . . ."

"What's the deal with Dr. Seiler?" Gregor asked. "Why did you tell us he had a crush on Yasemin?"

Amelie blushed and studied her hands with great interest. "Didn't he?"

Gregor didn't say anything.

"Why else would he have stuck his neck out for her all the time?" she finally said. "She wasn't the only mastermind with family problems."

My God, again with the life-is-unfair whining. This chick was not nearly as cool as she pretended to be.

"But she fit the stereotype, right?" Gregor said softly. "The poor Turkish girl from a strict, patriarchal environment, prevented from becoming what she wanted in life all because of tradition. Hmm?"

Amelie nodded.

"What does your father do?"

"He's a businessman. International, cosmopolitan, modern. Being the daughter of a man like that, you don't need to worry. You've got everything you need."

The crybaby was holding back tears only with great effort.

"Don't call people crybaby," Bülent mewled.

"You've been spending too much time with Edi," I snapped back at him.

"Level with me," said Gregor. "Have you ever noticed Dr. Seiler selling colorful pills?"

Amelie regained her composure and put her poker face back on. "No. But he's also the career counselor, not just the principal, which is why he has a separate office where lots of kids can go talk to him in private. He'd have no problem selling drugs there."

THIRTEEN

Tuesday, 10:15 a.m.

"What were you doing between Monday afternoon and Tuesday night last week?" asked Gregor.

Jenny and he were sitting by Tristan's bed, looking at him expectantly.

Tristan blinked with confusion. "That's the period when Yasemin was murdered, right?"

Gregor nodded.

"Uh, both days I arrived at school at seven thirty in the morning. Monday I worked until four, Tuesday I did prep for a faculty meeting to discuss graduation requirements, and I stayed fairly late . . ."

"Who can vouch for that?"

Tristan stared at Gregor. "You don't think I . . . ?"

Gregor and Jenny remained silent. Jenny had dug up a cluster of cases of drug abuse associated in one way or another with the Nelson Mandela Comprehensive School. Several students had suffered drug overdoses, and there'd been plenty of other drug-related phenomena: heart arrhythmias during gym class, circulatory collapse at the school festival, nervous breakdown during a class trip. The situation looked only slightly better at other schools, but a minor irregularity in the statistics was better than nothing, Jenny had said.

"Did Yasemin figure out that you were dealing drugs at school? The 'smart pills' kids were using to cram for tests?"

"Sorry?" Tristan whispered.

"And then Yasemin wanted to turn you in, and you killed her. And Zeynep became suspicious after Yasemin's death. Which is why you sold her a fatal dose."

"Y-you can't believe that," Tristan stammered. "I . . ."

"You still haven't told us what you were doing late Tuesday."

Jenny wrote something down in her notebook. Since Tristan wasn't talking, I zoomed over to read it. Shit, just another psychedelic shorthand doodle. But maybe she was jotting down the question that I was also wondering about: Did Tristan have a car? How big was it, and was it dark? Could evidence be found from Yasemin's clothes and body that connected her with the carpet in the trunk of Tristan's car? Why in the hell hadn't all of those questions been asked yet?

Tristan sat in his hospital bed, pouting under his ridiculous-looking medical turban, gapped teeth, and blackened eye.

"Mr. Seiler—" Gregor started to say.

"*Doctor* Seiler," Tristan corrected him in an icy, slightly shaky voice. "And I protest any accusation of this sort. If you don't have any leads better than the first teacher you see, then it's no wonder so many crimes go unsolved in this country."

On this point, the pedagogue was quite mistaken, because more than 95 percent of all murders are solved in Germany. But I've said that before.

Tristan wasn't done ranting. "We have to do everything ourselves. People drop children off at our door, unwashed, unfed, and without the slightest notions of social behavior, and we're supposed to fix it all. We're supposed to teach them how to behave like human beings, how to eat with fork and knife, how to leave the bathroom clean after using it, how to express oneself in complete sentences, and how not to lay a punch into other students just because they look different or have a different opinion. Meanwhile, we're supposed to drum whatever educational nonsense into their heads, material that doesn't interest them and that will never be even remotely helpful to them in life. And once we've achieved all of that, we get beat up on top of it all. I'm so fed up with it."

He'd gotten beat up, if I'm not mistaken, for a completely different reason, but in his state of massive self-pity, it was easy to forget. Now the man was crying.

"So embarrassing," Bülent whispered from beside me.

That was something we could agree on.

"Well?" Gregor asked casually. He wasn't irritated by the drama or sympathetic from the whining. He was pure business, the way a cop should be.

"I plead the Fifth," he said. Actually, we don't have a Fifth Amendment in Germany. We say we're making use of our *Zeugnisverweigerungsrecht*, but you get the idea.

Gregor opened his mouth to say something when a nurse came in.

Ignoring Gregor and Jenny, she rushed to Tristan's bed. "Please clear the rrroom!" she said with a heavily trilled *R*, throwing back Tristan's covers.

Gregor turned to Tristan. "I would normally take you in to HQ now, but since you're bedridden, I'll have to make do knowing you're safe here. When you're ready to talk, please let me know. A colleague will be outside your door to make sure nothing distracts you from your recovery."

In the corridor, Gregor took Jenny aside. "I'm going to get a warrant to search his apartment, car, and offices at school."

Jenny nodded.

"Can you head directly over to the school and seal his office? Then see if his alibis check out?"

Jenny nodded again, her cheeks flushed.

"I'll handle the paperwork and get someone assigned to guard this door. I'll try to catch up with you at the school—and I'll call as soon as I know anything."

I naturally decided to follow Jenny, since Gregor's phone calls to his higher-ups were bound to be utterly unexciting. But I didn't follow her through stinking hallways and crowded elevators. Instead, I left the hospital through the roof to see what my assistants were all up to. I hadn't seen Niclas in ages, and Edi and Joe were still hanging out with Mariam in detention or wherever, but Bülent was on me like a shadow. So far, so good—until I heard Martin's call for help.

"Pascha! The doctors are bringing the children out of their comas!"

It took me only a second to get what that meant: the bonsais were being woken up. Their souls needed to get back to their bodies lickety-split so that their reunion or merger or whatever you wanted to call it would work. At least, that's how I hoped it would work.

"OK, Bülent! Where is Niclas?" I asked.

Kebab Boy couldn't read Martin's thoughts, but he could read mine, and he started flying in circles around me, all excited. "I don't know!" he burbled. "Will it hurt?"

It took a moment for me to get what he meant. "No idea," I had to admit. "We need to get the others."

We had left Joe and Edi back with Mariam after Gregor had finished questioning her, but that was twenty-four hours ago. I still didn't know if Mariam was sitting in a cell somewhere or was at large or had been deported. We zoomed over to police HQ as fast as we could. No one was there. Shit.

"Maybe Mariam went back to the church asylum," Bülent suggested, so we zoomed over there. *Nada* again. "Immigration holding cell at the airport?"

"We don't have time to search the whole city for those two," I said. "Plus, we still haven't found Niclas. You fly over to the hospital. Maybe the others are there already—let me know. But you stay there in any case, right by your body, no matter what happens. I'll keep looking."

Bülent was about to talk back, but then he thought about finally being able to eat his mother's pita and *börek* and *köfte kebab* and *lokma* . . . and he reconsidered. He took off like a jet, leaving me all on my own. And I didn't have the foggiest idea where to start.

I wandered from police HQ to the airport and back to the spot where Yasemin's body had been found, where there now stood a shrine of dozens of candles, teddy bears, flowers, and other stuff on the cobblestones. No Mariam, no Joe, and no Edi. I was never going to find them this way. I needed help.

Martin is exactly the right person for this kind of help. He is the ultimate and rare example of a man who can understand women. If there's anyone who can put himself into the pubertal mind-set of a sixteen-year-old Iranian girl and deportee, it's him. So off to the Institute for Forensic Medicine.

I arrived at the same time as a colleague, by which I mean the delivery of a body. Martin was playing receptionist.

"Put him in here, OK, thank you. Papers? Thank you."

The newcomer stank like hell. Likely because he'd been dead for a while already. The fresh ones—even though they are considered *muy dangeroso* in terms of infectiousness for technical hygienic reasons—don't stink nearly as bad. But the stench of this one kind of crossed the line, although when he was alive, I'm sure he must have stunk that bad too. His clothes, his worn-out shoes, the newspapers layered between his two winter coats, and the matted hair were all signs that we had a bum before us today. Not one of the homeless ones who has a BahnCard 100—which lets you ride the train in a velour seat all you want to anywhere in the republic. No, this was one of the old-style, troll-under-the-bridge bums. This was the start of what we call dead-bird season, because it was the first time this fall it had gotten down to subfreezing temperatures overnight. But I wasn't here to philosophize about the plight and mortality of homeless people; I was here to draw out Martin's feminine side. So . . .

All at once I took a big breath, although you might think that was something I didn't actually need, but instead of exhaling or talking . . . I just kept the virtual air in. Out of surprise. The bum on the stainless-steel table below me was missing both ears.

"True," Martin said after he had finished the paperwork and was looking at the body a bit more closely.

When it comes to his work, Martin is totally on the ball, which is why his brain also flipped on at the realization.

"The ears we examined yesterday!"

Although the coroners normally have plenty of vacancies in the morgue drawers, they generally are pretty stingy when it comes to use of refrigerated space for small bits like individual ears, which are not stored in a morgue drawer. Which is funny. Instead, small bits get a little corner in the refrigerator used for items procured in court as evidence. They call it the "court cooler." Obviously the ears and things don't lie around all willy-nilly in there; they are instead packaged properly in evidence jars. I'm sure you have an evidence jar in your refrigerator as well, bought at one of those parties where you can't pick up any babes but instead can purchase overpriced plastic dishware with names that are ironic when used in forensics, such as Modular Mates, right? So Martin was about to pull out his breakfast jar when a question occurred to me: "Where did they find this guy?"

To help you follow this train of thought, please reactivate the part of your brain that may have paid attention to geography in school now. See, Cologne is in the middle of the Rhineland and thus, obviously, straddles the Rhine. When she was examining the ears yesterday, Katrin had theorized that the earless body had been tossed into the Rhine for disposal purposes. The Rhine flows, generally speaking, northward. So the next big city downriver from Cologne is Düsseldorf, although technically it's only half the size of Cologne. But don't get me started on the whole Cologne–Düsseldorf rivalry thing. Düsseldorf has its own Institute for Forensic Medicine, though. So if, as Katrin suspected, the body was thrown into the Rhine in Cologne and was washed downriver to Düsseldorf, it would be very unlikely that that body would turn up in our inbox here in Cologne. It would have flowed to our colleagues downriver.

Martin looked at the toe tag. "Schleiden."

"Where in the hell—"

"In the Eifel Mountains."

OK, I had to process that a bit myself.

"Before you process anything, you should see to the children," Martin said.

I was a bit distracted, thinking, but I managed to update Martin on the kids' situation: Bülent was where he was supposed to be (i.e., at his own beside), Niclas had totally disappeared, and Joe and Edi were likely still with Mariam. Then I explained

Mariam's current situation and asked the critical question, "Where can she be?"

Martin thought for a moment, supported by the professional, scientific half of his brain and by his empathy-enabled bacon belly, and said, "At Yasemin's parents'."

I didn't have the faintest idea what she would be doing there, but since I could flash over there within a fraction of a second and back again, I decided it was worth the effort to check.

And she was there. Mariam and Mehmet were sitting on the couch, Yasemin's father was in his armchair opposite them, and their mother was clattering around in the kitchen. And the most important thing: Joe and Edi were buzzing around the couch too.

"Hey, you two, come on. You're being taken out of your comas today," I yelled.

Mehmet was crying. "I didn't know anything, Father. I really didn't."

"Yasemin was always very closed off," Mariam whispered. "That's what I liked about her. She never betrayed a secret, and she never told anyone anything that would or could hurt someone. I'm so sorry."

"I'm staying with Mariam," Joe announced.

"I'm staying with Joe," Edi chimed in.

This was going to be a hoot. What should I do if they just refused to go?

Below us, the secondary drama was in full gear.

"Did you give her the phone number for that teacher?" the father asked.

Mariam shook her head. "No, but Sibel's number was easy enough to find. She went to the schools and asked everyone to get in touch with her if they ever needed help. Yasemin may have gotten the number from the main office at school. She may also have visited the church asylum and found it out there."

I was starting to feel nervous. "You two good-for-nothings haven't quite grasped what I just told you," I said. "If you don't hightail it right now back to your little bodies, you will be dead! And this time permanently!"

"Nonsense," Joe said absentmindedly. He was flitting around Mariam as though he wanted to become one with her.

"Uh, Joe? Maybe we should . . ." Edi carefully began.

Well at least Edi Einstein had figured out what was going on here.

"Who killed my daughter?" the father asked.

"I don't know," Mariam said.

Mehmet didn't say anything, but he sure knew something. Since the earless bum had been found in the Eifel Mountains, Mehmet must have had the same perpetrator in mind as I, but that didn't matter at the moment, because I had a wholly different problem. If I couldn't stuff the bonsais back into their bodies, they might be stuck hanging out with me for all eternity. I would never have any peace and quiet! And if some hella hot chick ever shows up here with me, a chick I might actually like to spend eternity with, she probably wouldn't stay with me as long as I had four whining snot-noses stuck to my ass.

"Joe, if you don't come now, you'll never see your father again."

"I can't leave Mariam alone now," Joe explained.

This guy was bound to be a priest or probation officer or the new messiah or something, but in order for him to become anything at all, I needed to get him to leave now.

"She doesn't know you're here. She doesn't even know you exist. And you *don't* really exist right now either. But if you come with me now, then you'll wake up back in your body again, and you'll be able to see her again. And the best part is: she'll be able to see you too. And talk to you."

Joe now felt ambivalent but still wouldn't leave his spot.

"Joe, come on. Otherwise I can't go either, and then I'll be dead, and my mom will be so sad," Edi urged.

And then came the fireball trick. Well, I don't know how else to describe it. But Edi suddenly expanded a huge soap bubble, except this bubble was open on one side. She literally sucked Joe in through the side and then closed the opening around him. Joe was inside the shimmering soap bubble, swearing like a used-car salesman who arrived at work to find that beech martens had chewed through the wiring in every car in the lot—that actually happens *a lot* in Germany—but Edi managed to keep him contained. She slowly moved to the window, panting.

"Wow," I said.

I was witness to a new law of nature and couldn't do anything but stare with my mouth virtually agape at the soap bubble as it disappeared out the window. I followed her.

"Let me out!" Joe yelled.

Edi was trembling. This operation seemed to require all of her energy, and she could hardly move forward. At this speed we'd be back at the hospital by next Tuesday. Maybe I could push? I approached the soap bubble, inside of which Joe was still pushing in the opposite direction Edi was trying to go.

"Don't touch me," Edi groaned.

Seriously? First of all, I didn't know how I could actually touch something since I didn't even have a hand. Second of all, I didn't know how to help Edi without—

"Just think 'wall.'"

Right on, man. I'll think 'wall.' I . . . I couldn't close my mouth anymore. I sensed Joe's thoughts and feelings ricocheting off me. He couldn't get through to his beloved anymore. I was a wall.

"OK, that's better," Edi said. She resumed course.

Halfway to the hospital, Joe gave up his resistance. "OK, let me go. I'll come with you," he whispered tearfully.

Yes, life can be brutal. To say nothing of the afterlife, or between-life, or whatever this was.

We made it back to the hospital room just in time. Two doctors and a nurse were in Joe and Edi's room. The nurse was preparing the new IV bag. This time, presumably, without the whole slumber cocktail that had been keeping the short shots sacked out thus far.

"OK," I said, relieved. "You two stay here, I need to—"

Bülent came storming in. "Is Niclas with you?"

Edi and Joe stared.

"We can't leave him behind," Joe said after a while.

"Yes we can," Edi said resolutely. "He's a puke pill."

The three of us stared at her.

"It's true," Bülent said. "He is."

"Then we agree." I said.

"But we need to find him," Bülent continued. "Otherwise we're just as crappy as he is."

Huh? Had I misheard? Bülent wanted to save Niclas?

"You're right," Joe said.

Edi shrugged. "Fine by me. Pascha, you can arrange for that, right? They just need to wait a little while longer."

The three nodded and cleared out. I was left floating there with my blabber flap hanging open and my skull empty. *Uh . . . well.* Now there really was only one person who could help: Martin.

"You need to keep the doctors from waking up the kids. None of them are there yet!" I roared the second I arrived at the institute.

But Martin wasn't there. Dammit, where was he? I rose in a huge vortex like a hurricane high over the skies of Cologne and yelled for Martin. His voice was nearby. That was a good sign, at least.

I found him between Birgit's naked legs. Martin and—with her head cocked in a questionable direction—Birgit were staring at a TV screen with an image full of interference. A woman in a white coat was pointing at a small, bright point. "Here, this is it."

I didn't see anything, but Martin and Birgit were studying that little pixel error as though it were a Lamborghini Sesto Elemento, which is a V10 that can go from zero to a hundred in two and a half seconds.

"Martin," I said loudly. "The kids aren't there, and you need to keep the doctors from waking them out of their comas!"

Martin froze.

"Isn't that wonderful?" Birgit asked, taking his hand.

Martin let her take his hand and said, "What?" His gaze zoned out to the infinite expanses of the universe.

"What's wrong?" Birgit asked.

"The children . . ." he whispered.

The doctor patted his arm caringly. "I don't think there is more than one. I can make out only one embryo."

"The kids, Martin. I found three of them, but they won't go without the fourth, and now they're all gone. You need to keep them in their comas."

"And how . . ." he started to say.

"I don't fucking care how," I roared.

He winced.

"Call the hospital, send in the cops, whatever you do—DO IT NOW!"

"Sorry. I urgently need to . . ." Martin mumbled, taking his hand back from Birgit and rushing out of the room.

"A lot of men aren't able to cope when they witness their first vaginal ultrasound. He'll get there with time," the doctor said, consoling Birgit. "What does he do for a living?"

"He's a coroner," Birgit mumbled, looking worriedly after Martin.

"Oh," was the last thing I heard, and then I took off. I could only hope that Martin could handle this, because I wanted to see how far along Gregor had gotten.

I zoomed over to the school and found Jenny standing in the main office, her notebook in her pocket, saying good-bye as she left the room. I couldn't tell from her good-bye or her face whether she had gotten good or bad news about Tristan's alibi. She left the building and went out to her car in the parking lot. As she fumbled in her bag for her key, she looked out over the lot and noticed a dark-green SUV just pulling out.

She craned her neck after the car. I had seen it from a different angle, namely, from higher up, but I also felt like I knew the driver. So I zoomed down behind the Jeep (a not-quite-new Cherokee) and instantly recognized Dominic Nolde.

Dominic Nolde in a large, dark SUV. Dominic Nolde, who had been on a class trip in the Eifel Mountains last week. In Hellenthal. About six kilometers from Schleiden.

All these puzzle pieces were suddenly starting to fit together. Dominic Nolde was the connection between Yasemin, Zeynep, and Mehmet. Yasemin and Zeynep were dead; Mehmet was hiding in fear for his life. My brain was far from getting all the details to line up, but one thing I knew fairly certainly: Gregor was totally on the wrong track.

Below me Jenny had finally opened her snot-green Beetle, climbed in, and started the motor. She didn't buckle her belt until her wheels were squealing as she tore out of the lot. She followed Dominic's Jeep about three cars back.

As I followed them, I tried to reconstruct the case. We had always assumed the people on the class trip couldn't be perps because they were up in the Eifel Mountains. All the other kids were presumably still minors, but we knew Dominic Nolde used to be in the same grade as Şükrü Bozkurt and then spent a year abroad. Bozkurt was now a student at the university, which made him and Dominic both eighteen, which is the age that Germans are allowed to get their licenses.

Ergo: Dominic could drive a car.

He must have crawled down from his climbing tower out in Hellenthal on Monday or Tuesday, driven to Cologne, and killed Yasemin and kidnapped Sibel. Then he raced back out to the youth hostel, and the teacher never noticed the guy had even been gone. Had Dominic run a second trip on Thursday and personally ensured Zeynep took a couple of pills too many? Of course! And during that murderous mission was when he delivered the first ear to Akif.

I followed Dominic, who had since reached his home, to the parking spot for his Jeep: right next to the front door and right in front of the garage door with the weeds growing along the bottom. He went inside, and I waited for Jenny. She parked fifty meters from the Nolde house on the opposite side of the street. She pressed a button on her phone, only to hear a message saying the caller was temporarily unavailable. She hung up and swore.

The door to the house opened, and Dominic stepped out, rolling a fairly heavy-looking pilot case behind him.

Jenny swore again and got out.

"No!" I yelled, but naturally she couldn't hear me.

Now, just between us: I'm not an overly macho guy, but Jenny-Bunny was the wrong person to singlehandedly butt heads with Dominic. One of the top bulls like Gregor could have done it, but a petite blonde mouse like Jenny—never. Still, she looked so determined.

"Hello, Dominic," she called across the street. "I'm so happy to run into you."

Dominic slammed the tailgate of his Jeep shut, his squat luggage case now inside, and slowly turned around. "I'm sorry, Detective, but I'm in a big rush."

He walked to the driver-side door and tried to get in.

"Don't move, Dominic."

He got into the car.

Jenny walked faster and reached the driver-side window.

Without warning, Dominic flung his door open with full force, hitting Jenny in the temple.

She fell to the ground.

"Ouch!" Niclas roared in my ear.

I winced like an electroshock patient. Holy oil pan, where did he come from?

"The whole world is looking for you, you clown. You need to get to the hospital, chop-chop. It's time to get back into your body," I snapped at him.

"Oh . . ."

"Don't say 'oh'—get a move on!"

Dominic got out and looked around cautiously, but apparently no one had noticed the little incident. He grabbed the unconscious Jenny under the arms and pulled her toward the backyard. Under her blonde hair I could see a thin trail of blood trickling down her face. Halfway to the gate, Dominic stopped and shook his head, turned around, and stuffed Jenny into the passenger seat. He buckled her in, got in himself, and started the motor.

Just as quickly, the motor died.

I heard crazy laughter from beside me.

"Awesome, right?"

"Stop that shit," I yelled. "Get to the hospital!"

Dominic turned the motor back on, and Niclas turned it off again.

"I've been practicing for days. I'm going to major in computer science at college, you know."

What? Oh, never mind.

"Nice work there, Bill Supergates, but now back to your resurrection."

"But I still want to—"

"That's enough!" I roared. "Go gather up the other grasshoppers and get the hell back into your pasty-ass bodies. This is your last chance!"

Dominic, who had now taken the key out of the ignition, shook it and rammed it back into the ignition. What kind of repair technique was that supposed to be?

"But you need me here," Niclas whined. "If I help you, we can stop the car with the electronic immobilizer."

"I can do that myself, you doughnut hole, so fuck off and get out of here."

Niclas pouted and took off. Good. Maybe now one of my problems could be solved. Now I just needed to save Jenny's life. But for that I was going to need my earthly helper, Martin, again, who was already busy with the bonsai-rescue operation. Hopefully the man was up to multitasking.

I flew as fast as I could and radioed Martin.

". . . problems . . ." is all I got in reply.

This couldn't be true. I looked down at Jenny and Dominic, memorized the teenaged murderer's license number, and went off to the hospital.

Martin had just rushed into reception at the ICU. He was looking around frantically.

"Can I help you?" the clerk at the counter asked.

"I'm looking for Dr. Urdenbach. I just called. My name is Gänsewein."

"Oh, yes. One moment."

Martin waited nervously for the door into the ward to open and the doctor on call to step out. He finally came.

The doctors didn't shake hands.

"Dr. Urdenbach, thank you so much for seeing me. Have you already started taking the children out of their comas?"

"No. I didn't understand what you were saying on the phone, but out of an abundance of caution, we have not started that phase yet. But now I would really like to know what you have to do with those children and why you think you need to intervene in their treatment."

Uh-oh. This guy was in a state of academic outrage, if I was interpreting his insulting formulation correctly.

"Um, yes." Once again, the second Martin left his own professional sphere, his eloquence left much to be desired. "I am, uh . . . I spoke with Ms., uh . . ."

He broadcast a question to me, Edi's mother's name.

How was I supposed to know that?

"... So, uh, with the mother of Edi, uh, Teuerzeit, yes. That's her name. Ms. Teuerzeit."

Dr. Urdenbach looked impatient and unwilling as he made a dismissive gesture with his hand. "Yes, yes. I've heard about that. It's completely new to me that the Institute for Forensic Medicine would ever examine an accident victim without seeking permission first, and it is surely even more unusual that it would happen without involving the attending physician and specialists."

"Yes, of course, it's just that ..."

I couldn't take all the squirming anymore. Martin's brain was a yawning void, so there was no way I could expect him to convince the good Dr. Urdenbach to put off the wake-up phase anymore. Niclas and the other three hadn't shown back up yet, so now it was up to me.

"Do you member the equipment problems last week?" I asked Martin. "I'm going to do a *Poltergeist* routine again."

I left him where he was, zoomed to Edi and Joe's room, found the nurse there hanging IV bags on hooks. And then I jumped into action.

First, just the way Niclas had gotten his monitoring equipment to flip out before, I did the same trick with Edi. The nurse leaped into frantic mode, checking the readouts on the machines, bending over Edi, taking her pulse, opening her eyelids, and flashing a light into her pupils. I changed venues and made Joe's machines glow, then I zoomed next door. I repeated the magic with Niclas and Bülent. All four alarms were beeping away, and the whole ward piled into the rooms like a pit crew at a Formula One race.

I went back to Martin and Dr. Urdenbach. They had now been joined by Edi's mother, who stood beside Martin with a giant paper cup of coffee in her hand.

"We swapped out the equipment, and there's no reason not to—" Urdenbach was just saying when the door flew open and the fattest of all nurses stuck her sweaty head through the gap.

"Code blue!" she roared and then vanished again.

Edi's mother slapped her free hand over her mouth. Dr. Urdenbach squinted at Martin and then turned around and ran off.

"For heaven's sake . . ." Edi's mother whispered.

"Don't worry," Martin whispered to her. "Everything will be OK."

"Martin, Dominic Nolde beat up Jenny. He has her unconscious in his car, and they left his house three minutes ago. Let Gregor know."

Martin was visibly confused. The rapid change in topics had overwhelmed him.

"Did you get that?" I asked.

"Uh, yes."

"This is important! Dominic's the killer, see? I'm going to go locate Jenny and Dominic again. You stay here at reception. And make sure the dwarf awakening is stopped until I've dug up the flea circus again."

Edi's mother set her coffee on the counter and gripped Martin's sleeve with both hands.

Before Martin could reply, I was off. I needed to stay with Jenny.

The Cherokee had disappeared from the driveway. Not unexpectedly. I checked the arterials in all directions and found Dominic heading toward the on-ramp for the A57. For the pedestrians: Autobahn 57 heads northwest out of Cologne, along the Rhine. I quickly tried to think what escape options that direction offered him. Düsseldorf, Duisburg, and over the border into the land of windmills, wooden shoes, and stoners. That's not a stereotype, by the way. But the thing is, the Dutch highway patrol drives Porsches, and our boy would land in the can there faster than he could order a *kopje koffie* and a joint of purple haze at the first coffee shop he drove past.

So, as appealing as stopping for a purple haze might be, running the border was not likely. Dominic would be wiser to take the A44 just north of Düsseldorf and then head southwest, perhaps straight to the Düsseldorf airport.

Where were the blue-light specials that were supposed to be following my fugitives? Where was the helicopter that the police so readily dispatch for any run-of-the-mill bank robbery just to find some junkie zoning out with his bag of cash? When would Gregor save Jenny-Bunny like a hero? God, did I have to do *everything* myself?

Back to Martin. He had since been joined by Joe's father, who was now serving as support for Edi's mother. They were both closely intertwined.

"Where is Gregor?" I asked. "Did you tell him about Dominic's car?"

"His cell phone is off," Martin said.

Oh, God, this could not be happening! Gregor was probably still in Tristan's room, because they make you power off your cell phones when you're in the ward there. In such cases I wished Gregor would release more of the anarchist he is at heart, but even the strongest cop apparently capitulates to the greatest threat known to man (after high-school janitors): nurses. "I called one-one-zero, but I have no idea how soon they'll be able to reach him. In any case, I left a message for him and with dispatch and with his boss."

Great. So back to Dominic. I had just left the hospital when my four bonsais had to swerve all around me to avoid crashing.

"I found them!" Niclas yelled.

"We're all here," Edi said with glowing cheeks. "I can hardly wait to—"

"It's going to have to wait," I said. "We need to save Jenny."

Sounds great, except I didn't have the faintest idea how the five of us could pull that off. The short shots understood that as well. With shocking precision and speed, they were now able to clue in to what I was thinking and feeling even before I knew myself. High time to unload them. But first we had to get something done.

I explained the situation to them.

"Why does he have Jenny with him at all?" Bülent asked. "Does he want to take her with him?"

"She's a hostage," Edi explained dead seriously. "So no one blows up his car."

Wow. That took my spit away. Our little Edi, antiterrorism consultant.

"Once he's at the airport, will he let her go?" Bülent asked.

In a best-case scenario, I thought. "Yes, that's what I assume."

"When exactly will he let her go?" Bülent asked.

"At the airport, brainless. Weren't you listening?" Niclas said.

That was a good question though. He needed to get rid of her before security, because no one can get through without a ticket. And definitely not someone unconscious with a bleeding head wound. In fact, taking her to the airport didn't make that much sense . . . did it? Then again, he was a teenager—and a desperate teenager at that. But, no, I didn't think so. He'd want to get rid of her before entering the airport. The question was whether he'd let her go or kill her.

"Kill her?" Joe asked, horrified.

"Of course," Edi said icily. "If he lets her go, she'll call the police first thing."

"Not necessarily," I said. "He'll probably lay a fist into her to keep her knocked out, and then lock her in a bathroom stall or drop her in the forest somewhere, where she won't be found until hours later. By that time he'll be long gone."

Bülent and Joe tried to believe me, but Edi knew better, and Niclas didn't seem to care one way or another. The main thing was to hunt down and nab Dominic.

By now, the Jeep was at the junction with the A44, but he didn't exit to drive to the airport after all. I didn't understand the world anymore. He was really planning to brave the Dutch police? Seriously?

"He's driving past the airport," I informed Martin, who was still at the counter at the ICU, watching everyone heading in and out of the double doors to the ward. Edi's mother and Joe's father were keeping a not inconsiderable distance between them and the nervous Martin, but with the code blue, they couldn't go see their kids either.

"I can try to reach Gregor again . . ."

He dialed, left another message, and shrugged.

I flashed back to my team.

"OK, the first thing we need to do is figure out where Dominic is driving to. It's important that we keep Martin up to date. As soon as he contacts Gregor, he'll need up-to-the-minute status reports."

Everyone nodded.

"Let's assign specific jobs," Edi suggested. "We need at least one surveillance team and one messenger who will keep Martin informed."

"No chick is going to boss me around," said Niclas.

"Yeah, one is, asshole," Bülent said. "Edi is a hundred times smarter than you."

"I think Edi has a good idea. If someone has a better idea, say so now," Joe said.

"I'll sabotage the car, then that guy won't be able to get anywhere anymore," Niclas declared.

"Oh, and how do you plan to do that?" Edi snipped.

I knew how, of course, because I'd tried it out once. But we still had one little problem.

"The car is driving a hundred sixty kilometers an hour," I said. "If you disrupt the electronics, there'll be an ugly accident."

"So what?" Niclas said.

"Then Jenny will be dead," Bülent said.

"Then make a better suggestion, dumb-ass."

"I think . . ."

"He's headed to Schiphol!" Edi yelled.

"Where did you—"

"I looked at his navigation system." Her voice was bursting with the bright sound of authentic female triumph.

Super lame that none of us had thought of it.

"See, my kids' mystery books aren't stupid at all," she whispered to Joe.

"Mysteries? You mean you have all those good ideas from books?" Bülent asked. "Wow. Will you lend me some?"

Edi nodded.

"What'd you say?" asked Niclas. "He's headed for a shit hole?"

"*Schiphol.* Another airport," Edi corrected him.

"Where's that one at?" he asked.

Awkward silence.

"Amsterdam?" said Joe.

Looking at the direction Dominic was headed on the autobahn, I thought that all fit. The question was why.

"If the police finally come and get him, they won't shoot Dominic, will they?" Joe asked.

"Of course they'll take him out," Niclas said. "And they should too."

"Um, but if Dominic is the one who kidnapped Ms. Akiroğlu . . ." Joe pointed out.

Shit! I had totally forgotten about her. We needed Dominic alive, and we still needed to get out of him where the teacher was hidden. If she was still alive at all.

Edi wailed.

"She's still alive, Edi," I said. "Calm down."

My team of assistants started peppering me with thoughts and suggestions. Everything from shooting him with tranquilizer darts, like Edi had seen them do at the zoo once, to Niclas's idea of mowing everyone down with machine-gun spray and seeing who remained alive.

"We need to let Akif know," Bülent said suddenly. "You can't do something like this without the family. The police can be much too dangerous."

He tilted his head at Niclas. I understood what he meant. If the cops had attitudes like Niclas's, then within two hours we'd find a huge bomb crater at the terminal with a hundred steaming corpses in there, and we still wouldn't know where to look for Sibel. But could Turkish family traditions really help us?

"Akif is a kind of policeman," Bülent pointed out. "And he won't do anything that will put his sister's life in danger. And he'll be sure to watch out for Jenny too. Better than anyone else will."

Apart from Gregor, I thought, although he's going to be kicking himself if he loses his partner in action even before he hears what's going on. And he still wasn't reachable at the moment. So Akif was our only option.

"OK, who will be our messenger?"

Bülent, Edi, and Joe stared at me.

"Oh . . . I—I was being rhetorical," I stammered. Obviously *I* had to be the one going back and forth with Martin since no one else could talk with him. *Duh.*

I updated Martin—who was still loitering up and down the halls at the ICU—about Akif Akiroğlu and his double life as an undercover drug enforcement agent, and I told him to tell Akif about the latest developments. Martin nodded and took his phone out of his coat pocket. Whenever he's in professional mode, you can rely on him. Evidently he had accepted the fact that he was going to have to spend the foreseeable future providing information to people he didn't know—people who in turn were going to ask him where he had the information from, and he wouldn't be able to answer—and that most such conversations were going to end awkwardly. But Martin seemed prepared to take on that role. After all, this was all about Jenny. And Sibel.

"And all the kids who will otherwise fall to these drug dealers in the future," Martin thought after a looking at Edi's mother and Joe's father with a grimness that I didn't know he had in him.

"Huh?" I asked in amazement.

"Fatherhood changes a man," he said simply.

My jaw nearly hit the floor. Virtually, obviously.

"I don't know that you'll ever get to know that feeling," he said with the wisdom of the ages, "but let me tell you, it changes your whole life."

I had seen this change coming, first with horror, and now with grudging respect. But right now I wanted only one thing, and that was for Akif Akiroğlu to get his ass straight to Amsterdam.

FOURTEEN

No idea how Martin got hold of Akif's number (via Principal Bieberstein, as we found out later), or Akif managed to get there in record time (a former classmate of his, Bernhard, a flight instructor and charter pilot at Bonn-Hangelar Airport), but in any case the Cessna 425 Conquest I touched down on the runway at Amsterdam Airport Schiphol at the very moment Dominic was exiting the freeway. We only knew that because Niclas was already hanging out in the tower, waiting to wreak havoc up there again. He heard them talking about the arrival of a private charter plane from Bonn-Hangelar, so he zoomed out to the runway to check it out and saw Akif crawl out of the plane with a crazed look on his face and a cell phone to his ear. And by crawl I mean he literally crawled. His shirt was covered in splotches whose origin was instantly clear if you considered for a moment the greenish color of his face. Akif the Terrible had been seriously boozing it up before Martin's wake-up call had reached him, or else he suffered from major motion sickness. Or both. No matter, at least he was here.

I assigned Bülent to actively surveil Akif, and Edi and Joe stayed on Dominic and Jenny—Niclas wouldn't take any orders from me anymore, anyway. I could only hope that he didn't pull any bullshit.

I was torn between the four kids and Martin, who was still keeping watch at the ICU but had finally made it through to Gregor.

"Dominic and Jenny are on their way into the terminal," Edi and Joe reported. "He's put a cap on her, so people can't see her wound."

Shit. There were thousands of women in caps flitting all around the airport on this cold-ass November day, and she wouldn't be approached by any of the workers, no one would point at her, and no paramedic would ask to help her. As of now, Jenny was basically invisible.

"He's going into Concourse 3."

"What's there?" I asked.

"Check-in counters," Joe said. "My family took a plane one time through here. You have to check in, and then they hand you your boarding card, and then . . ."

"What destinations?" I specified.

"Uh, Pari . . . uh, Paromoriba," Joe stammered.

"Paramaribo," Edi corrected him effortlessly. "That's in South America. Other flights are for Port of Spain on Trinidad, Curaçao, and Aruba. Those are all in the Caribbean."

"Of course."

"Oh no. There are pirates down there. You should remember, we learned about pirates at school during the Summer Pirate Fest . . ."

"Where else?" I asked sternly.

I had always thought Curaçao was a drink that looks like a dissolved urinal cake—and tastes about the same—but Miss Smart-Ass naturally knew it all, and better.

"Iran, Morocco, Indonesia, Cuba," Edi fluently read off various departure boards.

"Hold positions—I need to tell Martin."

By this point I had perfected what I like to call the Blitz Shift as I raced back and forth at light speed between Martin and the airport in Amsterdam. I could have given the transporters in *Star Trek* a run for their money now.

"How much longer do we need to wait?" Martin asked worriedly. "The doctor wants to have security throw me out, and then they'll start waking the children . . ."

"I'll know that in a second," I said. Then I turned to do another round of mischief with the sensors on the monitoring equipment all up and down the ward. Once all eleven machines were beeping their alarms at once, I zoomed back to Amsterdam. Before too long the constant back-and-forth was really starting to piss me off.

Dominic and Jenny were now walking with their arms intertwined through Concourse 3. No idea if Dominic had given Jenny some pills or if she was suffering from a full-on concussion, but she was hardly conscious and just let him lead her anywhere, constantly leaning on something the whole way. Mostly on Dominic, unfortunately.

Meanwhile, Akif had made it into the airport building. The color of his face was again its usual night-shadow white. He had one of those miniheadsets at his ear and looked more alert than I'd ever seen him before. His stride was dynamic, his gaze furtive. Even though his barfed-up clothes looked shitty and his excessive stubble was too thick to look cool, for the first time I suddenly could imagine how dangerous this guy was. Dangerous to his opponents. And right now he was Jenny's only chance.

Dominic took a position at an airline counter listing multiple destinations. Miami, Havana, Ulaanbaatar. Where in the hell was that? There were about ten people ahead of him in line, but it was moving relatively quickly. I nervously kept an eye out for Akif.

And then suddenly everything happened real fast. Akif made Dominic, but Dominic hadn't seen him. Akif came from behind, pressed something—I couldn't tell what—into Dominic's lower back, and whispered into his ear, "Game over, asshole."

Dominic froze.

My four assistants swirled around me all excited. "Why doesn't he just shoot him?" Niclas asked.

"Because he still needs to find out where his sister is being held, you bozon," Edi said.

Joe giggled. "Bozon! Good one, Edi. Real good."

"He doesn't have a gun in his hand at all," Bülent said, voice trembling. "Why not? He has a gun though, right?"

"He does," I confirmed. "No idea why he doesn't have it with him though."

"Let go of her," Akif demanded.

"You're not a cop," Dominic said after looking over his shoulder. "So fuck off."

"I'm the drug squad cop who's been busting your balls," Akif said.

"Oh, the elder brother. Nice to meet you," Dominic said with a grin. Relieved even, I thought. "Give me your cell number and let me go. As soon as I'm where I want to be, you'll get a text message telling you where your sister is."

"Who said anything about my sister?" Akif said. "Let the nice blonde lady at your side go, and you'll come out alive. They'll prosecute you as a minor, and then in ten years you'll be out of jail again and can start all over again. If not, your story ends here and now."

"And you'll never see your sister again."

"She's not my sister anymore. She dishonored the family."

Dominic's face showed signs of cracking. "Bullshit," he bluffed.

"Wanna bet?" Akif asked.

"Oh no, how terrible!" Edi said.

"He's bluffing," Bülent said casually. No idea how he knew that; maybe he had an antenna for Turkish family crises, but I believed him. The others did too.

And then it happened. None of us had seen it coming. We only saw Dominic suddenly fall to his knees. It took a moment for me to get how. Jenny had taken her left hand and firmly clamped it onto his balls. Dominic gasped for air and collapsed centimeter by centimeter under the pain.

Blood was now seeping through Jenny's cap, her face was white as chalk and contorted with pain, but she didn't let go. Instead, she slowly knelt down with Dominic. Akif seized Dominic's left arm and turned him around.

"*Hebt u hulp nodig?*" the Dutch woman behind the three of them asked, wanting to know if they needed help, since Jenny was bleeding and Dominic and she were on their knees. "*Ik ben namelijk ziekenzuster . . .*"

"Thank you, but we don't need a nurse," Akif replied in English. "We just need to sit down for a moment."

He pulled Dominic out of line, which forced Jenny to let go of his balls. Dominic straightened up and laid a serious punch into Akif's chin with his free arm. Akif tumbled and lost his grip on Dominic's arm. Dominic got loose and sprinted off, running into Jenny—who was now able to stand on two feet—while grabbing his crotch and wobbling like a Weeble toward the exit. Akif quickly got his head back on straight and starting running after

Dominic. The security guards preening everywhere in the concourse suddenly took notice and got on the move as well.

Akif was just a fraction of a second faster than he needed to be to throw himself onto Dominic before he made it out the exit. Both men thrashed around in a tangle of arms and legs, beating each other like crazy. By which I mean, Akif was beating Dominic like crazy, and Dominic was trying to have a high-school fist-fight. Damn, Akif had so many surprises up his sleeve. He knew exactly where to land each blow. And this despite his still-fresh gunshot wounds! And a pretty nice elbow from Dominic, which made Akif's cheekbone give way with a crunch. But Akif kept whaling on him. Dominic's right fist made a cracking sound when it hit Akif's chin; Dominic moaned but kept swinging.

Meanwhile, a whole mob of chattering Gouda grazers had gathered around the wild boars, and the security guards were resolutely scurrying toward the show. Jenny passed them. With a stern look in her eye that sent chills down my spine, she walked like a zombie straight through the concourse, pushed a child out of the way along with a woman and a stroller. She beat the security guards. She grabbed the first vanity bag she noticed draped over the top of one of the spectator's luggage carts. Aluminum, ribbed. Pricey as hell. And very manageable. Jenny grabbed the vanity bag, swung it in the air, and thundered it down onto Dominic's skull.

The chick whose luggage it was yelled something, and Jenny tossed the now severely battered bag back to her with a swing that itself could have been considered assault. Then she grabbed Dominic by the hair and pulled him off Akif while she held out her hand to the battered Turk.

"Jenny," she said. "Pleased to meet you."

"Akif. Shit, you're dangerous."

Jenny looked at him for a second, and then the zombie look in her eyes disappeared, and she began to grin. Then she laughed—until the tears started. Once the tears got going, she was crying like a little girl.

"Watch it," Edi threatened me.

OK, fine. Jenny was crying like a little boy.

"Is that it?" Bülent asked almost whiney.

Oy—you can all bite me!

My three companions were smiling. They had apparently taken an oath against me. Wait—three? Where was Niclas?

At that moment, the airport's security alarm went off.

Now that the fight was over and there was no further danger, all of the other guards had come to check out the scene of the brawl and chat with each other. But they all froze with the alarm. Then their pagers and phones all started beeping at once, and they ran off.

"Fire alarm," Niclas crowed as he appeared out of nowhere. "Awesome, right?"

"That's our cue to bail," I said. "Chop-chop. Your folks are waiting."

We whooshed back at Mach 3 to University Medical Center in Cologne. As we flew, the bonsais started painting vivid pictures, imagining what they were all going to tell their friends at school. Niclas could mention his decisive experience as a computer hacker; Joe had saved a damsel in distress from the cruelty of the German immigration service; Edi had tracked down a dangerous drug dealer—while attending enough classes at school that she'd hardly missed anything in her absence. Only Bülent was quiet. What he had learned about his fellow Turks in Germany was weighing on his chubby little soul.

Once we were within ten kilometers of the hospital, I started picking up Martin's urgent calls that we needed to hurry. The doctors had decided to wake the children up immediately.

We arrived just in the nick of time. Dr. Urdenbach was standing at Edi's bed, a new IV bag hanging on the stand next to her, and the valve letting it drip into the line going into Edi's hand was already on.

"Bye, Pascha," Edi said. "And thank you for taking care of us."

"You're welcome," I said. If I had said "Happy to help," it would have been a bald-faced lie.

"That's not true," she contradicted me. Shit, she'd seen through me again. A wide grin revealed the sparkling metallic grille over her teeth. "Fortunately my mom doesn't know my babysitter continuously used swear words and stole cars and . . ."

I smiled back. "Stay cool, Edi." I was going to remind her not to be such a smart-ass and not always outdo the boys and, above all, not to forget what I had said about eyeglasses, braces, and clothes. But she was gone. Just like that. The next moment the figure below us started moving in her bed, and then Edi opened her eyes.

"Cool!" Joe whispered.

"Does it hurt?" Niclas asked.

"Hi, sweetheart. My name is Dr. Urdenbach," the doctor said. "You're at the hospital. Can you tell me your name?"

"Edi," she replied in a whisper, and then her eyes fell shut again.

Meanwhile, the nurses turned to Joe.

"I had so much fun with you," Joe said. "And I learned a lot."

"Stealing cars, hitting on women . . ." I said.

"Uh-uh," Joe said, shaking his head with a grin. "That most people are really different than they seem. Akif isn't a dealer, our teacher is a Protestant, and you . . ."

"Careful," I said.

"You're not the asshole you pretend to be."

"Don't say asshole . . ." I called after his fading ghost face. With a hardly audible, "Hey, Pascha, take it easy," he vanished.

The three of us watched Joe twitch his eyelids briefly, mumble his name, and fall back to sleep. The doctor and nurses were satisfied with his vitals as well, so they moved to the next kid. Now it was Niclas's turn.

"I'm definitely going to try stealing some cars," he shouted, and then he was gone.

Bülent sighed loudly. "Man, he is such a jerk."

"You'll be able to belt him on the jaw here in a couple of seconds when you're flesh and blood again," I said.

Bülent nodded. Then he hesitated, embarrassed. "Pascha?" he began. "Will you still be our guardian angel?"

That staggered me—the Kebab Boy from Team Turban coming at me with cherub blather. I swallowed the lump I suddenly got in my throat. "Sure, man. And you become a detective, Bülent. You've got real talent."

Bülent nodded. "*Görüşürüz*, Pascha!" And then he was gone too.

I looked down again at Edi and Joe. Her mother and his father were weeping in each other's arms. Then I took off.

Alone again at least! No one was jabbering into my thoughts, no one was squabbling, no one was asking stupid questions. Heaven.

I trundled all relaxed over to Martin, who was still waiting at the double doors to the ICU.

"The snot-noses have all been successfully brought back online," I announced.

Martin nearly collapsed with relief.

"How did you convince Akif to fly to Amsterdam?" I asked.

Martin's face locked up. "That's my secret."

I would find out one way or another.

"No you won't," said Martin, the man with the steel heart.

"It'll be a moment when you're boasting about your son."

His steel heart melted into mushy, warm baby food. "How's my son doing, actually?" Martin asked. "Can you tell me? Did he make it through his first ultrasound all right?"

Should I confess I had just made it up, my ability to communicate with the cluster of cells?

"It tickles a little, but it was fine," I said.

You have to save your favors for hard times when a bribe might be required. But before Martin could ask me more on the topic, I took off. I needed to take care of another teacher.

First, though, I needed to find Akif, Jenny, and Dominic, because without Dominic's confession, there could be no rescue team for Sibel.

"Come on, people, we need to—" I began, until I realized my assistants weren't there anymore. Hmm. It was pretty quiet without them . . . Well, OK. If my choice was between constant chatter or silence, I'd take silence. Happily so.

It took a while, but I found the plane Akif had taken to Amsterdam—with Jenny, Akif, and Dominic contained cozily inside. As the pilot landed at Bonn-Hangelar, Jenny was asleep, Akif was puking, and Dominic was whining (while buckled into a seat and handcuffed) about the stench of the puke and about being detained illegally.

Gregor was already waiting at the landing strip. He carefully hugged Jenny, shook Akif's hand, and carted Dominic off to the backseat of his car, the hands of the suspected kidnapper and murderer, now in police custody, still cuffed behind his back.

The drive took way too long because, as usual, Cologne was one huge traffic jam. But finally Dominic was sitting in an interrogation room. Dominic on one side of the table, Gregor on the other, and Akif and Jenny next door, watching through a one-way mirror.

"Where is Sibel Akiroğlu?" Gregor asked.

Dominic didn't say anything.

"We'll talk about everything else later. Right now, we can handle the whole situation graciously or unpleasantly. I'm happy to go either way. It all depends on how fast we find Sibel Akiroğlu—alive."

Dominic didn't say anything.

"You're only making your situation worse by not telling us about her, kid."

"I would prefer it if we could speak to each other as two grown men," Dominic said.

"I'm happy to address you as 'sir' or 'governor' or 'poo-bah,' whatever you want—so long as you tell me where Sibel Akiroğlu is. *Sir.*"

"I don't know what you mean. How should I know where that woman has gone to?"

It went like that for a good long while, with Dominic digging in his heels.

"OK, we'll have to find her without him," Gregor finally said with a sigh after he had given up and come in to see Akif and Jenny. "Let's go into my office and see what we can do."

Gregor rushed off. Akif offered Jenny his arm for support, and she took it. I got the impression she was less in need of something to lean on than she was pretending to be, but that's women for you. Maybe it was because Akif had taken off his puke-covered shirt and was flaunting his flabby naked upper torso, with the slightly bled-through bandage on his right side, under his open jacket. Akif himself should have gone to the hospital ages ago, because the whole left side of his face was now a shimmering dark purple, but he apparently didn't want to leave the party prematurely.

Gregor was already sitting at his desk, talking on the phone. He needed an arrest warrant and a search warrant, and he wanted a cell-phone data list—the whole thing. Jenny dropped into her desk chair, Akif pulled up a chair next to her.

"Maybe he just kept her in the basement. It doesn't seem like the father has the slightest interest in the son," Jenny said. "He wouldn't notice gorillas coming in and out of the house."

Gregor hung up. "I'm driving over to the Nolde house and turning it upside down," he said. "The father will let me in, but just in case, can you have the search warrant delivered in a patrol car?"

Jenny nodded. Then she picked up her phone. "I need a list of properties owned by Schiercks. Specifically, uh . . ."

Jenny rattled off Dominic Nolde's personal data. Name of father, name of mother . . .

". . . Gerlinde Annemarie Schiercks. In addition . . ."

I left Jenny and Akif. There was too much adrenaline-doped hormonality polluting the air between them. Instead I followed

Gregor, who was already on his way to the Noldes'. He needed to ring five times before Dominic's father opened the door.

"Kreidler, Criminal Investigations, Cologne PD. We've met before. May I come in and look around all the rooms in this house that you haven't been in yet today? Including the basement."

Mr. Nolde studied Gregor with an annoyed expression. "Why?"

"I'm looking for a young woman whom your son may have, uh, kept here."

Nicely worded.

"I haven't seen anyone."

"That's the point."

"Oh," Nolde said, thoughtfully. "Please. You won't need me?"

Now Gregor looked irritated. "No."

Nolde shuffled back into his study. Gregor watched him go, then he shrugged and started searching the house for any trace of Sibel. Nada. But he did find a safe in Dominic's bedroom.

"Mr. Nolde, there is a safe in your son's room. Can you tell me the combination to it?"

Again it took several attempts to get Nolde Senior into his time machine to travel back to the present.

"It was my wife's," he said. "It hasn't been used for a long time."

Gregor nodded tentatively. "Does your family own any other properties?"

"I don't own anything at all, young man. My ex-wife's family owns quite a few properties, so many one loses track."

"How can I reach your ex-wife?"

"No idea. I haven't had anything to do with her in many years."

"Dominic's car is registered to his maternal grandfather. Could that grandfather have . . . ?"

"Maternal grandfather?" Nolde asked. "He's been dead for ages."

"Yes. Apparently Dominic forged his signature and awarded himself full powers of attorney. Did the grandfather have . . . ?"

"Dominic has a car?"

Gregor closed his eyes. "Thank you for your help."

Nolde shuffled away again. Gregor took his phone out of his pocket. "Hi, Jenny. I found a safe. As soon as we get the warrant, we'll need the tank buster. Oh, and try to see if you can locate Dominic's mother."

Gregor left the house and got into his car but didn't turn the key in the ignition. He stared through the windshield into space, looking as though he might burst into tears at any moment. I could see why. If Sibel was still alive, they had to find her before she died from lack of water. They didn't have much time. He started the car and drove back to HQ.

Jenny was waiting for him with a two-page list.

"What's this?" Gregor asked.

"The Schiercks family's real-estate holdings."

"Shit. Did you reach the mother?"

"No. She's out of town. Her attorney will apparently contact us."

Gregor scanned the list of properties. Various apartment buildings in Cologne, plus some in Frechen, Hürth, Erftstadt, and then also single-family homes, vacation homes, cabins to rent to hunters, and one castle. (Yes, we actually do have real castles in Germany.)

"Sibel will be dead by the time we work down this list," Gregor said.

The look on Jenny's face meant she doubted Sibel was still alive at all.

These people needed help, that was clear to me, but I didn't know what I could do for them. I couldn't read Dominic's mind. I couldn't contact Sibel. I had to think of something else.

I could check the properties. Gregor had tossed the list onto his desk, and the single-family and vacation homes were on top. I thought those were better candidates anyway, because it's easier to hide a kidnapping victim in a freestanding building than in an apartment building. I tried to memorize the list, but my memory has never been that good, hence all of my problems. Shit, I could really have used the Onesies crew again to search multiple addresses all at once. But maybe I didn't need to remember all the addresses. There had to be a way to narrow the possibilities down. I needed to think. When Sibel was kidnapped, Dominic had actually—officially, anyway—been with his school up in Hellenthal. He kidnapped Sibel in Cologne. Assuming he didn't want to drive too much out of his way with his kidnappee, Sibel's prison cell had to be on the way from Cologne to Hellenthal. I went through the list . . . Shit. The apartment buildings in Frechen, Hürth, and Erftstadt were all on the A1 southwest to Hellenthal. And so were the towns with smaller buildings.

OK, more narrowing down of the list. If Dominic had left Sibel with everything she needed to stay alive for a few days, then he could have used any of the properties because he would never have needed to return. However, if he needed to regularly drop supplies off for his victim, he'd need a property near the youth hostel.

I had to refresh my memory about the geography of the Eifel Mountains. From Cologne, you take the A1 to Mechernich, where you exit onto the state road through Schleiden and on to Hellenthal.

The list gave one vacation home in Schleiden, and a cabin in Gemünd. OK, it was worth a shot. I left Gregor, Jenny, and Akif in their desperation and took off.

The vacation home was easy to find but empty. It didn't look like it was being used at all. There weren't any living souls—or dead ones—here. It smelled musty from an extended lack of ventilation, so I left it behind and moved on, now looking for a forest cabin in the Schleiden district, plot 007, parcel 08-15.

I spent a half hour looking among the trees, shrubs, and blackberry hedges that had no blackberries on them. Duh, it was November. It was a mystery to me why human beings ever voluntarily set off into the forest—even by daylight. Why would you then also want to sleep in a cabin with rabid foxes lurking around at night only to wake up to the buzzing of skeeters and gnats everywhere? That makes no sense to me.

I finally found the cabin. Still warm. What was left, that is. I felt sick. I flew over the charred remains of the wooden house. The roof and walls had crashed in. Only the fireplace made of fieldstones still stood in what had been the middle of the cabin. It too was black as coal. A stench of smoke and, yes, burned meat hung in the air. I didn't need to look closer to know no person could still be alive in those ruins.

At first I was horrified.

Then came the questions:

Why had this hut burned down? Had Dominic quickly set the fire last night? But why? To destroy evidence? But if Sibel was in the smoking rubble, Martin would be able to ID the body through DNA analysis, so the fire wouldn't prevent the police from connecting the property to Sibel.

There were lots of possibilities. Maybe Dominic was stupid and hadn't thought ahead. Unlikely. Maybe Dominic took Sibel somewhere else and burned the cabin just to hide any evidence she had been there. Matches are faster than wiping everything down. That was more likely. Third option: Sibel hadn't been here at all.

I flew another circle, looking for a body in the hopes of finding none. But I was disappointed. Lying in the bed was a burned corpse in the usual defensive position. Technically it's called a "pugilistic pose" or "stance," which occurs when someone dies in a fire because flexor muscles are stronger than extensors, so the burning arms and legs bend on their own, leaving the corpse in such a pose. It can also cause dislocated joints, which can be misinterpreted as torture, but I knew better. All right, admittedly, I couldn't even tell if the barbecuee here had been a man or woman, but who else besides Sibel Akiroğlu could it be?

I was ready to fly off and wondered if I should go follow Gregor and Jenny's frantic search or just switch off completely for a while. I needed a vacation. I was sure people were partying on Majorca, even in November. I had never been to Majorca, but it wouldn't be a problem zooming over there now . . .

How did I get on the topic of Majorca again? Oh, yeah. The empty bottles in front of the burned bed.

Bottles?

Hmm. Now how likely was it that a kidnapping victim tied to a bed would have a set of *schnapps* bottles lying around that bed? The glass was all exploded, the labels mostly burned off, but the letters . . . All I could make out was ". . . bean ru . . ." I did recognize the shape of the bottle. And I could thus tell it had probably been a cheap bottle of spirits. Glorified rotgut, to be precise, which burns pretty big holes in brains.

So that threw all my theories out the window. I subjected the rest of the cabin to a much closer inspection, trying to detect anything that could help me, but there weren't any carbonized handcuffs or ropes on the bed, and the walls didn't have any cries for help scratched into them either. The only thing remarkable I found was some charred moose or deer heads, or whatever you call those animals with the horns, but that was only a matter of personal curiosity and had nothing to do with the case.

For as stupid as it sounds: if I was lucky, I had found the wrong cabin.

Hold that thought, I told myself and got going.

After a half hour more of searching—eureka! A different cabin but in the same area. Now, I hadn't ever seen Sibel Akiroğlu in person before, and the person rolled up on the bed looked only marginally like the chick in the family photo I had seen, but how many Turkish women do you find inside hunting cabins in the Eifel Mountains lying bound and gagged on a bed?

She was hardly moving, but she was alive. And freezing. The cabin wasn't heated, and Sibel lay on top of the covers, not under them. Her lips were blue, her skin was blue, and her hands, tied down on either side of her body, were blue too, and she had peed her pants. There were a few lethargic flies circling around her, but she didn't react to them. Help was urgently needed here, but how could I summon Gregor and Jenny to this spot before they started working down the list of properties?

There was only one way and—you guessed it: Martin. Who was in Edi and Joe's hospital room.

Edi's mother was sitting on Edi's bed holding her daughter's hand.

"And you have no memory of your time here in the hospital?" Martin was just asking.

"No. I was in the car, and then it crashed, and then the man came, and then I woke up here."

"Hey, Brace-Face!" I couldn't help calling to Edi, just in case she could still hear me. "You haven't completely forgotten me, have you? Remember what I told you about your clothes."

"You're here?" Martin asked.

"I found Sibel," I said. "You need to get Gregor on the right track. Otherwise it might be too late."

"I'm sorry. I need to go," Martin said to Edi's mother. "Take care."

They shook hands, and Martin would have shaken Edi's too but her eyes were closed.

"Bye, Martin," Edi said softly.

Martin froze. I froze.

Edi's mother said, "No, mommy's not going. I'm staying with you, sweetheart."

"Didn't she just say 'Martin'?" Martin asked me privately.

"That's what I heard."

"But her mother thinks she said 'Bye, Mommy.'"

"But she didn't," I said. I was certain of that.

Wasn't I?

We left the ICU and went to the cafeteria. Martin needed some tea. Ridiculous, conventional tea bags. *Eew.* But he was friendly about it. The cashier at the self-service counter couldn't help it that they didn't serve eco-socially responsible teas.

"I found Sibel. She's tied up in a hunting cabin that belongs to Dominic's mother or grandpa. No matter. But you need to call Gregor and tell him to skip all the properties in Frechen, Hürth, and Erftstadt."

Martin opened his mouth.

"And before you ask how to explain why you know this, just say you talked with Edi, and she said the kidnapper mentioned something about a forest cabin where they would never find her."

Martin didn't look convinced. I could sense it too, but I didn't have a better idea to offer him, so it would have to do.

Martin took out his phone and recited his speech for Gregor.

"OK, we'll start there," Gregor said after a pause, during which I imagined that he'd closed his eyes to suppress any thought of me.

Then he hung up.

FIFTEEN

Saturday, 7:40 p.m.

For the first time since Yasemin's body had been found, I saw Gregor not only smile but also beam.

"Really?" he said. "Godfather?"

Birgit and Martin nodded in unison.

Gregor stood up, walked around the table in the Turkish restaurant, and pulled Birgit up from her seat. He hugged her, kissed her on both cheeks, and nodded solemnly. "I'd be honored."

"When are you guys gonna talk about the case?" I asked Martin.

"Maybe not at all. We all have the night off for once."

Stupid-head.

"You must have picked that word up from the kids."

Stupid-head again.

"So," Gregor said, resuming his seat next to Katrin, "Dominic is still refusing to make any statements."

Finally!

"But it won't help him. We found Yasemin's blood and the blood of the homeless man on his knife, we found fibers in his car from Yasemin's clothes, and when our experts cracked his safe, we found a huge store of various kinds of pills. We found the rest of them in the sewer line—the technical consultant estimates Dominic tried to flush approximately fifty thousand pills."

"What kind of pills?" Martin asked.

"Smart pills, which he apparently became familiar with in the United States. But also ecstasy, speed, and the stuff Zeynep died from."

"Where did he get the drugs?" Birgit asked.

"Our clever Dominic would have done better to flush his hard drive instead of the pills, because otherwise I couldn't answer that question. But it was amazingly simple: he ordered the smart pills online. The harder stuff came from a Dutchman of Ukrainian origin he had met while he was in America. Akif and the Dutch police knew the guy and were finally able to nab him and his backers with the evidence from Dominic's computer."

"But why?" Katrin asked.

"Why what?" asked Gregor.

"I think what she means," said Birgit, "is why would a young guy like Dominic *do* all this?"

Katrin nodded her agreement.

"Money and hurt pride, I'd say," said Gregor. "He was pissed that his mother left him behind to go jet-setting with her new husband. She's been living it up while his father lived hand to mouth, and Dominic himself often went for weeks without a euro cent in his pocket. He got tired of being poor and wanted to be rich like his mother."

"Dealing drugs to kids?" asked Martin.

"Yep. And it worked. We found his Swiss bank account numbers in that pilot case he took to Amsterdam. He was already a millionaire several times over from his drug dealing."

"So he was the Mr. Big that Akif was after"—as I've said before, Birgit is one smart cookie—"and naturally Akif never suspected him because he wasn't your typical dealer," she concluded.

"That's right," Gregor said. "Akif had suspected the fat guy that his undercover colleague, Gina, was working on. But the fat guy thought Akif was the new dealer on the scene, which is why he sicced his gunman on him."

"Why did Dominic kill Yasemin and kidnap Sibel?" Birgit asked.

"Yasemin suspected Dominic was selling drugs. She talked to her brother about it, but Mehmet had no idea, and he didn't want to pin anything on Dominic. We know that from Mehmet, who finally started talking. After that, Yasemin called Sibel for help."

"Why didn't she just go to the police?" Martin asked.

Naturally Martin, my little goose, would have gone to the guardians of peace and justice and off-loaded all responsibility onto them.

"That's what the police are for," he shot back at me, "and you see what happens if you try to take matters into your own hands."

"Well," said Gregor, "Yasemin had no proof, which is why she asked Sibel what she should do."

"And how did Dominic find out that Sibel and Yasemin wanted to meet while he was up in the Eifel Mountains?"

"From Zeynep. We checked her phone data, and she texted Dominic. It's not clear how she knew, but she was probably keeping an eye on Yasemin on Dominic's orders."

"Did Zeynep know that telling Dominic was a death sentence for Yasemin?" Katrin asked.

Gregor shook his head. "I don't think so. Zeynep wasn't the brightest—and she was so in love with Dominic that she wouldn't have imagined that he'd do anything bad."

"Was Zeynep's death an accident, suicide, or murder, then?" Martin asked.

Gregor shrugged.

"But at least Mehmet is innocent, right?" Birgit asked.

"Yeah, but he feels guilty as hell. He's had a deal with his sister for years. Yasemin's parents didn't allow Yasemin to be out and about at night alone, but Mehmet worked out a way to give her some freedom. They'd arrange what time to go home and would meet up and walk the last couple hundred meters home together. When Yasemin didn't show up Monday night as planned and didn't answer her phone, Mehmet got scared. He tried her all night, and when he didn't find her, he went to the church asylum, which he knew about from Mariam. He was just as afraid of his father as he was of Dominic, incidentally."

"So Dominic killed Yasemin to protect himself, but why kidnap Sibel?" Birgit asked.

"During the day on Tuesday, Sibel had called Yasemin's phone several times to arrange to meet with her. Dominic had taken the phone and didn't know how much Sibel knew, and he wanted to keep her from going to the police. He waited for her at school, saw her drive off with the kids, and then he got the idea to cause an accident. Unfortunately for him, she survived, and he took her."

"Were the children able to identify him?" Martin asked.

Naturally Martin was now way more interested in children than just about anything else in the world.

Gregor laughed. "That's a funny story. The girl said the kidnapper smelled like chalk. We really racked our brains about that for a long time, until we asked about it at the youth hostel where Dominic had been staying. The kids were using chalk on their hands there to get a better grip while climbing. We even had the girl do a smell test with school chalk, gypsum, and climber's chalk. Her nose picked out the right one."

I was so proud of my little Brace-Face. All the bonsais, in fact. Under my tutelage, they had learned so much.

"Would he have let Sibel go in the end?" Birgit asked.

"That's not entirely clear to me," Gregor said. "Apparently his getaway was imminent. He had applied for visas for a whole slew of countries and bought a ticket he could use to fly around the world for six months. Yasemin started getting suspicious a couple of weeks too soon. But instead of taking off right away, he still wanted to sell off his fifty thousand pills. So he took his car up to the Eifel Mountains so he'd be mobile, even though he was on a class trip."

"He was pretty gutsy to stick around town so calmly while you were on the case," Birgit said.

Gregor nodded grimly. It can really piss a cop off when a bad guy seems not the least bit threatened by an investigation.

"He didn't think we were onto him until he saw Jenny at school on Tuesday. He drove home, packed up his cash and account numbers . . . and the rest you know."

"And what happened to Mariam?" Martin asked.

"The chief of police started a petition, which he sent out to all police departments nationally. We have almost five thousand signatures already. Combined with the murders and the media reports on Dominic's arrest, the political pressure is mounting for the government to give her the right to stay. That doesn't solve the underlying problem, of course."

After a short pause Katrin turned to Martin and Birgit. "On another subject altogether . . . Have you thought about names for the baby?"

Martin was about to open his mouth when Birgit jumped in.

"I think I'm going to be—" she muttered, pressing her hand over her mouth and scurrying off to the ladies' room.

307

EPILOGUE

She wore a white dress and held a candle in her hand. She was back in the church again, but this time at the side of a man you might mistake for a basketball player.

"Will you, Sibel Akiroğlu . . ."

You know how the rest of it goes. I zoomed over to the first pew on the left. Sitting side by side there among a whole heap of other bonsais were Edi, Joe, and Bülent. Niclas was in the second pew. Technically, he was hunkered down under the first pew, tying Edi's and Joe's shoelaces together.

The bedrooms of these four kiddos were now a part of my weekly rounds. Bülent had pinned a newspaper article on his wall with a picture of Gregor on it, Niclas had taken his computer apart and reassembled it—with very few leftover pieces—and Joe was studying Turkish so he could better understand the four million people of Turkish descent who live in Germany. Edi was finally doing what all girls her age regularly do: watching *Germany's Next Top Model* on TV and practicing catwalk modeling in her mother's shoes. But only when she thought no one was watching. Hey, it was a start.

After more organ noise and some warped vocals, Sibel and Thomas Bieberstein walked side by side out the front door of the church, followed by Akif and his beaming parents, who he had taken under each of his arms. He wore a black suit and had a clear, alert look in his eyes. Without his devilish goatee, you might even say he looked good. At least he wasn't wearing those balloon pants.

The school kids all joined the procession. Except for Edi and Joe, who tripped, stopping the others, and were run over by Bülent, who chased Niclas through the church.

Out in front of the church, everyone gathered: Edi in broken glasses, Joe with ripped suit pants, Bülent with a bloody nose, and Niclas with a black eye. Sibel called all the women up to stand behind her. Then she turned her back to them and tossed her bouquet.

Edi's mother caught it. She laughed as Edi hugged her and Joe congratulated her, and then she looked around for Joe's father. When she met eyes with him, she held the flowers up a little as she subtly raised her eyebrow. Joe's father beamed—and nodded.

The cop who was casually leaning against the wall of the church, watching the whole spectacle, smiled. Then his phone rang.

"Kreidler," he answered, stepping away from the wedding gathering.

I looked from Gregor to the celebrants, then back again. For me, the choice was clear. If I had to choose between squabbling kiddos and sickeningly sweet wedding speeches or a proper murder, I'd go for the action.

But that's another story.

THANKS

My thanks for support of various kinds this time goes to:

The team who put on the Children's Vacation Games in Eicken, run by Wolfgang Mahn and Patricia Mangold-Jütten, as well as all the kids who duped me while playing, peppered me with questions, took me through dangerous forest trails, and provided me with information and answers to my questions.

Dr. Frank Glenewinkel, who—in addition to the hoped-for answers to my myriad questions—is always telling me real-life anecdotes that are so offbeat, any bit of fiction would pale in comparison. In addition, he of course informed me that only the German public prosecutor's office can order a coroner to examine a victim of a violent crime, not the attending physician. But it was too cumbersome otherwise, and at some point a novelist must take creative license.

Claudia Kook, for whom I have my favorite Pascha expressions to thank.

Marcus Winter, the pseudonym of a colleague who is a detective in real life and who helped me out with some applied understanding of the theoretical chaos of storing telecommunications data.

My colleague Ilka Sitz and her husband, Mann Fevzi, who provided linguistic support for Bülent (the only things I can say in Turkish have to do with food).

All of my supporters on Facebook who have repeatedly given me encouragement (and commiseration during rough patches) and have helped me with the wording of a few things.

My editor, Karoline Adler. No book would be long enough if I had to write out everything that she has meant for Pascha.

Production director Bernd Schumacher, who drew up a production plan, the sight of which turned the faces of many parties involved pale—and who in fact implemented that plan.

Lisa Helm and Dieter Brumshagen who design book covers in the graphic arts department. Again and again, they make the invisible visible.

ABOUT THE AUTHOR

Jutta Profijt was born in 1967 in Ratingen, Germany. After finishing school, she lived abroad working as an au pair, an importer/exporter, a coach to executives and students, and a business-English instructor. She published her first novel in 2003 and today works as a freelance writer and translator. Her first novel featuring coroner Martin Gänsewein, *Morgue Drawer Four*, was shortlisted for Germany's 2010 Friedrich Glauser Prize for best crime novel.

ABOUT THE TRANSLATOR

 Erik J. Macki worked as a cherry orchard tour guide, copy editor, web developer, and German and French teacher before settling into translation. This career was probably inevitable, as he has collected grammars, dictionaries, and language-learning books since childhood—and to this day is not above diagramming sentences when duty so calls. A former resident of Cologne and Münster, Germany, and of Tours, France, he did his graduate work in Germanics and comparative syntax. He now translates books for adults and children full-time, including works by Kerstin Gier, Mirjam Pressler, Jutta Profijt, Carina Bartsch, and Sara Blædel, among others. He works from his home in Seattle, where he lives with his family and their black Lab, Zephyr.

Printed in Poland
by Amazon Fulfillment
Poland Sp. z o.o., Wrocław